Secret of 8

by

Cristal Sipple-Underwood
&
Andrew Underwood

Acknowledgements

We would like to thank our families for their support and encouragement in this lifelong dream- Richard Sipple, Tiffani Sipple-Kirik, Josh Tronoski, Lorraine Underwood, Judy & Rich Brunson, DeeAnn & Bruce Johnson, Terry Underwood, Scott Underwood, Jason & Stacey Underwood and our children, Megan, Jordon, Camron, Shelby, and Blake

Special thanks to Grandma Hazard Underwood & Blake for being the first of our family to read it and become our first fans. Thank you to April Burger-Wygant for her photography and artistic talent used for the cover of our book. We also want to thank Joe Zentis, our friend and author, for his help and encouragement. Thanks to our editor, Molly Mckitterick, for her knowledge and suggestions that turned our first draft into a final book, ready for the public. Last of all, we want to thank a few friends we grew up with in our neighborhood - Matt & Paul Boyd, Teddy Williams, April Burger-Wygant, Jim & Joe Gavio and Alan Bennion.

This Book is Dedicated in Memory
of
Georgiann Shenk-Sipple
&
Don Underwood

"Okay, I confess - I got really hooked, and read the whole rest of the novel from the manuscript you originally sent. The story line, characters, incidents, and climax are really excellent. For me, it is one of those rare books that you just have to stay up to the wee small hours of the morning to finish."

Joe Zentis- Owner, Writer & Editor for EpicGrampy.com-Past Owner of The Greenstreet Press, Freelance writer for Sharon Herald

"Thank you so much for letting me edit your book. I have seldom, if ever, had so much fun editing a book. I don't know how you plotted it but you have a wonderful imagination (s) and the book just rollicks along from one scary scene to another."

Molly McKitterick- Editor at Voice of America, 1st American Winner of the Japanese Suntory Award for Mystery Fiction, Author of "The Medium is Murder" & "Murder in a Mayonnaise Jar"-

How To Read This Book

This unique book was written with two points of view. The two main characters alternate views between the girl's (Sarah) and the boy's (Ben) unique perspective. You will notice small symbols at the beginning of each section or chapter signifying ♀= Female or ♂= Male to make it easier to keep track of who is speaking. Since this story is set in the 1980's, there may be words or phrases that are unfamiliar to our younger readers. We have underlined these within the chapters so they can be looked up on our "Secret of 8 Book" Facebook page. We supply photos, videos and descriptions to help the reader visualize, while also teaching a little history at the same time.

We hope you enjoy our first book in the series and look forward to the second book, soon to be released.

Keep an eye out for "The Wandering"
To Be Released in 2019

Chapter 1
Wary Watcher

♀ Something exciting was happening in my neighborhood. New kids were moving in, and we didn't know anything about them. It looked like a <u>gypsy caravan</u>. Pick-up trucks and trailers had heavy tarps pulled tightly over the mounds of furniture and boxes. It was the summer of 1980, but we learned about caravans in U.S. history class in school. Kinda made me want to build one and travel across the country looking for adventure.

Hiding behind the old tree stump across the street from the house, I was waiting to get a glimpse of the new kids. Every other kid in the neighborhood was too afraid because the new family was moving into a haunted house. The old house had stood empty for five years. The last owners, Mr. and Mrs. Jesperson, only lived there for nine months before Mrs. Jesperson mysteriously disappeared and her husband skipped town in a hurry, leaving behind most of their belongings. I know this because my dad is an antique and collectibles dealer. He bought out the entire contents of the house at a public estate auction. When we went to load his truck, I remember the kitchen table still had breakfast sitting on it. Something that looked to be the shape of toast, sat on a napkin. It was mossy green in color and furry like my wool socks. A cup of black coffee had a spoon still perched on its rim. Smelled pretty bad too, like something dead.

Rumor had it, Mr. Jesperson killed his wife and buried her in the basement, though the police inspected every inch and couldn't prove it without a body. When you live in a small town like ours, Grayson Mills, Pennsylvania, rumors spread like wild fire. If something out of the ordinary happens, everyone knows!

My name is Sarah Ann McNally. I am thirteen years old and the leader of our neighborhood gang. Not really, but I should have been. I have all the qualities a leader needs: intelligence, bossiness, humor, bravery, speed…and the ability to see ghosts. Yeah, you heard me right. I see ghosts.

My dad told me the new family used to live here years ago

before there were any kids in the picture. He ran into his high school buddy at the hardware store this morning and found out the family was moving back because of a job transfer. I guess they have a couple of boys, one my age. I'm not much of a welcoming committee.

I made my move at the precise moment, when the moving guys had gone inside. Looking both ways for traffic, I quickly crossed the chipped tar road. Hedges ran the whole length of the driveway, which gave perfect cover. Crawling on all fours, I made my way toward the rear of the house. Loud music was coming out of the garage. Once I reached the end of the hedge, I quickly jumped to the left wall of the garage and peeked through clouded window glass. A tall, tousle-haired boy was rummaging through a crate of what looked to be parts. Standing, I tried getting a better look, but the top pane of glass was covered with an old newspaper. With my back against the wall, I shimmied along the side of the garage toward the door.

Another boy, who was much younger, was drawing in the dirt of the driveway with a stick. He seemed to be talking to himself. I'd be talking to myself too if my parents moved us into the scariest house in town.

The back of the house didn't look any better than the front. It was a disaster. The white paint was cracking and falling off the wood siding, windows broken or clouded to the point no sunlight could get through, shutters hanging loosely by their corners, and shingles dangling off the gutters. Dad said they were nice people, but why would you buy a house like that? The little boy continued to play in the dirt, until I heard a woman's voice from inside the house.

"Michael! Can you give me a hand?"

He threw down the stick and ran up the back steps. When the coast was clear, I crept around the front of the garage and peeked in. He sure was making a mess. The crate was empty by this time; its contents were scattered all over the workbench. Suddenly, the boy jumped as if something bit him.

"Eureka!"

♂ Two old lawn mower wheels. Just one more set of wheels and some boards, and I'd have everything I needed for a soapbox derby racer.

This old garage was a gold mine of stuff. Carboard boxes were stacked along every wall, leaving the center open to park cars. My dad, who was an electrical engineer, said it was all junk. There was an old record player my dad called a Victrola. You had to wind it up because they didn't have electricity back when it was made. The speaker was a large horn type thing.

I moved here from out west, southern Utah to be exact. Coming from the desert to the east, was going to be a real change. We now had something called a yard. That meant there were boundaries. Back home, you could get lost in the wide-open spaces.

I hated this place already, a lot of houses and grass. My dad had been cussing since we got here. He wanted more of the house done and ready to move into, but each contractor he called, quit about a week later.

This new house of ours was a run-down creepy place with two big trees in the front yard, an oak tree in the back yard, front and rear porches, and a stone foundation. The house was over 100 years old, and the wallpaper in my room must have been at least that old.

It wasn't just the house; I was going to miss my two brothers and my two older sisters. I came from a large family. Now, just me and my little brother, ten-year-old Michael, were going to be at home. This was new for us.

I had read about soap box racers in the latest edition of my Boy Scout magazine, Boy's Life. They have some cool plans in it that I could tweak a little bit to make it go faster. All I had to do was find two more wheels.

After searching through a dozen tattered and smelly boxes of mason jars full of screws, old cabinet hinges and rags soaked in furniture stain, I came across a little wooden box with some carvings on the lid. It looked old; it had the kind of corners called "dove tail." My grandpa had told me when you saw those types of corners, you could be sure it was quality work. The box was locked, so I took it over to the old workbench in the far back corner of the garage and shut off the radio. As I was reaching to turn on the light, I heard something that made the hair on the back of my neck stand on end. I half expected a large rat to jump out behind me.

Chapter 2
Awkward Affair

♀ The boy froze when he heard the crunching noise. My last step gave me away. Somewhere hidden beneath a half a foot of grass, my foot had found the only stick in the yard. The boy stood like a mannequin, head tilted, ear to the air. Just when I thought I was a goner, he pulled the string to an overhead lightbulb, huddled into the back corner, and focused on a box that was sitting on a workbench.

With the light on now, I got a better look at him. His back was toward me, but from what I could tell he looked normal enough. Listen to me, talking about normal. There is no easy way to bring up the fact I see things, so most of the time, I blame the little lies I tell on a daily basis entirely on self-preservation. Without them, I would simply look like a nut case.

In third grade, my teacher said I needed some extra attention due to the fact that I didn't play with other students. After a few months of testing to determine if I had a hearing problem or a learning disability, they placed me in a special needs class. It was obvious I was in the wrong place, although I did find the kids more accepting of my weirdness than my previous classmates, who teased me endlessly. I was eventually returned to my original group, where I forced myself to participate and worked on ignoring the pesky ghosts.

At thirteen, I had learned to hide my talents. My only struggle was with being bossy. My mom said that was why I have a hard time making friends with other girls.

The back door of the house swung open, and the little boy named Michael flew down the steps. I froze in place like a deer in the headlights of an oncoming car. The boy looked past the garage and raced around the driveway side of the house. Still afraid to move, I waited for my chance to run. Just when it was safe to bolt, Michael returned carrying a large potted cactus that looked extremely dangerous. It had to be at least a foot tall with spikes as long as my pinky finger. He smiled broadly as he concentrated on the pot. He turned toward the steps yelling proudly, "Maaaaa! I got it! I didn't prick myself even once!"

The back door slammed shut. Relieved he didn't notice me, I leaned lightly against the garage door and exhaled. The rusty old hinge behind my head gave out a loud creak. Spinning around, I looked back into the garage. The older boy froze once again, momentarily, before whirling around to face the door. His hazel eyes, framed by almost invisible lashes, scanned the area. "Who's there? Come out with your hands up!"

With nothing to lose, I stepped into the garage and removed my sunglasses, trying to get a better look at him. You could tell he was grasping for words as his lips moved, but nothing came out. He was holding a screwdriver and looked petrified! He was tall and extremely skinny. He reminded me of Ichabod Crane from the headless horseman story! His knees looked as if he'd skinned them climbing somewhere, and he had straight teeth compared to mine. My two front teeth were longer than the rest and angled out slightly. I hated them. Kids in school called me "Bugs." after Bugs Bunny. His face was extremely round, and I imagined if he smiled he might be kinda cute. It was the sparkle in his eyes, though, that captured me.

Realizing I was staring, as his eyes pierced a hole through me. I shuffled my feet and forced myself to look away. My heart fluttered a bit, but I paid no attention to it. He was just a stupid boy, after all.

'What's your name?" I asked.

"Ben," he mumbled. "Ben Whiting."

"I'm Sarah."

It was an eternity before Ben cleared his throat and asked, "So, do you have any brothers?"

I couldn't help being disappointed. Maybe I was being unrealistic in hoping Ben could be my new best friend. Why would he want a girl for a best friend? I crossed my arms. "No, just my little sister Stephanie. She's nine."

"My brother, Mike, is ten. He's a pest most of the time, but we get along okay." A crooked smile crept across his face.

"Steph is spoiled rotten, so we don't get along real good," I admitted, almost ashamed. Mom lectured me about getting along with my sister. "Steph is the only sister you've got, and someday you'll appreciate her!" But Steph was always getting into my stuff and following me around, setting me up for trouble.

Ben dropped his screwdriver on the floor. When he bent over to pick it up, the suspenders attached to his shorts, sprang loose from the waistband in the back and shot over his head.
I giggled. He needed someone to give him fashion advice.

Ben turned a deep shade of red as he stood. He removed the suspenders and threw them into a box near his feet. He reached for the parts on the tool bench and held them in the air while shrugging his shoulders. "Wanna help me build something?"

♂ Did I just ask her to help me build something? My mind was in a whirl. What did I do that for? She looked normal enough, was cute in fact, and she did come to see the "new kid." Her red hair was long and pulled back in a ponytail. She had on pants, a t-shirt with the sleeves rolled up, and sandals.

I wished she hadn't laughed at my suspenders. I couldn't get pants to fit me. My older sisters always teased me about not having a butt. They said I looked like a frog in a pair of pants.

Gaining a little bit more confidence and trying to keep my voice from cracking, I said,

"I'm going to build a T-frame soap box racer!" I quickly looked for the two wheels I found earlier.

"It is just a skeletal frame racer. I am going to modify some plans I saw in a Boy Scout magazine. If I can make it wider in the front and narrow in the back, it will be more aerodynamic. I just need some wood, a way to steer it, a way to stop it, and something to sit on."

I did it. I was talking to a girl and not mumbling. This was turning into the best day of my life. I know how to use words but talking to girls is something I can't generally do, and this was a girl.

When I was nine, a blonde-haired little girl moved into my

school. She was all ribbons and bows and beautiful. It was Valentine's Day. I had made a nice little heart that said, "Be My Valentine" on it. I walked up to her during recess. She was with some other girls on the playground.

"Cathy," I said, "Will you be my Valentine?"

All the ribbons and bows and beauty turned into something mean and evil. I was taught never to hit a girl. I wish someone had been there that day to warn me, because this was not a little girl but a <u>Tasmanian devil</u> hiding in a little girl's body. I was scratched, kicked, and bitten.

Without saying a word, Sarah walked over to look at what I had in the box. She held up each piece like a detective, trying to solve a case, made funny shapes with her lips and saying, "Hmm," and "I see."

Any moment now, she would make that girly sound "Ewwwwww" in regard to the dirt and grease. This short friendship would be officially over.

I am good at making and fixing things. My dad calls it tinkering, but I call it fun. There were days when I would have traded being smart, for having a personality like my brother Mike. But I wasn't good at sports. "Okay, I guess we'll take Ben" should have been my name when it came to being picked for a team. The only reason some of them even let me play, was because I could make stuff that worked.

After sorting through the box of junk, Sarah wiped her hands on her clean white t-shirt and picked through my little tool kit. Mostly it was just a hammer, a few screw drivers, a couple of box wrenches, and my prize Craftsman adjustable wrench. She must have sensed the adjustable wrench was my favorite, because it was the one she spent the most time with.

"Yeah, I will help you build it." She looked at me. "But there is something you're gunna need, before you can do any of those things you went on about."

My look of confusion must have been hard to ignore. With one eyebrow cocked higher than the other, she continued,

"You are going to need another set of wheels, right?"

My face was hot, but I didn't care. This girl was awesome. I just grinned and nodded my head.

She grabbed my hand. "Come on. My dad has a bunch of stuff we can look through, and I bet he has some wheels we could use."

We ran out of the garage toward the street. I skidded to a stop and yelled, "Mom! I'm going over to Sarah's house. I will be back in a few minutes."

As we reached the sidewalk, I heard my mom yell out the kitchen window, "Hi Sarah! Ben, be home before supper!"

Chapter 3
Trains & Treasure

♀ We cut through Mr. Hannah's back yard and headed down the sidewalk, toward the old railroad yard. Along the way, I pointed out many of the well-known landmarks. The houses in Grayson Mills were close together, but not too close. Your back yard always connected to the neighbor's back yard one street over. We passed the volunteer fire department, which also served as our local police station, and stopped briefly at the community park. The park had a basketball court, playground, and public pool.

Just past the playground we ran into Marcus, the town bully, sitting on a bench. Fifteen, Marcus pretty much ruled the school. Tall and chubby, he had the worst attitude ever.

"Well, lookey here, it's Sarah Scare-ya." Marcus smirked.

I told Ben to look straight ahead and ignore him. Marcus stole my journal in the hall last year. He read enough of it to discover my secret, before he gave the journal back. Marcus yelled a few insulting remarks as Ben and I walked. He would have followed us, if one of the local police cars had not passed by. Once we got far enough away, I looked back at him. He was standing with his arms crossed in the middle of the sidewalk. "See you at Casper's house!" he screamed.

Around the corner, Ben asked, "Who's Casper?"

I looked at the sky. "No one. He was just joking around."

We reached the old train yard before Ben could ask any more questions. The yard was fenced in with a chain link, six feet high. Barbed wire coiled around the top of it. A few summers ago, the local police tried to secure the train yard so kids wouldn't vandalize the old locomotives. The barbed wire worked until the fence started to fall apart, and the police gave up. Now, the gates hung open, and the yard was littered with paint cans. It just happened to be my favorite shortcut. Ben slowed when we reached the train graveyard section. He seemed to be in a trance, looking at the old engines, caked in coal dust.

"Come on! You want your wheels, or what?" I asked. He just stared. Finally, I pinched him back to reality.

"What did you do that for?" Ben rubbed his arm.

I stuck my tongue out and made an annoying whiney sound, mocking him. "How old did you say you were?"

"I didn't tell you? I'm almost fourteen, why?"

I rolled my eyes. "I thought boys quit whining around ten."

We took off running toward my house and reached my dad's barn in record time. Ben leaned against the weathered planks. The old <u>Mail Pouch advertisement</u> was still readable on the barn's backside. One end of the roof leaked last winter, but for the most part, it was in decent shape. I lifted the latch to the door, and we stepped inside.

My dad had been collecting antiques for almost fifteen years. He started when my mom was pregnant with me. By now, he had filled the large weathered barn with gadgets, furniture, lamps, and unexplainable wonders. The smell was musty, with a faint hint of sawdust.

♂ I could have spent the rest of the day, or better yet, the rest of my life in the old train yard. The vines that climbed the chain fence on the outside, hid treasures I might never have known were buried there: old steam engines, large diesel engines, cabooses, passenger cars of all types and ages. The best part was, it was all just a stone's throw away from my new house.

In the barn, Sarah took off as if shot out of a cannon and disappeared up some stairs. I was winded from chasing after her, but didn't want her to think I was a wimp. At least, I hadn't had an asthma attack. That was the last thing I wanted her to find out about me. After resting a moment at the top of the steps, I stopped dead in my tracks.

Sunlight filtered in through the barn slats and hit a small mobile made of colored glass. Each colored piece of glass, hanging by fishing line, made the barn loft come alive with color.

A smile slowly took over my face. This was her place. The way the boxes were stacked and the way she had positioned mirrors to catch the colored glass, told me this was where she came to dream. Hidden between the boxes I could see old machines, gears, pulleys, wheels of different sizes and types. In one corner, was a huge old <u>cash register</u>. I had seen them before in museums back home. This one was still showing the words, "NO SALE" in the small glass window.
Spinning around in a circle, she asked, "Well, what do you think?"

I wandered around for a minute, ending next to Sarah. "This place is great." I softly punched her on the arm. "You're pretty cool for a girl."

I had turned away when I heard her say, "Geez, if that's how you show you like me, I better keep my distance!"
I didn't bother looking at her, because I knew she was still smiling.

"Hey, look at this," I said as I walked over to a box. It had wheels in it. "Wow, these are real wagon wheels from a <u>Radio Flyer wagon</u>." I turned one of the wheels over and over in my hand, as I continued. "They made them with real brass bushings and not the plastic stuff the new ones are made of!" Holding the wheel, I spun it with just barely a whisper of noise. "These wheels make the best racers. You put just the right amount of oil on the brass, and they will spin forever."

It had gotten quiet in the loft. Sarah was watching me with an amused look on her face. "Sorry, I get carried away when I talk about building things. My dad says I have a one-track mind."

She stuck out her tongue and crossed her eyes. That did it; I laughed, which gave me the courage to ask the question that was burning a hole in my mind. "Man! Where did this stuff come from?"

Chapter 4
Haunted History

♀ "From auctions, garage sales, and dead people's houses!"

Ben's eyes grew wide as he raised his eyebrows. "Dead people's houses?" he stuttered as he took a step backwards, hands in the air.

"When people die, my dad buys all the stuff they leave behind. You can't take it with you, ya know!"

I pointed to a pile of boxes near the stairwell. "Those came from Mrs. Boyer's house. She was a widow, who died a couple months ago at the age of 93. She had no children." I nodded at another grouping of boxes. "Those came from a storage locker near the tracks. I guess the items were unclaimed when the owner died suddenly in a car wreck." I walked over to the pile next to Ben. "And those came from your house. Mr. and Mrs. Jesperson used to live there a few years back."

Ben looked at the boxes. "What happened to them? Did they die, too?"

Not counting Ben's family, the Jespersons were the fifth family to move into the house in ten years, I explained. Mr. Jesperson was a retired schoolteacher, and his wife was the town gossip.
Ben spun the wheel in his hands as he listened.

"According to the cashier, Mr. Jesperson had an argument with his wife at the market the day before she disappeared. It was something about her stealing his private stash of money."

"What do you mean, she disappeared?"

I tapped my homemade mobile and sent a rainbow of color across his curious face. "On June 17th. Mrs. Hannah, who still lives across the street, said she heard yelling coming from the house early in the morning. She saw Mr. Jesperson open the side kitchen window to let out a black cloud of smoke. Mrs. Jesperson ran out the back door and tried to leave by getting in the car. Her husband dragged her back into the house by her hair! No one ever saw her again. The neighbor behind your house, who is our mailman, saw Mr. Jesperson unloading bags of cement into the basement early the next morning. I believe he killed his wife and buried her in the basement, and her ghost haunts your house to this day!"

Ben, who had been biting his nails, sighed. Pulling a cardboard box, he plopped himself down, crushing the box under his weight and sinking into it. I had to giggle at how comical he looked trying to get out of it while maintaining his cool.

After extracting himself he asked, "So, there might be a ghost in my house right now?"

I nodded.

"Cooool!" he said excitedly. "That is why no one ever lives there long."

Ben nodded. "That might be why the contractors left in such a hurry without telling us why!" A bead of sweat ran down Ben's forehead. I suggested we head back outside where it was cooler.

Ben grabbed the two wheels as we went. Outside, he gave me a blank stare. I recognized the stare. Mom had told me whenever Dad gave her that stare, it meant he was thinking hard and would most likely not hear a word she said. I decided not to take any chances and make sure he heard me, so I pinched him again.

"Whaaaaat!" He furrowed his brows.

♂ Sarah motioned with a wave of her hand toward the tree in her front yard. I followed and asked for a drink of water.

"Sure, I will be right back."

Sarah ran up the steps to her house, while I sat with my back against the tree and looked into its leaves. This was one of my favorite kinds of tree, big leaf maple, and it was old. There were plenty of places to build a tree house in it.

Sarah's home was a two-story, clapboard sided house. There was a huge wraparound porch with a large porch swing on the side that faced me. The house was white, and of course it had a white picket fence, like the one <u>Tom Sawyer</u> got his friends to paint for him.

A cold spray of water hit my face.

"Hey… Ben, wake up." Sarah was leaning over me, trying to

hand me a glass of water. "You must be a deep thinker," she said as I grabbed it and drained it in one gulp.

I sat the glass on the ground next to me. "Ahhhhhhh, that was good. Thank you."

Sarah plopped herself on the ground straight across from me and told me about the trees in the neighborhood, which ones were good to climb and the ones I should stay away from. One of the trees she pointed out, was at the other end of the block. It was a large old oak tree with one long, dead branch that hung out over the road. "That is called the hanging tree," she said. "Back when my grandpa was my age, there was some trouble with a couple of immigrant boys and the theft of a bank roll for the railroad. They hung the boys there on that tree." I stared at her as she relayed this wild story. "But I did some investigating at the library and I asked some of the old people in town. They just needed a scapegoat. The money was never recovered and the boys had just come in on the train looking for work, when the money vanished."

She pointed over our heads. "This tree is special. My great-grandfather planted it. It has always been a good tree to climb."

I thought about the stuff in the barn and the story Sarah had told me about my house being haunted. "Sarah, do you *really* believe in ghosts?

Chapter 5
Ghostly Gab

♀ I could see how much he wanted me to say yes. Most of my life was spent not talking about ghosts, for fear of being teased, and now this kid wanted to talk about them. "Hmm…I don't know. What do you think, Ben?" I played it safe.

He jumped to his feet, knocking my glass of water into my lap. "Are you kidding? I totally believe!" he practically shouted.
I gasped as the ice water soaked into my jeans.

"Umm, sorry Sarah, I get a little excited sometimes."

Nothing could have made me happier. "Don't worry about it.

It's so hot today, I'm sure it's gonna dry in no time."

Ben threw himself down next to me once again and crossed his legs Indian style. His mouth moved a mile a minute, which made it hard to tell when one sentence ended, and another began. He threw out words like "paranormal" and "phenomena." When he ended, he stopped, sighed, and looked embarrassed.

"Boy, you sure know a lot of stuff about ghosts." I said.

He nodded, "I read a lot of books. I'm kind of a nerd that way."

"So, you ever seen one?"

Ben lowered his head. "Never have. I've always wanted to, though. It would be cool if I could ask questions and find out why they are hanging around. What about you?"

I could not hold back my grin as it got wider. "YES! Ummm... All the time." I put my finger to my lips. "Don't tell anyone. Dad said it should be a secret."

Ben stared straight at me, no expression in his face. Like a robot, he abruptly stood and held his hand out to help me up. I reached and grasped his greasy, nail-bitten hand. He lifted me to my feet quickly, wrapped both of his arms around me, and hugged. I don't know how long we stood there, but it seemed like a long time.

I finally squeaked, "You're crushing me!"

Ben let go, realizing what he had just done. He pushed me back quickly, so I was an arm's length away. "I'm going to be late for dinner! See you tomorrow!" He spun around and ran toward home.

♂ I finally got tired of staring at the ceiling and decided to get up. I don't know how late it was but everyone in the house – the house I now knew was haunted – was asleep.

I had been thinking about the stuff in the garage and remembered the little wooden box with the etched top I had found. I needed to get the box and find out what was inside.

Creeping down the unfamiliar back stairs, I found each and every loose board. Everyone was tired from unpacking, or I would have woken up the whole house. Once I got to the back door, I eased it open and stepped outside into the cool night air. The garage was only ten or so feet away and there was enough moonlight outside to see where I was going. The yard was a jungle of tall grass and weeds, casting eerie shadows across the dirt of the driveway. It was way too quiet.

  I dragged my feet through the darkness, hands in front of me feeling for the bench. I pulled the string on the light, after I stubbed my toe. Reaching to the shelf, I carefully brought down the box. The brass latch was stuck. I had to pry it open with an old screwdriver. Inside, the box was lined with faded red velvet. Lying in the middle was an oval, the size of a half a dollar. Picking it up, I discovered it was a piece of jewelry, what my mom would call a <u>cameo pin</u>, with a figure of a woman carved in ivory against a pinkish background. Turning the object over – it was thicker than I expected – I saw it had a gold clasp and bumps along the side edge. Looking more closely, I saw there were hinges. The cameo was a locket; it opened. Fumbling with the latch, I pried it apart. What I saw inside almost made me drop it.

Chapter 6
Midnight Mystery

  ♀ I wiped the sleep from my eyes and looked at the two little pebbles resting on the sill of my window, the ones that must have hit the glass and woken me. Moonlight shone across the lawn below, casting a bluish tint to everything it touched. Ben's round face resembled a blueberry. Wearing his silly grin, he was standing in the middle of the lawn, holding a small flashlight, dressed in a light jacket and pajama bottoms.

I leaned out of the window, sighed loudly and told him to stay put.

  Jumping into a pair of jeans, along with my favorite sweatshirt, I quietly made my way downstairs, being careful to avoid the third step from the bottom. That one always squeaked and gave me away. I could hear my sister as I passed her bedroom. Steph was talking in her sleep again, muttering something unrecognizable. Sometimes it sounded like she was speaking a different language, and there was a lot of thrashing around and blankets being thrown to the floor. Those nights were the ones when no one, except Steph, slept. You'd swear she was auditioning for a part in a horror movie and she never remembered a thing! Tonight, was just an ordinary dream night.

When I got to the back door, I slipped on my flip-flops and crept across the enclosed patio. Sandy, our dog, stood, stretched, and yawned from his bed near the corner.

"Go lie down. It's not time to get up yet!' I whispered to him.

His perked-up ears fell with disappointment and he plopped himself back down. I blew him a silent kiss and slowly opened the screened storm door.

The grass was cool and wet with dew, making my rubber sandals squeak with each step I took. I grabbed Ben by his jacket sleeve and pulled him under the shadows of the oak tree.

His eyes were wide with excitement and I could tell he had some kind of adventure in mind. I just wished he didn't wake me up out of a sound sleep to do it.

A sudden breeze picked up and blew against my back. I had neglected to put my hair up. Keeping my hair under control was not an easy task, so most of the time I pulled it back. I had someone tell me once it resembled the mane of a lion.

Ben stared at my hair, while shifting his weight from one foot to the other. "You're not mad at me, are you?" he stuttered.

Wrinkling my nose, I shook my head. "But if you don't tell me what was so important you had to wake me out of a sound sleep for, I *will* be mad!"

♂ I reached into my pocket and withdrew the cameo I found in the garage and handed it to her. "I couldn't sleep and so I went to the garage to… "

She grabbed the cameo out of my hands. "You woke me to give me this? You could have waited until tomorrow!"

I knew that tone of voice. It meant someone's Ben-o-meter was on overload and it was time to go home. I reached over, opened the locket and shined the flashlight on it. "Sarah, did you have any relatives who lived in my house, maybe an aunt or an uncle – someone who lived there like fifty or sixty years ago?"

I paced back and forth while she looked at the photo inside the locket, keeping pace with my runaway mouth. "I tried to go to sleep, but I kept remembering the scary story about the guy burying his wife in the basement. I was wondering about ghosts and if her ghost haunted my house. What would I do if my house was haunted? Maybe I could catch a ghost with my dad's camera or even better I might be able to record the ghost talking. Did you know you can record the sound of a ghost talking on a regular <u>cassette tape</u>?"

Her hand touched my arm. "Ben, slow down." She had a bemused look on her face. "Wow, had I known telling you that story about your house would keep *me* awake at night, I would have never told you."

Chapter 7
Shooting Star

♀ I brought the photograph closer to my face, as Ben held the flashlight on it. Her hair did look long and unruly like mine, although I could not tell what color it was because the picture was black and white. The dress she wore was beautiful, trimmed with lace and feminine. She looked to be roughly 18 years old. A cameo – this cameo? –was pinned to the high collar directly beneath her chin.

"The face...gosh!" It was like looking in a mirror! My hands trembled and I dropped the cameo. Ben leaned down at the exact moment I did, and we conked heads pretty hard.

"Ouch! I think I see stars!"

Ben rubbed his forehead. "She could be your twin sister."

The cameo was the same one in the picture. I ran my fingers over the raised ivory face and admired the delicate gold lattice around the edge of it. "As far as I know, none of my relatives lived in your house. I've seen the old family albums and this person is not in them. The only relative I looked like was my great grandpa." I pushed the cameo deep into my pocket. "Well, except for the beard." I paused.

"Maybe, we need to look in your garage tomorrow and find more clues!"

Ben's eyes were large and owlish. "Maybe, you're reincarnated. Maybe, this was you a hundred years ago and you're coming back to warn yourself of impending doom." he announced.

We giggled and couldn't stop. We laughed so hard, my stomach hurt. I even snorted a couple of times. Ben's face turned beat red at one point and no sound came out. He was laughing one of those silent laughs. I patted him on the back. Finally, he exhaled.

"Wow," I said. "This is going to be the best summer. We have a mystery to solve."

I walked out from under the oak tree and lay on the grass on my back. Putting my hands behind my head, I looked at the dark night sky. Ben plopped beside me and did the same. The stars were bright and plentiful, filling the blackness with a million pinpricks of light. Now that we were quiet, all I could hear were the peepers and Ben's sigh. This silence was not awkward or uncomfortable. It was nice. Turning my head, I looked at his profile. I'm kinda glad he didn't notice me staring. I might never have noticed the fine hairs on his top lip or realized how long his eyelashes were. I sighed and said something I don't normally admit.

"You were right, Ben."

Ben turned his head to face mine and looked confused. "Right?"

Biting my bottom lip, I continued, "You were right about not waiting until tomorrow to show me the cameo and photo. I'm sorry if I yelled about you waking me."

He smiled. "That's okay. I guess I forget not everyone processes information like me and maybe I'm being a pest."

I shook my head, stumbling with my words. "You're not a pest, just – well, different. There's nothing wrong with different."

"Speaking of different, you never did tell me about the ghosts you see."

"Oh look, a shooting star."

"Where? Where?" he asked a little too loudly.

The upstairs light in my parent's room lit up, as I tried to shush him by putting my hand over his mouth. I removed it when the light went off.

"I better get going soon." Ben whispered nervously. I nodded and agreed.

He reached over awkwardly and grabbed my hand. It was warm and fit perfectly in my own.

♂ I glanced out of the corner of my eye and caught Sarah staring at me. Her hand felt small inside mine. She was most likely thinking about what a weird kid I was. I imagined being examined like a bug, just before having a pin pushed through my body, and put on some display board. I cringed and smiled when I realized it would make a great horror story.

It was just the two of us and the sounds of crickets and frogs. I was getting nervous now. She kept staring at me. I was not sure what to do. I hope she didn't want me to kiss her. Not that there was anything wrong with it. I was sweating and my hands were getting clammy. I hoped she didn't notice. Was this where I was supposed to kiss her? I had never kissed a girl before. I mean, I didn't even know how. What if I mess it all up? Or worse yet, what if she doesn't want a kiss, and she is just one of those girls who like to stare at you? I wish my sisters were here to tell me what I was supposed to do.

The way the street light and the stars were shining on Sarah, made it look like she was leaning in for a kiss. I felt sick in the pit of my stomach. Please don't let me throw up, please don't let me throw up, I prayed silently.

"Ben's got a girlfriend! Ben's got a girlfriend!" In his Batman pajamas, my little brother popped up from the bushes and made kissing noises.

I jumped as if a bee stung me. "Sarah, this was the best day of my life, but I got to take care of this little brat before he gets home."

Sarah was already standing. She looked kind of sad, but a lot relieved.

"See you tomorrow, I hope!" I yelled and covered my mouth when I noticed how loud I was. I turned around to chase after my little brother.

Chapter 8
Fast Friends

♀ What just happened? One minute we were holding hands and the next he was looking at me like I had some rare disease that was going to infect him. Thank goodness Mike interrupted when he did. Maybe I shouldn't have let him hold my hand. Was it possible he believed I was going to kiss him? Giggling at the thought, I shook my head. "Silly boys!" Tomorrow, I needed to let Ben know, best friends don't kiss.

Halfway up the stairs, I heard someone in my room. Peeking around the corner, I saw my mom sitting on my bed. Not sure what to do, my mind raced with a million little lies I could tell to explain where I had been. Mom was staring straight ahead at my closet door and waiting patiently. I watched quietly as she turned her head and ran her finger across my nightstand, leaving a clean trail in the dust. She smiled and shook her head. My mom was the most beautiful mom in town. I couldn't count how many times she was mistaken for my older sister. We looked nothing alike, but we had the same beauty mark, a small mole under the left cheekbone. We called it our <u>Marilyn Monroe</u> beauty mark.

I must have sighed too loudly, because she spotted me and motioned with her finger to come in. Patting the spot beside her, she smiled. I reluctantly sat next to her on my tattered quilt, as she put her arm around me. "Honey, I saw you in the yard with your new friend," she said softly.

I opened my mouth to explain, but she put her finger to her lips to shush me.

"No, just listen," she said. "I want you to know if you ever need to talk to me about anything, anything at all, I'm here for you." She paused. "Whatever you tell me will be our little secret, okay? I will not tell Daddy."

I nodded but said nothing. She stood, kissed me on the forehead, and told me how grown up I'd become, and how proud she was of me. I smiled at her. "I love you Mom."

She whispered, "I love you more. You'll always be my baby."

She headed down the stairs, her knees cracking with each step. Her knees made strange noises for some reason. She said it was because she was getting older. "Just like old houses. They creak!"

♂ I caught up with my little brother about twenty feet in front of the house. Mike had short legs but he sure could run fast.

"Hey you, get back here!" I grabbed the back of his pajama shirt and swung him around to face me. "What were you doing?" I growled in the most ferocious voice I could come up with.

With a little grin, he whispered, "Ben's got a girlfriend!" He kicked me in the shin and bolted for the stairs again. I tackled him before he got there.

"She is just my friend." I whispered fiercely as I put him in a headlock and gave him a <u>noogie</u>. "Promise me you won't say anything to Dad!"
He tried to roll out from under me. "Ben's got a girlfriend!"

Sitting on his chest, I grinned because I had him pinned to the ground. "Okay. You asked for it." I tickled him. Mike was extremely ticklish just under his arms, and if you tickled him just right, his laugh went high like a whistle. I clamped one hand over his mouth just in case he squealed loudly. Leaning in close, I said again, "Promise you won't tell?"

If Dad found out I had snuck out of the house in the middle of the night to see a girl, they would never leave me alone, and all I needed was for Dad to think it is time to have the "talk." I heard about the "talk" from my older brothers.

I dug my fingers into Mike's ribs again. "Promise and I will let you go." I could see in his eyes he was ready to agree, so with a nod I released him.

We sat on the wet grass, looked at each other, and laughed at the same time. It hadn't been easy for either one of us to just pick up and move out to the middle of nowhere. I grabbed a handful of grass and threw it at him. "You're a dork."

He stuck out his tongue, crossing his eyes. "No, you're a dork!" He threw grass back at me. "Ben, are you still mad at Dad for moving us out here?"

Good question. It hadn't sunk in we had moved; so far, it felt like we were on a vacation. I looked at the stars. "I don't know how I feel at the moment, Michael."

With a big sigh, I got to my feet and bent over to help him. Walking towards the porch, I put my hand on his shoulder. "We will be okay."

Chapter 9
New Normal

♀ An annoying bird woke me, squawking at the top of its lungs. Rolling over to my side, I stretched my arm to the window and shut it with a slam. I closed my eyes to go back to sleep, but I could still hear that stupid bird. "CAWWWWW! CAWWWW!"

Disgusted with the fact that sleeping in was out of the question, I sprang from bed and threw open the window. I grabbed the closest thing, my sneaker, and threw it at the black bird perched on the tree limb across from my window. With a flutter of its wings, the bird took flight, as my shoe flew into the tree and stuck between the branches.

"Great!" I said with attitude.

Since I was already dressed from the night before, I decided not to bother changing clothes. Ben would never notice anyway. Boys don't pay attention to clothes. I grabbed my right shoe and headed downstairs. Stephanie was at the kitchen table, with her hand all the way inside the cereal box looking for the "prize" advertised on the front.

"Don't even think about it! It's mine!" She threatened me.

It never ceased to amaze me how you could love someone but not like them much. I dropped my shoe. "I don't want your baby toy anyway."

Grabbing the loaf of homemade bread and pulling a knife out of the dish strainer, I cut a piece as thick as I could. Not too thick, so it wouldn't fit in the toaster, but thicker than normal store-bought bread. I pushed one piece into the slot. When I heard the popping noise and the toast didn't come out, I picked up the toaster and caught my reflection in the shiny silver surface. What a mess! I had grass sticking out of my hair and it looked exactly like a bird's nest. I carefully pried my toast loose and ran my fingers through my hair.

"See ya!" I ran out the door with my shoe in one hand, while stuffing the toast into my mouth with the other.

"Wouldn't want to be ya!" yelled my sister.

I climbed the tree with ease and retrieved my shoe. Once back to the ground, I slid both shoes on without untying them and ran as fast as I could down the street. Once Ben's house was within sight, I stopped. Out of breath, I had a stabbing pain at the top of my leg. Reaching into my pocket, I realized the pin on the back of the cameo was stabbing through the material of my pants. I pulled it out and went to close the pin latch, when I noticed something I had not seen before. There were initials and a date engraved on the back.

"Boy! Wait till Ben sees this."

Ben's little brother, Mike, was sitting on the ground in front of their house, putting on <u>metal roller skates</u>. They attached to your shoes with straps around the ankles and metal toe pieces. Mike was having a hard time getting his attached to his sneaker. "Hi! You need help with that?"

Mike shook his head and turned away a little as he continued to attempt to cram his foot into the skate. Kneeling, I grabbed the other one sitting on the dirt beside him and adjusted the wing nut on the bottom to make the skate bigger.

I handed it back to him. "You're trying to put your foot into something too small, ya know!"

Raising an eyebrow, he reluctantly took it from me and tried it on. When it fit perfectly, he looked at me with his mouth open in amazement.

"Wow, I never met a girl who could fix things."

I giggled and showed him how to adjust the size.

"It's easy, see. Must have been a long time since you used these, huh?"

He looked a little sad. "Yep, two summers ago. Gosh, my feet got bigger."

I pointed to my own gunboats. "Not as big as mine, size 9 ½ women's shoes."

His face broke out in a wide grin.

I smiled back and reached out to shake his hand,

"You must be Ben's brother, right?"

He nodded and shook it. "You must be Ben's new girlfriend."

♂ Before he went to work, Dad had left me another list. Not a "Hello Son," or "Good morning," all it said was what to do. Just once I would like for him to talk to me about what he wanted done, and not leave it on a piece of paper.

I ate my toast and drank the last of the milk straight out of the jug; something that upset my mom. I took the list and headed out back to see what my dad had in store for me today. I was still not awake when I stepped outside, but that changed when I saw Sarah out in the backyard talking with my little brother. A little self-conscious about the wild mop of hair I had on my head, I quickly reached through the back door and grabbed one of my hats. Pulling it tight on my head, I turned back around. "Hi," I said without a stutter.

"Hey," Sarah smiled.

"How are you?" I asked, as she stood.

"I am fine!" My little brother mimicked a girl's voice and giggled.

Sarah grabbed the list out of my hands. "What's this?"

"Oh, it's just my dad's way of saying 'I love you, Son'."

She handed the list back to me. "Well, do you want some help with it? You can get done twice as fast if I help."

All I could do was grin. "Sure. I guess we could start with sweeping the garage. I can show you where I found the cameo."

Chapter 10
Helping Hands

♀ Ben slid the doors to the garage open, letting in as much sunlight as possible. The floor was covered in partially, unpacked boxes. It looked like his Dad had already begun organizing.

"Did your Dad's note say to sweep around the boxes or move them and sweep?" I asked.

Ben was already picking boxes up and setting them on top of the workbench, near the back of the garage.

"I better do it this way just in case. I don't want to have to do it again. Knowing Dad, he will give me a nice, 'Do it right the first time' lecture if I rush."

I grabbed two of the nearest boxes, stacked one on top of the other, and carried them toward the back. As I strained to lift them to the bench, I got a stabbing reminder of what I had in my front pocket. "Ouch! Not again!" I screamed, dropping both boxes with a clunk. Dust flew into the air and left a cloud of suspended particles, hovering in the streams of sunlight. Reaching deep into my pocket, I pulled out the cameo once again.

"You have to see this!"

I turned the cameo over and explained to him how I discovered the engraving on the way over. Ben grabbed the cameo out of my hand and quickly ran to a rusty steel toolbox sitting near the door. He dug frantically, throwing tools left and right. Mumbling and talking to himself, kind of like the way my dad does sometimes when he can't find something. "Eureka!" he screamed.

In his hand, was the biggest magnifying glass I had ever seen. It had to be eight inches in diameter and had a fancy carved wooden handle.

"Whoa! Where did that come from?" I asked, as he held it up to one eye.

His eye looked the size of a saucer and reminded me of a Cyclops movie I saw last summer. "My Dad bought it for me when I was five. I carved the handle last year on one of my first Boy Scout camp-outs, as a Tenderfoot."

We moved closer to the window and flipped the cameo over. Cramming our heads close together, we held the magnifying glass over it.

"It looks like the initials E-V-H and a date of 1924!" he shouted. "Let's hurry up and finish this; I have to show you something."

♂ Between the two of us, we made quick work of stacking the boxes marked "storage" in the far-right corner of the garage. It looked like the floor of the old garage was hard-packed dirt, but once we swept, we found it did have a layer of cement underneath decades of grease and grime. We had to stop several times to let the dust settle, but within two hours, we had the first chore on the list complete.

I leaned the broom against the wall. "My dad wants to hold a rummage sale next month, once we get things moved out of the basement. I'm surprised your Dad didn't buy it all."

Sarah turned around. When the sunlight hit her, she had this golden halo of dust. I laughed. "What are you laughing at?" she asked as I laughed harder. "You look like Pigpen from the Snoopy cartoons."

She walked past me towards the door. "Well, you don't look any better."

"Hey wait up, I was only joking."
I caught up to Sarah as she reached the back yard.

"Sarah, I am sorry. I was teasing. I should have said thank you for your help, instead of laughing at you."

When I held out my hand, I noticed I was about as dirty as she was. I was surprised, when she did something I had only read about in a Tom Sawyer book. She spit in her hand. "Best friends?" She extended her hand for me to shake. I was a little grossed out but I was not going to let her know about it. I spit in my hand and said, "Best friends," as we shook on it.

"Let's get washed up, and I can show you the basement."

We walked to the back- porch, side by side, until we reached the door. Sara stood, as if waiting for me to open the door for her. I had to smile. She acted like one of the boys, but liked to be treated like a lady, too. I opened the screen door and followed her into the house.

"Mom!" I yelled a bit too loud.

"You don't have to yell, I'm not deaf yet," she said in a calm voice, as she peeked out of the pantry.

My mom was your basic stay-at-home mom, like you saw in the old sitcoms of the 1950s. She was pretty cool for a mom. She loved playing board games, liked to talk about cool stuff, and let me pick out my own school clothes without trying to make sure they were going to fit me. "Mom, this is my new friend, Sarah."

"Oh. She is a cute one," Mom said with a smile on her face. "And what did you do to her? You are both filthy." She wiped the dust off my face with a wet rag.

"Mom, you're embarrassing me."

She stopped. "I guess you're getting a little too old for that, aren't you?" Mom turned to Sarah. "It is a pleasure to meet you, young lady. I hope my son has been treating you with respect."

"Yes Ma'am," Sarah said.

My mother shook her head. "Show Sarah where the wash room is, and you come back and clean up here in the sink."

I walked Sarah down the hallway to where the bathroom was. It wasn't much of a room, just a little place under the stairs with a sink and a toilet in it. "I will meet you back in the kitchen when you're done."

I walked back to the kitchen sink and removed the layers of dirt from my hands, arms and face.

"Ben." Mom had one of those I-am-about-to-deliver-a-lecture looks on her face. "I am glad you have found a new friend here in town, but I want you to remember the house rules."

The house rules: *no* friends over to the house unless Mom or Dad are home, *no* girls are to ever ("and I mean ever") go into our bedrooms, under penalty of death or something worse, etc. etc. "Yes, Mother, I remember the house rules."

I had just finished cleaning up and drying off, when Sarah came around the corner. I almost dropped the towel I had used to dry my hands. I was still in shock she wanted to be my friend, and my mom was right. She was cute.

"Thank you, ma'am, for letting me use your wash room."

My mom couldn't have smiled any wider. "She has such nice manners. I like her already!" Looking at me, she said, "I hope you learn something from her."

I walked to the fridge and got out a couple of Popsicles. "Would you like one, Sarah? We have red, green, orange, and yellow. Wait, we have one purple left."

I held out the five colors like I was holding five cards to do a magic trick. "Pick a color, any color."

Sarah picked the red one, and I picked the green one. We both headed through the living room, out to the front porch. I held the door open and followed Sarah outside. Just after the screen door went shut, I could hear my mom say. "I will make gentlemen out of them yet."

Chapter 11
Panicked Promise

♀ Ben's front porch needed a little work. It was large, wrapping around one side of the house. The white paint was peeling. You could see bits of older green paint underneath. On the driveway side, an old porch swing hung from chains. It was lopsided but seemed sturdy. Ben plopped himself on the higher end of the swing, so I was left with the lower end. "Your mom seems nice. She's pretty too."

Ben nodded as he chewed on the end of his plastic wrapper. He was having a hard time getting it open.

"Don't you have any scissors?"

"Yeah, but they're still packed somewhere in a box."

"Where's your knife?"

He gave me a funny look. "How did you know I had a knife?"

"Well, I saw the carving you did on your magnifying glass handle, and you said you were a Boy Scout. I just figured."

He looked sad.

"I lost it somewhere during the move. It was my favorite knife, too. My grandpa gave it to me a couple of Christmases ago. A Boy Scout knife, better than any I had ever seen."

I grabbed his Popsicle and tore at the end with my teeth,

growling like a ferocious dog. The sadness left his eyes.

We sat on the swing quietly for a few minutes while we ate. Ben kept sliding downhill toward my end of the swing. We ended up elbow-to-elbow, swinging and talking.

A faint little voice came from behind the hedge. "Ben's got a girlfriend!"
Ben looked at me and counted with his fingers.

"Ben's got a girlfriend."

On three, we both jumped off the swing and ambushed his little brother in the hedge. Ben sat on top of him as I tickled him, the three of us laughing hysterically. Michael squirmed out from under us and made for the backyard, screaming as he ran, "Wussies!"

We headed around the other side of the house but we never made it. The wooden double doors to the basement were wide open. I stopped abruptly and Ben just about plowed me over. "Geez, warn me next time," he said with a green-tinted smile.

"Sorry! I told you I was a fast runner. Guess I forgot to tell you I was a fast stopper!"

We both peered down the cement steps. It looked pretty dark at the bottom, and I could smell the mustiness.

♂ Each step was like descending further into a liquid cooled bath. The air temperature changed, so by the time we had gone halfway, we both shivered. The door at the bottom had at one time been painted white. The white was peeling away, and the bottom edge was gone. The whole door looked like a set of ancient teeth, rotted with age. I reached out to the latch. A spark jumped from the hasp into my fingers. I quickly pulled back with a small squeak. "Sorry, I guess I was charged up or something." I reached forward once more, and this time, I didn't receive a shock. I pulled the hasp to the side and shoved hard. At first the door wouldn't budge, like there was something on the other side pushing back. When Sarah pushed as well, the door flew open and banged against the stone wall of the house foundation. The noise echoed throughout the tomb-like basement.

"Sarah, maybe I should go get a flashlight."

I headed to the stairs when Sarah grabbed onto my arm. "Don't go," she whispered.

Her grip was strong. She was staring past me into the darkest part of the basement. A soft glow was coming from the back wall. I knew from earlier, there were no windows in the back, just the old coal storage room.

"Sarah, are you okay?"

Not taking her eyes off the glow, she walked forward into the darkness. "Shhhhh, listen. Do you hear that?"

I was beginning to hear what sounded like an old music box, when Sarah grabbed my hand and ran back towards the stairs. The door to the basement was drifting closed. It looked like it was picking up speed and going to shut us in. We both reached out for the handle at the same time and struggled to pull it back open. With more effort than should have been needed, we slipped through. The door slammed shut and the hasp slipped into place. Hand in hand, we ran up the stairs and out into the sunlight, stopping only when we were at the back of the property.

Sarah let go of my hand. "Don't go back down there alone. Promise me Ben!" I had never seen her this serious.

"Okay, Sarah, I promise." Promising was easy, I had no desire to go back. Sarah was still pale.

"What did you see, Sarah?"

For a few minutes, she said nothing. She just stared at the back of the house.

"I have to go home."

She walked to the path that led through the old train yard. "When you get your chores done, come by my house," she said over her shoulder.

Chapter 12
Basement Ben

♀ Pushing my way through the tall weeds, I picked up my pace as I got closer to the train yard. Past the old coal car, I sprinted down the road to my house. The faster I ran, the more the tears burned my eyes. I hadn't wanted to cry in front of Ben, and I had to get as far away from the basement as possible. When I reached the mailbox at the foot of my driveway, I wiped my face with the bottom of my shirt. My heart was still racing, but not from the running. Was it possible for a thirteen-year-old to have a heart attack? Overwhelmed, I sat on the edge of the driveway and sobbed into my hands. My crying stuttered as I tried to calm myself.

"Why me?"

After ten minutes, I was done. Staring blankly at the wildflowers growing beneath the mailbox post, I sighed. How could I tell Ben what I saw? I finally make a friend and now I was going to scare him away. I needed to figure out how to tell Ben.

"Oh, by the way, I'm a freak of nature! Wanna hang out?" No, that wouldn't work. I had told him I saw ghosts all the time, but it was only a small part of it. How do I tell him I saw *his* ghost, as if he were dead and haunting his own basement?

♂ Rooted to that spot. I watched Sarah disappear into the distance. I could swear she was crying.

Okay, list. Where was the chore list? I soon found it in my front pocket. Garage, check. Okay, mow the front and back lawn.

"Check oil level before mowing the lawn," I read out loud. "Gas can is in the tool shed." It was going to take me the entire day to mow this mess. I dragged the old lawn mower out of the tool shed and onto the driveway in front of the garage so I could check the oil. The fuel level was low. "Damn! I forgot the gas back in the tool shed."

Turning, I took one step and fell flat on my face. I had tripped over the gas can. Wait a minute! That was not here before; I hadn't brought it with me. "Michael!" I waited for a few minutes and yelled louder. "*Michael*!"

He came running around the front of the house to the garage.

"Whaaat?" His face was covered in peanut butter and jelly, reminding me I had not had lunch.

"Did you put the can there?" I asked. He shook his head and took another bite of PB&J sandwich.

"Are you sure?"

I picked it up. The five-gallon gas container was full and I was having a hard time lifting it. He nodded his head and ran back into the house. This was getting weird.

"Ben, are you going to have some lunch?" Mom called.

Standing, I wiped my hands on the rag just inside the garage door. "Yes, Mom!" I would get to this right after lunch.

"Don't slam the door." I heard as I opened the screen door. "And take off your shoes. I just swept the kitchen floor. I don't want you tracking dirt across it."

Rolling my eyes, I walked backwards, looking for a place to hide the dirt I had already brought in with me and decided under the throw rug was the best place. After taking off my dirty shoes, I proceeded into the kitchen.

Sitting at the table were my Mom, Michael, and some old man I had not seen before.

"Son, I want you to meet Mr. Wilkerson."

I reached out to shake his hand. He only looked at it.

"Mr. Wilkerson used to take care of the lawn here for the last owner," Mom said cheerfully.

Mr. Wilkerson was pretty old looking, with wild hair that stuck up in odd places on his head. His eyes had deep wrinkles around them. The frown he wore seemed to be the only emotion his face was capable of.

"Mr. Wilkerson came to tell me about the old train yard out back."

The old man fixed me with a stare that could wilt flowers.

"I don't want you to go out there, young man," he grumbled. "You and your friends stay out of there. It ain't safe."

He stood. He was as tall as I expected and skinny. He wore an old pair of overalls with a long sleeve flannel shirt and dark brown, leather, work boots. I was about to remark he should have taken his boots off, but I decided I didn't want to see what was in them. As he reached the door, he looked back at me and did something that scared me more than the basement had. He smiled. There was nothing friendly about that smile.

"You remember what I said, Boy. Stay out of the train yard," he repeated even louder as he slammed the back door and went on his way.

"Mom, that guy gives me the creeps. Why did you let him in the house?"

Placing her hands on her hips, she looked sternly at me.

"That is not a nice thing to say about the poor old gentleman. If he was still here, I would make you apologize to him."

I took a bite of my sandwich and said, "Eeeastheepy ole aann!"

Putting down the dishes she was cleaning, she turned around and glared at me. "Benjamin, you do not talk with your mouth full!"

I took a large swallow of milk and put my glass down a little harder than I should. "Sorry."

"What are you sorry for?" She prompted.

"I am sorry for saying he was a creepy old man and for talking with my mouth full."

My mom had learned a new form of discipline from one of her family books. It was called benching. It wasn't enough you had to say you were sorry, but you had to know why you were sorry. I would have rather had my butt paddled.

Two weeks ago, before our move, I had gotten into trouble for letting my little brother mess with Mom's new Avon make-up kit. I had to sit on the edge of the bathtub and think about what I had done wrong, why I did it, and what I was going to do to make sure it didn't happen again. First of all, I didn't do anything wrong. It was Michael! I must have sat in the bathroom three hours, before I finally told her I was sorry. I guess, watching my stupid little brother put make-up on his stuffed animals, was wrong. I should have stopped him from being stupid, and the next time I saw him being stupid, I was going to hit him. What I said was, "I am sorry, Mom. I will watch my little brother closer and make sure he stays out of trouble."

Once lunch was over and we had cleaned off the table, I went back to my chores. It was shaded in the front yard, so I would start with that first. I was just ready to pull the rope, when I remember my dad saying, "Walk the lawn first, to make sure you don't run over something that will become a missile and kill or maim someone." I walked the overgrown jungle of a lawn. As I rounded the rose bush, I noticed something gold and shiny to the right of it. I bent to pick it up. It was the cameo I had given Sarah the night before.

How had this gotten here? Sarah hadn't been by the roses. I looked up and down the road to see if by chance she had come back. But I didn't see her.

I put the cameo in my pocket and made my first cut of the foot-high grass. I raked the grass and made the second cut. If nothing else, I had learned to cut lawns like a pro. I had just finished, when Dad pulled into the driveway.

"Did you get the list done?" he asked as he got out of the car.

"Yes, Dad."

I put the mower away and went into the kitchen.

"Mom, I got my chores done. Can I go to Sarah's house?" I asked.

My mom smiled. "Sure, just come home in time for supper. Supper will be a little bit late. The stove isn't working."

From the living room, I could hear my dad. "For crying out loud, what is wrong with the stove?"

Chapter 13
Silent Sidekick

♀ I picked myself up and dragged my feet toward the house. Pushing my hands into my pockets, I realized something was missing. The cameo. In a panic, I retraced my steps to the end of the driveway. Getting on my hands and knees, I searched in the grass. "It has to be here. It has to be here." I mumbled. I had it when I ran through the train yard. I knew that for sure. I felt a stabbing pain in my leg right before I passed the old coal car.

Just when I was about to head back, I heard someone call my name. "Tarah! You dweeb! You not my friend no more?" Nate lived across the street from me. He was the oldest of six children, all of whom were named after famous places his parents visited on their New York City honeymoon. Nathan, the only boy, was named after <u>Nathan's Famous Hot Dogs</u>. His sisters were named <u>Tiffany, Liberty, Macy, Madison</u> and <u>Ellis</u>.

Nate was deaf. He wore a hearing aid with a battery pack, which hung from a knitted sack around his neck. He could talk good but relied on reading lips for the most part. I signed the symbols for "How are you?" as I dusted myself off.

He shrugged, "Where you been?"

"Just been busy with stuff lately, sorry I haven't been by."

"You're getting 'tuck up on me."

"No, just have a lot of chores," I lied.

I found it hard to tell the truth when it meant hurting someone's feelings. Like when Mom asked me how her hair looked. She used to have long beautiful hair that went all the way down to her butt. She would lie on the couch and throw her hair over the end like Rapunzel. I would sit there forever and brush it. She cut it short six months ago. Ever since, then I have to lie when she asks how it looks. I hate it short!

I stood at the end of the drive for another five minutes, talking to Nate, until he spotted his dad pulling in their driveway.

"Catch you later!" he yelled as he ran across the street.

I walked back to the house and decided to rest in the hammock for a bit. Seeing ghosts and crying took a lot out of me. I must have fallen asleep.

♂ Just for good measure, I shook the hammock one more time.

"Hey you, are you going to be okay?" I asked, concerned.

With a little stretch and a yawn, Sarah just looked at me.

"Uh huh, I guess I needed a nap."

Sitting, she rubbed the sleep out of her eyes and shivered like she was cold, despite the late afternoon heat. She looked exhausted.

"I got the list done, so I thought I would come and see if you were okay."

Sarah slowly got off the hammock and walked to the front porch of her house.

"Sarah, you're making me a little nervous. Are you okay?"
She sat on the steps and looked at her hands.

"Ben, I'm not sure how I feel at the moment. Something is not right in your basement. I know it isn't safe for you to be there."

I sat beside her and reached out to grab her hand, but she pulled away.

"Hey, it's me, the new kid, remember?" I was a little hurt, and I didn't understand the sudden mood changes.

"Sarah, listen, if I did anything or said anything wrong, I'm sorry."

I stood, when her hand reached out and grabbed my arm. I almost pulled back. Her hand was ice cold. "Don't go," she pleaded.

I sat again but she still didn't say anything. I figured it must have been something terrible, or my new friend would have found the words to tell me what was wrong. I was about to ask again, when she broke the silence.

"Ben, I lost the cameo. I had it with me when we were in the back yard, and I felt it while I was walking in the train yard, but I don't know where it is."

I reached into my pocket. "You mean this?" I said as I handed it to her. "I found this in the front yard by the old rose bush."
I tilted my head, trying to see her face. She was crying.

"Hey, it is okay. I found it. It is not worth crying about. See, it's right here." I put it into her hand. "Now, are you going to tell me what is going, on or should I play twenty questions?"

She sat and continued to stare at me. I reached over and wiped one single tear that had run down her face.

"Okay, you asked for it. Is it larger than a cat – no, wait, a bread box, or a cat in a bread box?"
Sarah smiled.

A little more confident, I continued. "Is it red or green? Is it a frog in a blender?"

Her eyes got big and round. "That is so gross," she said, but she laughed anyway.

I smiled at her. "I got you to laugh, and you can't feel so bad if you can still laugh."

I decided to change the subject.

I launched into the whole meeting with Mr. Wilkerson, how creepy he was, and how my mom wanted me to apologize for calling the old guy creepy.

At that part of the story, Sarah spoke up.

"Mr. Wilkerson would take it as a compliment to be called creepy. None of the kids in the neighborhood like him." She was tracing the lines on the pin.

"Did he really mow our grass?"

Sarah had stopped tracing the cameo and was pushing on the face of it. "Yeah, I guess. I don't remember seeing him much. We didn't go that way, if we could help it."

I was ready to ask her another question about Mr. Wilkerson, when I heard a faint click. The cameo face opened, to reveal a compartment. Sarah reached inside and withdrew a carefully folded piece of paper. She placed the cameo on the steps beside her and unfolded it. I slid over closer to get a better look. It was a letter. I was reading the first line, when Sarah's little sister flew out the front door.

"There you are! Mom has been looking for you."

She glanced at me.

"Oh, hi," she said as she raced down the steps and around the side of the house.

I turned around to look at the letter again, but Sarah had folded it and put it into her pocket. "I have to talk to my mom. I will be right back." Sarah walked into the house. I picked up the cameo and looked inside. Scratched on the back, was a series of letters and numbers. "E.V.H. 12S, 16E, 4N"

Chapter 14
Wistful Warning

♀ Mom was sitting in the easy chair with the <u>hair dryer</u> on her head. She was going out tonight with dad for their anniversary. As soon as the pink foam rollers went into her hair and the blue plastic case came out, I knew I would get roped into babysitting my sister. The dryer looked like a regular shower cap, attached to a long hose. The snake-like ribbed hose, stretched to a small motor inside a plastic case. Once the cap was in place and the switch was turned on, the cap blew up and resembled a mushroom. Dad always said, "Look out! Mom is headed for Mars, keep your distance."

"What did you want, Mom?" I screamed.

She didn't look up from her magazine and continued to wiggle her slippered feet atop the footstool.

"Maaaaa!" I screamed again.

She jumped, and noticed I was standing in the doorway. "Oh, Honey, sorry, I didn't hear you!" she yelled. She leaned and turned off the hair dryer. "Sarah, I just wanted to tell you I met Ben's mom at the grocery store today," she said with a smile. "I told her what a lovely boy he was and he was welcome at our house anytime."

I smiled.

"She also offered for you and Steph to come over to their house tonight, so you won't be home alone. Wasn't that nice?" she remarked while raising her eyebrows.

I commented on how I didn't need a babysitter, when she held her hand up, palm facing me, to stop me.

"Young lady, I did not ask for your approval. I am the parent. Keep your opinion to yourself."

I sighed and said, "Okay, Mom, whatever."

Walking toward her chair, I decided to ask her a question.

"Mom, if you knew someone might be in trouble, would you tell them?"

She looked me in the eye and wrinkled her nose. "I guess it depends on what kind of trouble."

"Life or death trouble!"

Her expression became serious. She was thinking. After fifteen seconds, she responded. "If something happened to this 'someone' and you didn't warn them ahead of time, would you feel bad?"

"Gosh, if anything ever happened to Ben, I would never forgive myself!" I blurted out. Realizing I gave the name away, I put my hand over my mouth.

She stood. "Why is Ben in trouble, honey?"

I lied. "Oh...well...um...it's just I heard some boys down the street talking. They said they were going to beat up the new boy."

Hands on her hips, she looked angry. "Sarah Ann, don't lie to me. You know what happens when you lie."

I cried. She walked to my side and guided me to the couch where we sat together. When she wrapped her arms around me, I broke down and told her what I had seen in the basement.

She tried not to grin as she patted me on the head. "Sweetie, you have such an active imagination. I'm sure there's a logical explanation for this. I bet you saw Ben's reflection in an old mirror."

I forced a smile. Well, I tried. I quickly hugged her, stood, and ran towards the back door. "Thanks, Mom. I'm better now," I lied again. Boy, was I going to H-E-double hockey sticks for this!

"I'm glad I could help." she called after me as I ran out the back door.

Ben was sitting in the hammock, slowly rocking it back and forth. I jumped from the top step and raced to sit beside him. "You never showed me what the letter said." he complained.
I pulled the letter from my pocket and handed it to him.

"Ben, you're my first best friend, and I don't want anything to ever happen to you, so I have to tell you. You're in danger!"

♂ "Does the letter have something to do with me?" My hands shook as I opened the fragile paper.

"No, that's not it," Sarah replied. "I haven't even read it yet. It has to do with what I saw in the basement."
I looked straight at Sarah. "What did you see?"

She looked at the ground, then at her hands.

"Follow me."

I followed her over to the old oak where she sat with her back to the tree. "I only told you a little about what makes me different."

She patted the ground beside her. I plopped down across from her Indian style. I have always had a hard time talking with someone if they were sitting next to me. I have to look them in the eyes. My grandma used to tell me, people say as much with their eyes as they do with their mouth.

Sarah looked at the ground. "Sometimes I see ghosts of people I know." She rubbed her hands the way adults do when talking about something unpleasant. "Usually, they are already dead. When we were in the basement, I saw you as a ghost."

I was not sure what to say. I kept waiting to hear "Gotcha!"

When I looked into Sarah's eyes, I could see she meant every word.

I rested my elbows on my knees and my chin on my hands. I had a hundred questions running through my mind, but not enough words to give each question a voice. What did my basement have to do with my ghost? What did the picture of the girl and her initials have to do with my basement? All these questions had no answers.

I looked back at Sarah. "We're going back into the basement tonight. You are going to have to sneak out and meet me in the back yard.

"I don't have to sneak out tonight because my parents are going out for their anniversary. Your mom has volunteered to watch me and my little sister."

My jaw dropped. My mom did that? That meant my mom was out and about in town today. Oh man, I hope she didn't have her pocket photo album with her. I hated that photo album. "Here is Ben sitting outside without a diaper, taking a bath in the sink and running outside without any clothes on. It was a phase I was going through. I prayed silently my mother was not going to bring out the baby books tonight.

Sarah was staring at me funny. "You look like you swallowed a bug or something," she said.

Wishing that was the only thing wrong, I replied, "I have to warn you, my mom is not normal. She has picture books I wish would have been lost in the move." I clenched my hands. "I wouldn't blame you if you don't want to be friends any more after tonight.

Chapter 15
Love Letter

♀ Under normal circumstances, finding the letter inside the cameo would have excited me to the point of extreme impatience. Yet, at the time of discovery, I was more worried about my best friend's safety. Now that I told Ben what weighed so heavily on my mind, I was ready to read it.

Ben carefully unfolded the yellowed piece of plain paper. The edges were tinged a dark brown. It looked as if it had been opened a hundred times. The creases were worn and see-through in places. He set the letter on his lap as I leaned in. Penned in black ink, each word flowed into the next, the bottoms of the y's and g's looped fancily around the words below them. The writing was ornate. It was not a long letter, just a few sentences.
Ben read aloud.

"My Dearest Elizabeth, I cannot bear to see you so unhappy. Please consider running away with me tonight. Meet me at the tracks at 10 p.m. If you do not come, I will know your love for me was never true. All my love, Henry."
Ben looked at me with disgust. "A stupid love letter."

"It's beautiful," I said thoughtfully.

Ben proceeded to stick his finger down his throat. I smacked him in the arm and pinched him.

"Hey, what's with the pinching anyway?"

Looking at his one arm, I noticed a bruise turning slightly green from the first time I pinched him.

"Sorry. You're such a...such a...*boy!*"

While folding the letter back into its neat little square, Ben stuck his tongue out at me, and laughed.

"Well, that wasn't as exciting as I imagined it would be," he said.

I disagreed. "We know the owner of the cameo's name. It was Elizabeth."

When returning the letter to the inside of the cameo, Ben pointed out the engraving.

"Looks like it might be some type of coordinates. S for south, E for east… Maybe the numbers are measurements in feet," he beamed.

"Maybe it's a secret code." I guessed.

I loved codes. My grandma had bought me the first two books from the <u>Nancy Drew Series</u>. *The Secret of the Old Clock* was my absolute favorite. Ben nodded. There he went again. Looking deep into my eyes and making me squirm. Why did he do that? I looked away to avoid his stare.

"Sarah, do you think I'm going to die?"

I looked back at him and said with pure conviction. *"Over my dead body!"*

♂ A smile slowly crept across my face. With a friend like this, I felt sorry for anyone trying to mess with me. I was ready to ask her what board games she liked to play, when I remembered I had a messy room back at home.

"Uh, Sarah, um, I, uh, got to go." I tried hard not to make eye contact so I didn't have to explain why I had to leave. "Promised my mom I would do something before supper tonight and, well, if I don't do it, I will get into trouble." I was telling a lie, but I wasn't. Mom had told me to tidy things yesterday and I forgot. "Sarah, I have to go home and clean my room. If I don't do it before you get there tonight, you're going to call me a slob." I stood.

"Hey, slob."

I turned and got hit in the head with a wad of grass.

Sarah smiled at me, standing with one hand on her hip. "What are you going to do about it?"

I bent to pick up my own hand full of grass and ran after her.

I hadn't gone more than a few feet when it became apparent she was much faster than me.

"See ya later," I yelled as I headed for home.

Instead of going down the street, I took the short cut through the train yard. It was getting dark and I had just passed an old boxcar. A skeletal thin hand shot out from the shadows and grabbed the front of my shirt. "I told you to stay out of the train yard, Boy."

I struggled to free myself from Mr. Wilkerson's grip but I couldn't budge his fingers.

"Let me go!" My voice came out more as a squeak than as a command.

"You're just like the rest of them brats in this neighborhood, always cutting through here, painting their names on the ole box cars." He coughed and spit out a big green wad of phlegm.

"Mr. Wilkerson, I just moved here. I didn't paint anything on the boxcars. I don't even know what you are talking about."

Pulling me close to his face, I caught a whiff of his breath. He had been drinking. "I'm sorry, please let me go. I won't do it again." I said.

"You will be sorry, son; you and your whole family will be before long. He looked at me hard. "The last family that lived there was sorry." He chuckled. It was not a friendly sound. It was one a person makes when they run over something in the road and you know they enjoyed it. "Yes sir," he continued, "they only stayed in the house for two years before she drove them out." At the mention of a she, I stopped struggling.

"What do you mean, *she*?" I asked.

Looking me straight in the eyes, he said, "She is a wild one, she is. She will make you see things and hear things."
He let me go but I didn't run away. "I don't understand."

"They say old man Wilkerson is gone off his rocker, but I know the truth," he grumbled, coughed, and spit once again. "I have seen her at night prowling the train yard." Old Man Wilkerson leaned back against the old boxcar and lowered himself to the ground.

"I don't understand. Who is she?" I asked again.

Wilkerson just waved me away, telling me once again to stay out of the damn train yard.

Chapter 16
Babysitting Bummer

♀ Mom's face was three inches away from her mirror. Her mouth opened like a baby bird waiting for a worm, she applied her mascara. I loved watching her put her make-up on, even though I didn't think she needed it.

She noticed me watching her up against the bathroom doorframe and said, "Are you going to change your clothes and clean up a bit?"

I glanced at my clothes. I was a mess.

"Maybe leave your hair down tonight," she said as she yanked out the elastic band and brushed my tangled red hair.

"Mom, am I pretty?"

"Oh, Sarah, you were born pretty," she replied with a soft look in her eyes.

We smiled at each other as we looked into the mirror.

"I better change my clothes. I don't have much time." I headed toward the hall. "You want me to help Steph pick something out to wear?"

"Good Luck! You know how your sister is about style."

Mom was right. Stephanie was high maintenance for a nine-year-old. Had to have her clothes a certain way and could spend hours in front of the mirror. If anything, I should be asking *her* for wardrobe help.

Once in my room, I noticed how messy it was. All the talk about Ben cleaning his room, made me realize how I'd been neglecting mine. I opened my closet door to find only two shirts hanging inside. I debated between the one with a bow and the one without the bow. I chose the bow. As I pulled my shirt over my head, Dad hollered up the stairs. "Sarah! Steph! Better get walking before it gets dark!"

In unison, my sister and I yelled back, "Okay, Dad!"

Mom came into the room, kissed me on the forehead, and reminded me to wash my face. I changed my socks and headed back to the bathroom. After washing, I noticed the make-up drawer had been left open. Instead of closing it, I pulled it all the way out and sat it on the edge of the sink. "Lip gloss, blush, and mascara." I mumbled to myself.

Carefully, I applied each one making sure not to overdo it. Mom hated it when women put so much make-up on, because they looked like clowns. The end result wasn't too bad. I admired my reflection as I quickly brushed my hair one more time. Mom and Dad had already left by the time I got downstairs. My sister was waiting on the back stoop. "Ooooo, you're wearing Mom's make-up! You're going to be in trouuuble!" she teased me.

"Shut up. Steph! It's just a little bit." I grabbed her hand, and we quickly set off for Ben's house.

We entered the train yard and spotted Mr. Wilkerson wandering inside the gate. "Eeewww, there's that weirdo guy again." she said.

I stopped and looked at her with concern. "What do you mean *again*?"

She proceeded to tell me she had seen him stumbling past our house before, in the direction of the train yard. One day, she had followed him to a rusty old caboose near the water tower. "It looked like he lived there."

I told her to never follow him again and to stay away from the train yard. "Just be careful," I whispered.

It was getting dark, and Mr. Wilkerson had disappeared, so we decided to race to Ben's house. "Last one there is a rotten egg!" Steph screamed.

We took off sprinting and I made it to Ben's back door in record time. Steph was huffing and puffing behind me, running as fast as her short legs could take her. "Wait up!" she pleaded.
I knocked on the door just as she reached the bottom step.

"They're here!" Michael yelled as he ran to the door. Without even pausing, he opened the screen door, grabbed my sister's hand, and dragged her into the front room. I didn't even get a chance to say hello. Ben's mom walked around the corner from the kitchen.

"Hi, Sarah, Ben is in his room. You can go get him. It's the second door on the left. Just make sure you both come right back. We have rules about that."
I bolted up the stairs and approached the bedroom door.

♂ I hadn't even lived here a full week and I already had things under my bed I couldn't identify. I spotted a small rock the size of a golf ball near the middle. It looked like the same type of stone the house was made of. I was just reaching it when I heard Sarah's voice. "Hello, anyone home?"

Grabbing the rock, I slid back out from under the bed. "Hi." I brushed the dust bunnies off my shirt. Looking at the rock I held in my hand, I noticed it had part of a letter engraved in it.

"What is that?" Sarah asked.

"Just something I found under my bed. I have no idea how it got there." The stone fell from my hand and hit the floor with a resounding thud. Sarah took a step back as I bent over to pick it up. The stone was warm to my touch, as if it had spent the day out in the sunshine. I set it on my dresser and looked back at Sarah. "Well, this is my room." I said with a sweep of my arm.

I wouldn't say I was a slob, but my room back in Utah reflected me. I liked to build plastic models and arrange them as if they were in real life. I built jet fighters and hung them from the ceiling as if they were in dogfights. The best and biggest model I had ever built, the USS Constitution, or <u>Old Iron Sides</u>, sat on my dresser. I hadn't lived here long enough to decorate my new room yet. The desk by the window was going to be my sanctuary. There, I would dream and invent. At the moment, I had the guts of an old radio spread over it. My dad had found it in our garage and thought I might want to fix it. I loved to fix old things.

"My dad has one just like this in his barn," Sarah said.

Most of the time, these old radios only needed to be cleaned and given some TLC to get working again, but I had been having problems with this one. I was hoping my dad would have some time to help me figure out why it didn't work.

"Why don't you bring it over to my dad?" Sarah suggested as if she could read my mind. "He can help you fix it."

"I would like that. I just don't know why it isn't getting any power. I did everything I normally do, but it just doesn't want to work."

My room was filled with boxes containing the normal array of scary books, science fiction, and my prize collection of <u>National Geographic</u> magazines that went back to 1970. Most kids had comic books, but I liked to read about faraway places and pyramids.

"Ben and Sarah!" My mom called from downstairs. "What is taking so long? Ben, you know the rules."

As we walked past the dresser, the rock fell to the floor and almost hit my foot. Weird, I had left it pretty far away from the edge. I picked it up and carried it with me out into the hallway.

Michael and Steph were playing with Legos on the floor of the living room. Mike was busy building a large structure and Steph was playing with the little Lego people. I almost laughed, when I saw they were playing house.

"Here is your person. You can be the daddy," Steph said to Mike.

Before I could say anything, Sarah punched me in the arm. "Don't stir up that bees' nest. They are playing nicely, and they're not in our way."

We walked into the kitchen, to where the large china hutch stood against the far wall. Although it was called a china hutch or cabinet, I didn't remember it ever holding much china. The top part with the glass display cabinet had little trinkets and souvenirs from different vacations my family had taken over the years. The cabinets underneath held our games.

Opening the cabinet doors, I absent mindedly put the rock on the top shelf. "Do you like to play board games? We have a few that are kind of fun." I rattled off a list of games we had: Sorry, Aggravation, Uno, Monopoly, and Life. "I'm not allowed to play Monopoly for the next month, so that one is off the list."
Sarah looked at me quizzically. "How come?"

"I don't want to talk about it." I rubbed the back of my neck.

My mother chimed in from the other part of the kitchen where she was washing the dishes from dinner. "Sarah dear, my son is not a good sport when it comes to playing Monopoly. He either has to win or he pouts."

Rolling my eyes, I looked in her direction. Sarah picked up the pack of Uno cards and walked back to the table near the kitchen

counter. "Are you any good at Uno?"
I smiled back; I could crush anyone at Uno.

One hour later, I never wanted to play Uno again. In fact, I was sure Sarah was cheating. How did anyone get the "draw four" and "draw two" cards so often? I finally admitted defeat and told Sarah about my little run-in with Mr. Wilkerson in the rail yard.

"What did Mr. Wilkerson mean when he said *she*?" Sarah was just as puzzled as I was. "We need to go to the library and find out who owned this house before the Jespersons."
We had just put away the cards, when my mom called out.

"Ben, can you go to the basement and get the ice cream out of the freezer?"
Sarah looked up sharply, and my blood ran cold.

"Mom, I don't want any ice cream," I said as if this little act of self-denial would keep me from going downstairs. From the living room, we heard the thundering feet of two kids and their screams for ice cream.

"Ben, please go get the ice cream for our guests," Mom repeated.

Getting up from the table, I looked over at Sarah who was also getting up. "Yes, mother." Together, we headed to the hallway door to the basement.

Chapter 17
Arctic Apparition

♀ Ben flipped the switch at the top of the basement stairs. I saw wooden steps painted grey with black rubber treads. The basement was pretty bright compared with the way it had looked earlier.

"My dad replaced every single light bulb this evening," Ben informed me.

He led the way with confidence. I reached for his hand half way and he seemed ready for it. He turned and smiled a hesitant smile, trying to make me feel better. It didn't fool me, though. I knew he was scared. At the bottom of the staircase, we surveyed the area. It looked like Ben's dad had done more than change light bulbs. The floor was swept, and the cobwebs were gone.

"Boy, it doesn't look scary anymore," I said hopefully.

Ben nodded as he led me to the freezer on the back wall. The white upright freezer sat near the washer and dryer with a large cement sink in between. Someone had stuck wooden shims under the front corner of the freezer to keep it level. The cement floor was uneven. I looked around to see if there were any spots in the floor where newer cement might have been placed. But the entire floor looked ancient. Maybe Mr. Jesperson didn't bury his wife in the basement. I didn't see any old mirrors anywhere, either.

Ben opened the freezer door, pulled out a tub of vanilla ice cream, and tucked it under his arm. "We better make it quick. If we explore too much the ice cream will melt, and Dad will think he has to fix the freezer, too."

I giggled as we turned toward the stairs. Ben walked one step before tripping and falling flat on his face. The ice cream flew from under his arm, across the floor, stopping short of a brick wall to the left. I looked at him with concern.

"You all right?"

I offered my hand to help him.

He pulled himself up, rubbing his scuffed chin. "Yeah, I'm okay. What did I trip on?"

Turning, we saw a gasoline can. I walked over to the can to lift it, but it was heavy.

Ben seemed to be processing what had just happened. "That was not there when we came down, and I left it in the garage this afternoon."

As I bent to pick up the ice cream tub, I leaned on the brick wall for support. "Wow! This wall is warm."

Ben shuffled his feet as he walked over to the wall. Pressing both hands on the bricks, he paused, listening. "Do you hear that?"

I could hear what seemed to be faint music. It sounded like it was on the other side. The brick was entirely different than the original stone used in the basement, which made it look like it was added at a later time. Yet, there was no apparent door or access point I could see from where I was. Ben walked around the corner as he pressed his ear against the wall methodically, every few feet. "No door over here," I heard Ben yell.

The music stopped. Ben came back around the corner and picked up the ice cream.

"There has to be a way in," he said. "We will have to come back later. Right now, the ice cream is melting."

He headed for the stairs and got half way there, before I realized my feet were not moving. I was frozen.

"Ben!" I said urgently.

As he turned to face me, the light bulbs over our heads began to go out one by one. They dimmed and went dark. In a matter of five seconds, all the bulbs were blown out, and we stood in complete darkness. Before I could say a word, a noise toward the back of the room startled me. The freezer door flew open with such force, the frozen vegetables inside catapulted across the floor. The light in the freezer shone brightly, as condensation vapor billowed out.

Ben's face was barely visible across the room, lit up with a yellowish cast. The cloud of vapor cascaded to the floor but it did not disperse. It accumulated in a cloud a few feet in front of the freezer and as we watched in terror, the cloud took shape. Slowly, the whitish translucent figure of a woman emerged. There were no facial features, only the basic outline of her body. My legs crumpled beneath me, and I fell to the floor. Clouds formed as each breath escaped my mouth. The figure moved toward me, floating inches above the basement floor. I heard Ben yell, "Run Sarah, run!"

But I could not move. What appeared to be an arm, protruded from the misty shape and pointed to the brick wall. As quickly as it appeared, the cloud was gone. When the light in the freezer went out, I sighed loudly. Once again, we were in total darkness.

"Are you okay, Sarah?"
I crawled in the direction of his voice.

"No! What do you think?" I said sassily. The floor was cold, and I could tell even though it had been swept today, I was getting dirty by crawling around on it. I knew I was close when I heard Ben say, "There you are. Boy, your hand is cold. "
I could hear him walking up the stairs.

"Wait! What about me?" I yelled.

Kicking open the door at the top of the stairs, Ben spun around and looked down the staircase. His outstretched hand was empty.

♂ From the dimly lit hallway, I could just make her out, crawling toward the stairs on her hands and knees. I made up my mind I was going to go back down, when the basement door slammed shut, cutting me off. I reached for the handle. It felt like I had grabbed a chunk of dry ice. I let go, wrapped my hand in my shirttail, and tried again. It wouldn't budge. The handle was stuck fast despite my pounding.

"Mom, Dad!" I yelled, "The door is jammed, and Sarah is stuck in the basement!"

I ran into the kitchen where Mom and Dad were sitting at the table, sorting through silverware. "Mom, Dad, hurry! Sarah is in the basement and I can't get her out!"

Still they sat, making piles of forks and spoons, as if I wasn't even there. I raced into the living room where Steph and Michael were still playing with their Legos.

"Help Me!" I screamed.
They didn't even acknowledge I was there.

I raced back through the kitchen, out the back door, and around to the right of the house to the stairs leading to the basement. I jumped down to the bottom. If I didn't get to Sarah, she would be lost. I hit the door with everything my thirteen-year-old body could muster. One hundred twenty pounds of sheer determination and fear crashed into it, tearing the hinges away from the rotting wood. For a brief moment, I was airborne, riding it until it slid to a stop just a few feet away from the stairs where I last saw her.

"Sarah, where are you?"

A faint cry in the dark led me to a small lump in the corner. I crawled to her side. "Are you okay?"
She whispered, "Yes."

I was standing, when the upstairs door to the basement opened and I heard my mom. "What is taking you guys so long to get ice cream?"

I was just getting ready to tell her the lights didn't work, when I heard the sound of a switch. Miraculously, the lights came on.
"Why didn't you turn the lights on?" my mom asked.

"I did, Mom. We were just getting ready to come upstairs when they all went off."

I was going to tell her what had happened, when Sarah gripped my hand and shook her head no.

"Make sure you shut the freezer door." Mom disappeared from the top of the steps.

"Why didn't you want me to say anything?"

Sarah only looked back towards the cellar door. I followed her gaze.

Sarah whispered, "I heard you crash through the door Ben."

The door I had crashed through was hanging back on the hinges just as it always had. We both stared at it for a moment in silence. The freezer door was closed and no frozen food was in sight.

Sarah and I walked together up the stairs. At the top, I reached out and flipped the switch several times. The lights in the basement went on and off without any problems. I pulled the basement door closed and went to the kitchen to give Mom the container.

"Would you like some ice cream, dear?" she asked Sarah.

"No thank you, ma'am."

Sarah didn't stop in the kitchen. I followed her back down the hallway. As she passed the door to the basement, she hugged the opposite wall. She continued out the front door to the porch steps.

For a moment, she just stood there. When she turned to look at me, she was crying.

"Sarah?"

She wiped the tears with the back of her hand.

"I was so scared when you went up the stairs. You were talking to no one and you acted like you were holding someone's hand." She shuddered. "When the door slammed, I couldn't see anything in the darkness. But I could hear things moving around me."

My hand lifted to the back of my neck and wiped off a cold sweat – a sure sign I was agitated. I told my part of the story, how the door handle went icy cold and no one heard my cries for help.

We sat on the top step of the porch, and Sarah leaned her head on my shoulder. "What is going on Ben? None of this makes sense."
"I don't know, Sarah, I don't know."
The fireflies were coming out, turning the front yard into a field of miniature shooting stars.

Chapter 18
Family Fluke

♀ The first ghost I ever saw was when I was six, right after my grandma died. We were at her funeral. My family was standing around the casket saying how good she looked, which I didn't understand. How could she look good when she was dead? It was when I saw Grandma standing by a pretty vase of flowers, I was confused. She had on her favorite dress, not the one she was wearing for her funeral, and she was smiling at me. She motioned for me to come closer, and of course I did. I was so excited she was still alive. She leaned and whispered to me,
"It's okay, Sarah. It is beautiful where I'm going."
Just as I was about to turn and yell for my mom, she disappeared.

Since that day, I have seen other ghosts. Usually, the sightings are quick, fleeting moments. Some just wave, smile, or give me a message to tell a person I've never met. I've never known who they were or the person they wanted to contact.

My dad figured out something was up when I wandered off, talking to imaginary friends. He was the only one in my family who knew about my curse. He recognized the signs. His grandmother had warned him, the first-born children in our family had this gift. She told him it was only temporary and would eventually disappear in my mid-teens. I've noticed my ability to hear the ghosts has slowly disappeared, as I get older. I honestly can't wait for the sightings to go away, too.

What happened to Ben and me in the basement was unlike any ghostly encounter I had ever had. I was not the only one to see things this time. Ben witnessed everything, too. It was also different because the ghost did not seem friendly. I felt a sense of evil.

As the air got chilly, I shivered. I lifted my head from Ben's shoulder. He looked worried. Reaching over, he took his finger and wiped under my left eye. His finger had a smeary black substance on it.

"Why are you crying black stuff?"

The mascara! I turned away in embarrassment.

"Oh, it's nothing – just make-up."

Ben stood and handed me a rag. "It's not much – just a rag I found in the garage. It's clean, I swear."

I took the rag and wiped under both eyes. Still standing on the top stair, Ben looked at me. "You shouldn't put stuff on your face. It covers up how pretty you are."

As I brushed the dirt from my clothes, I was careful not to look directly at him.

"Thanks, Ben."

It was the nicest thing a boy ever said to me.

When my parents came to pick Steph and me up after their night out, Ben's dad had his head in the stove. My dad offered to give him a hand. Our moms talked about recipes and how nice it was to go out once in a while. I overheard my Mom offering to return the favor and watch Ben and Michael some time.

At home in bed, I was still clutching Ben's rag which was comforting. Before I turned out the light, I opened it and spread it across the quilt on top of my bed. It wasn't a rag, but an embroidered handkerchief. Not frilly or feminine looking, it was just plain white, with two rows of stitching along the edges. Diagonal on one corner, were three letters in faint silver threads: H .W. E.

Could Elizabeth's Henry have owned this? Maybe he gave it to her when she was crying and she forgot to give it back. Why would she be crying? As I played with the fabric, I finally allowed myself to drift off to sleep.

The following morning, I was heading out the back door when my dad stopped me. "You okay, Kiddo?" He was sitting in the patio putting on his work boots.

"Yeah, Dad, I'm okay."

"Did you have fun last night?"

"Lots of fun. Hey, Dad, where in the library would I go to find out who owned Ben's house in the late 1800's?"

He stood, laughed, and shook his head. "What kind of ghost hunt are we on today?"

I looked around to make sure no one would overhear, which could be difficult with Steph in the family. "Just curious about a girl named Elizabeth," I whispered.

He suggested looking at old newspapers in the periodical section.

"If you see Mrs. Campbell at the library, she can direct you to the <u>microfiche machine.</u>"

"Thanks, Dad, you're the best!" I rose on to my toes and kissed his cheek.

The library was a brick two-story building that smelled of musty old pages and Lemon Pledge. It housed the best adventures you could find. The double doors were solid walnut with swirls of burl that took on different shapes every time I saw them, and they had polished brass handles shaped like eagles. Mrs. Campbell, the librarian, practically lived there. I swear she had a sleeping bag somewhere behind the counter. The more I thought of my fondness for the library, the faster I walked. I yawned, the lack of sleep catching up with me. Did Ben sleep last night? I hoped it was the one night he *didn't* sleep like the dead.

♂ During the night, I heard sounds in my closet. Once, I got up to see what was making the noise but saw only a nearly empty closet with a few clothes and boxes. I spent most of the night watching the time go by on the digital alarm clock, the red numbers slowly moving time forward as I puzzled over what happened in the basement. Did it happen? If not, why did I have a bruise on my shoulder from where I hit the door? When I finally did sleep, the dreams were just replays of the same stuff.

By 7:30 in the morning, I was done with dreaming and determined to find out what was going on. I found Dad in the kitchen. Dressed for work, he was drinking his orange juice and reading the newspaper. "Hey, Champ."

"Hi, Dad."

My dad could be like two different people at times. In the morning, he was a person you could talk to. At night when he got

home, he just wanted to be left alone.
"Dad, can I ask you a question?"

The corner of the paper went down as Dad peered at me with his glasses part way down his nose, a grin on his face.

"Is this about girls?"
At the mention of girls, I stammered.

"N-n-nooo!" Rolling my eyes, I continued. "What do you know about our house?"

Putting the paper on the table, he pushed his glasses up on to his face and got a faraway look. I thought I was going to have to repeat the question when he answered.

"Well, according to the bank, it was built in the mid-1800's. Sarah's dad told me the old place was used to throw wild parties back in the 1920's. They called it a <u>speakeasy</u>."

"What is a speakeasy?"
It sounded like a type of telephone.

"Was there something in particular you were looking for?"

I knew his tone of voice. It was the tone that let me know I was going to be asked the question.

"Have you done your homework yet?" Dad asked as I grinned.

I grinned not at what he said but because I knew he was going to say it. "Have you done your homework" has nothing to do with school. It means, "Have you studied out what you want to know first?" My dad was more than willing to help someone who had studied out the problem or question first.

"I guess I need to go to the library." I admitted.

He finished off his orange juice and got up from the table. "Good thinking, Son." He gave Mom the normal goodbye kiss. As he walked by me, he ruffled my hair. "See ya, champ."

The library wasn't too hard to find. It was a big two-story brick building right in the middle of town. As I pushed the doors opened, I couldn't help but question why they needed such heavy doors. I walked towards a lady sitting behind the front desk. Her appearance screamed "librarian." I had read horror stories about librarians like this. I'm sure she was a nice lady, but the way she stared at me was scary. I approached the desk as if I was approaching some pagan altar on which I was going to be sacrificed.

The librarian looked over the eyeglasses that were chained to her neck.

"Young man, are you lost?"

If I was a boy, and it was summertime, then I must have made a wrong turn and found myself in her library.

"No, ma'am," I said without so much as a crack in my voice. "I am looking for the microfiche readers to learn some history of a home I recently moved into."

She stood slowly, and for a brief moment, I saw images of flying monkeys coming to tear the straw from my scarecrow body. As she smiled, a magical transformation happened. She reached her hand across the counter. "My name is Mrs. Campbell, and you must be the young Mr. Whiting."

Grinning, I shook her hand. "Yes, Ma'am. My name is Ben."

She led me to the back of the library where the microfiche readers were and directed me to the large card catalog. She showed me how to look up different dates for property records and old newspaper articles. She instructed me to bring her the card for the ones I wanted to view, and she would get them for me.

I looked through the property listings by street. I soon found our house. It was designed and built in the late 1800's by Hans Brinkenhofner. The original owner was a man by the name of Jackson Hilliard. I figured this would be the best place to start, so I took the card to the front desk. As I approached, I recognized the red ponytail waiting to talk with Mrs. Campbell. I tapped Sarah on the shoulder. "Hey, why are you here?"

"I'm here to see the little fish machine."

I tried to not laugh out loud, but she was clearly not joking, which made it even funnier.

Chapter 19
Cryptic Clues

♀ Ben handed Mrs. Campbell three index cards. She looked over her glasses at me and smiled. "Well hello Miss McNally, are we renewing your book today?"
I shook my head and pointed to Ben. "No, I'm with him."

She gave me a look of approval and raised her eyebrows while looking at Ben. I knew what she meant but was hoping Ben didn't catch it. She knew my interests; I checked out a lot of mysteries and romances.

Mrs. Campbell went over to a large oak cabinet that took up the entire back wall. It looked to have a hundred drawers of different sizes. She opened one of the larger drawers and pulled out three translucent sheets the size of a notepad. "There you go, young man. Now, please be careful to hold these by the edges to minimize fingerprints."

Ben carefully took the sheets and led me to a room in the back of the library. The room was dimly lit, but I could see a row of what appeared to be televisions on a long counter. Alone in the room, we pulled two chairs up to one of the machines. Ben pulled out a pad of paper and a pen from his back pocket. It looked like he had a few pages of notes already.

"Gosh, what time did you get here? Looks like you've been here for hours."

Focused on what he was doing, Ben pulled a tray out from underneath the television screen and lifted a piece of glass. He laid the first clear sheet on the tray and put the glass back on top. He pushed the tray back into place and hit a switch on the side of the screen, which lit up to display a large picture of a newspaper page from 1927. "Ta-da!"

"Shhhhhh!"

I rolled my eyes and shook my head. Boy, it was hard to control Ben when he was excited about something.

Ben slid the tray to the right and down as I tried to read each page on the screen. He moved so quickly, I could barely focus. Just when I started to complain and ask him to slow down, he stopped and pointed to the screen.

"There! There's Elizabeth...Elizabeth Hilliard."

I leaned in closer to get a better look. The picture was the front of Ben's house. Two teenage girls were perched daintily on the front stoop. Both were well dressed from head to toe. The older girl with her hair in a tight bun – I recognized right away as Elizabeth. She did not look as much like me as the first photo, but there was still a resemblance. Her face was pleasantly smiling at the camera. The younger girl in the picture was a little on the plump side with ringlet curls pulled to the top of her head. A few strands hung around her ears and the nape of her neck. She was pretty, but not as breathtaking as Elizabeth. She had a slight frown on her face.

We read the caption under the photo:

"The Hilliard sisters, Elizabeth, age 16, and Katrina, age 14, are sponsoring an ice cream social at their home on Saturday at 1 p.m., to raise funds for our new library."

The ghost haunting Ben's house helped to build our precious library?

Ben removed the sheet and replaced it with the second one. We didn't find a picture, but we did find a small article stating the ribbon cutting ceremony for the new library would be postponed due to the tragic death of its benefactors, Mr. and Mrs. Jackson P. Hilliard. This article was dated only three years later, in 1930. Elizabeth and Katrina were orphaned at the ages of 19 and 17.

In Ben's eagerness to switch films, he dropped the last remaining sheet on the floor. He leaned to pick it up, when an old tattered brown boot stomped on top of it, just short of crushing his fingers. The resounding thud of the boot against the wooden floor and the sound of crinkling plastic startled us both.

We should have smelled old man Wilkerson coming. His breath traveled in waves and crept into my nose. He was furious. His eyes were bloodshot and his brows furrowed to the point that he appeared to have one eyebrow instead of two. His stained and wrinkled clothes looked as if he'd slept in them for months and were permanently attached to his fragile body. Reaching with his bony hand, he picked Ben up by the front of his shirt. His toes were just skimming the floor as he kicked frantically, knocking over his chair. I heard Ben gasp for air as the collar of his shirt dug into his neck. An evil hissing sound came from the old man's lips as he whispered,

"Puttin' your nose where it don't belong can be hazardous to your health, Boy!"

♂ I am not sure what Mr. Wilkerson said, but I got the gist of it. Our noses were almost touching and his eyes were full of hate and fear, when we heard the hard-tapping sounds of Mrs. Campbell's shoes as she approached the back of the library. Mr. Wilkerson let go, and I fell to the floor. I was not expecting the sudden drop and landed on my butt. Just as Mrs. Campbell came into the room, Mr. Wilkerson bent over and acted like he was helping me.

"You have to be more careful; these floors can sometimes be slippery," he said as he slid the microfiche from under his shoe and crumpled it with one hand, while helping me up with the other.

"What is going on here Mr. Wilkerson?" Mrs. Campbell asked in a stern voice.

"Nothin' Ma'am, I was just coming by to tell young Mr. Whiting here that he is not allowed to trespass through the old train yard."

Looking at Sarah, he continued, "I must have startled him and he fell."

I was just going to argue he was lying, when he put his hand on my shoulder and applied a vise-like grip.

"I wouldn't want anything bad to happen to young Mr. Whiting here or his little friend. You know how dangerous the old train yard can be."

Mrs. Campbell grabbed me by the arm and pulled me away from Mr. Wilkerson. Standing in front of Sarah, she said, "Yes, yes, I am sure these kids will not trespass on the train yard again."
Under the stern gaze of the librarian, he slunk out the door.

"He is a liar!" I exploded. "That is not…"

I felt Sarah's hand in mine and she was squeezing it hard. Her eyes were big and round. She looked scared, and she was shaking her head.

"Yes?" Mrs. Campbell asked.

I looked at my feet. "What I meant to say was, we didn't cut through the train yard."

"Are you sure that is what happened, Ben?"

"Yes, Ma'am."

"Okay, you two, if you are done with this reader you must turn off the lamp. They can get hot, and we don't need any more heat in the library today." She turned away and went back to her desk.

As soon as Mrs. Campbell was gone, I turned to Sarah.

"Why didn't you let me tell her what was going on?"

I picked up my chair and sat.

Sarah just stared at the floor for a long moment before whispering, "She was right there, Ben."

At first, I didn't understand what she was saying and I asked her to repeat it. This time Sarah looked me right in the eyes.

"Katrina was standing right behind Mr. Wilkerson."

I could feel the hair on my neck stand on end just like it was statically charged.

Sarah continued. "She looked at me and grinned."

Chapter 20
Sticky Situation

♀ "Katrina, not Elizabeth?"

Ben visibly shuddered as he turned off the microfiche machine light.

I rubbed the goose bumps on my arms, hoping to warm myself. It didn't work.

"Katrina was here the whole time?" Ben asked.

"I didn't notice her until Mr. Wilkerson had you in the air. Are you okay?"

I reached over and touched the red mark on Ben's neck. He flinched and grabbed my hand. "Your hand is freezing, Sarah."

I explained to him I usually got cold when a ghost was nearby. Call it my early warning system. I was born with it.

"Did you notice when Mr. Wilkerson was talking, you could see his breath?"

"No, I just noticed the smell of it." He grimaced and pinched his nose with his fingers.

"The light on the machine went out, just like in the basement."

As we walked out of the room, Ben grabbed my hand and held it tight. We paused briefly at the water fountain where he splashed cold water on his face. With water dripping from his chin, Ben looked directly in my eyes. "Are you okay? You look pale."

I told him how drained I was and how it reminded me of the basement when my legs collapsed. It was as if all my energy was sucked out of my body.

"Maybe it was Katrina we saw in the basement." I suggested.

Ben shook his head. "Maybe it was both of them, the one in front of the freezer and the one holding my hand."

We stood near the drinking fountain in silence. Ben suddenly looked panicked.

"What are we going to tell Mrs. Campbell about the missing film?"

I had forgotten Mr. Wilkerson crumpled it up and put in his pocket. I took the other two sheets from Ben.

"Let's wait a minute, until she's busy. I'll take care of the rest."

We circled the desk like vultures looking for road kill. When two people formed a line, I put my plan into action. In one smooth, calculated move, I bypassed the line and threw the films so they fell between the cracks of the counter.

"Oh no! I'm sorry Mrs. Campbell. The films fell between the cracks."

Mrs. Campbell spun around, while I looked as regretful as I could. She patted my hand. "It's alright Sarah. I'll get Frank the janitor to fish them out for me." She giggled. "Oh my, fish the fiche out." I gave her a weak smile and turned to Ben with a triumphant grin.

As we stepped out of the library, the sun blinded us. Ben took his baseball cap and placed it on my head. My head swam in it.

"Boy, you sure have a big head." I teased.

He knocked on his skull with his knuckles while opening his mouth wide. The hollow sound was extremely loud. I laughed at the thought of his pea-size brain, rattling around inside his big ole' head. It was highly doubtful, though. He was possibly the smartest person I had ever met.

As we approached the pharmacy, I made a quick right turn through the front door. "Put your turn signal on next time." Ben shouted as he changed course to follow me.

I grabbed a pack of watermelon bubble gum from below the counter and pulled a couple quarters out of my pocket. The girl at the counter barely smiled as she gave me my change. I handed Ben a piece and shoved two pieces into my mouth.

"So, what's the plan, Stan?"

♂ "I need to rest for a minute," I said, rubbing the spot on my neck where my shirt had cut into my skin. My head was a little fuzzy. Spotting a park on the other side of the street with some trees and benches, I stepped forward.
Sarah grabbed my arm and pulled me back roughly. I heard the sound of a car horn and a voice yell out, "Hey, Stupid, watch where yer going!"

Sarah's hand was waving in front of my face. "Earth to Ben, come in Ben. Houston, we have a problem!"

I had to grin. She didn't yell at me like some people do. This time I looked both ways before we crossed.

We found a bench that was back away from the street. As I sat, I felt something in my hand. I looked and saw a piece of gum there. I had to remember where I had gotten it. I guess the look on my face was enough of a push for Sarah to speak up. "Uh, Ben, it is called gum – you chew it."

I unwrapped the gum and decided this would be a good time to show Sarah I had a sense of humor too. Instead of putting the gum in my mouth, I put in the wrapper and chewed on it.

"Hey what are you doing? Haven't you ever had gum before?"

I couldn't hold a straight face any longer and busted out laughing. I took out the wrapping paper and put the gum in my mouth.

"Gotcha."

I pulled out the little notebook and flipped back a couple of pages. "Okay, here is what we know so far. There were two sisters who lived in my house, a cute older one and a kind of dumpy looking younger one. Their parents died in a tragic accident. The article didn't mention what happened. Maybe it was on the other piece of film old man Wilkerson took."

Sarah was blowing a large bubble with her gum. I was surprised at how big it got before it popped. She spun it around her finger and tossed the whole thing back in her mouth.

"I bet I can blow a bigger bubble than you can," she taunted me.

I couldn't blow bubbles like that.

"Nah, let's not and say we did," I mumbled.

"Come on, I bet you a quarter I can blow a bigger bubble than you."

She wasn't going to let this drop, so I finally admitted I couldn't blow bubbles.

She looked like she was going to laugh until she saw I was serious. "Want to learn how?"

What the heck, I might as well do this so we could get back to important stuff. "Okay, show me."

"Okay, first you push the gum with your tongue and kind of mush it to the front of your mouth. Get it flattened out against the inside of your teeth like this." Sarah worked the gum in her mouth. She eventually took it out of her mouth and showed how it looked. "Then you open your mouth a little and push your tongue into it and blow air."

I flattened the gum against my teeth, pushed my tongue into it and started to blow. Just as a small bubble formed, the worst possible thing happened. The wad shot out of my mouth and landed in Sarah's lap.

"Ah crap!"

Sarah's hand went to cover her mouth.

I didn't know if I had made her sick until I heard her snort and bust out laughing. I joined in when she handed me my gum back. "Sarah, I need to ask you a question. I was going to ask you last night, but things got a little weird."

"So, what is the question?" Sarah mumbled between smacks of bubble gum.

"Do you have an old camera I could borrow? I would use my dad's, but he can't remember what box it's in." I hated to borrow things, because my dad had a long-standing rule about borrowing something from someone: "If you don't have the money to replace what you borrow, don't borrow it."

"I need a camera to take pictures of the soapbox racer we're making. I want to send pictures of my design to the scout magazine." Sarah didn't say anything for a moment and her face lit up.

"My mom takes pictures all the time. If I take the pictures, I'm sure she will let me borrow her camera."

Chapter 21
Picture Perfect

♀ Ben and I raced down Main Street in the direction of my house. As we approached the train yard, Ben came to a complete stop.

"I...don't know...Sarah."

I leaned against the fence as I spit the gum from my mouth and stuck it to a rusty post. "It's okay Ben, we can go around."

Following the perimeter of the fence would take a little longer. Peering into the train yard, I told him how Steph had seen Mr. Wilkerson go into the old caboose. Ben nodded and gulped loudly as he swallowed his gum.

By the time we got around the west side of the yard, my hands were finally warming up. I turned to tell Ben. He was ten feet away, looking into the train yard. With his hands entwined in the chain link and his face practically pressed into the mesh, he stared. Here we go again, I readied my pinching fingers.

I turned and saw what had caught his attention. Twenty-five feet away, inside the fence near an old burn barrel, Mr. Wilkerson was sitting on an old railroad tie with his back to us. His hands were covering his face and his fragile old body was shaking. At first, I thought he was laughing, but he was crying. His muffled sobs barely reached our ears, but he was definitely crying. We stood motionless and watched, quiet as field mice. Realizing we were invading the old man's privacy, I motioned for Ben to follow me. We treaded lightly through the tall grass and weeds until reaching my street.

Ben grabbed the back of my shirt and pulled me beneath a large maple tree. I let out a sigh of relief.

"I'm glad we didn't cut through the train yard."

Ben had a perplexed look on his face. "I never imagined Mr. Wilkerson having feelings. Why is he so sad?"

I was just taking off Ben's hat to give it back to him, when Mike flew by on a big bike.

"Hey Loser! Dad said I could have your bike! You lost the deal!" he yelled as he sped by us.

He had the sleeves of a red jacket tied around his neck and the rest flapped in the breeze behind him, resembling Superman's cape.

"Dang it, I left my bike at the library."

Obviously upset, Ben told me about his dad's rule. Because Ben had a tendency to misplace things, forgotten items became Mike's for a week. This was supposed to cure Ben. He looked at his feet in disgust as Mike made another circle around us.

I nudged him with my elbow and tried to make him feel better. I showed him my best impression of Marcus-the-bully, picking his nose.

Mom was <u>canning</u> tomatoes in the kitchen. The large blue speckled pot sat on top of the stove with a dozen canning jars and lids boiling inside of it. Mom had her hair wrapped in a red handkerchief and wore the apron I made her last Mother's Day. It had bold letters on the front that said, "Kiss the Cook." She was obviously busy, which was the best time to ask her permission for something. Distraction was my friend.

"Hey, Mom, I have a question," I said as she placed the funnel in the neck of a hot jar.

"Oh hi, Honey. Well hello, Ben!" She quickly glanced in our direction. "I'm busy now. Is it important?"

I winked at Ben as I pulled a chair to the overcrowded table. I leaned on the one end of the table. Since the leaves were in, it would tip slightly. "I was hoping we could borrow your camera," I politely asked as the jars shifted and slid my way.

Mom reacted with great speed as she leveled the table and shooed me away with her other hand. "I don't care, Honey. Just use my older one. It's beside the developer in the laundry room."

Mom was an amateur photographer. She had taken some classes at the art museum last year and begged my dad to make her a <u>dark room</u> for developing her pictures. Dad joked if she spent time in the laundry room, maybe she would get caught up on the actual laundry. So, our laundry room was packed with equipment, trays, and bottles, making it resemble a chemist's lab. If it were not for the washer and dryer hidden underneath, you'd never guess we used it for anything else. I jumped from my chair and headed toward the basement door. "Thanks, Mom."

Ben followed but didn't seem overly anxious about going into our basement. I turned his baseball cap sideways and leaned in close to his ear. "Don't worry. Our basement isn't haunted."

♂ The first thing I noticed as we headed down the stairs, was how dark it was. It was like the darkness had weight and substance. This was one basement I didn't want to be in if the power went off. I looked to where Sarah was reaching to turn on the lights and saw a handmade cardboard sign. "Please call down stairs first before turning on the lights. Love, Mom." I looked at Sarah.

"Oh," she explained, "my mom has her stuff to develop the pictures there. It's her dark room."

The lights came on and the basement lit up in sections. From the stairs, it appeared it went on forever. Sarah headed downstairs and turned around. "Well, are you just going to stand there?"

As we walked through the basement, there were boxes, bigger boxes, and more boxes. Some had names like "Jorgenson house" or "Peterson Auction," and others were labeled with different names like developing agent and so on. The basement had a warehouse look to it.

"My mom said the camera is right over here by the developer." We walked through the maze, to an area much different from the rest of the basement. This area spoke of cleanliness and order. Measuring cups and bottles lined little shelves. There was also something that looked like a clothesline with black and white pictures clipped to it. Most of them were of Sarah and her family. I was surprised to see one of Sarah and me walking on the street together. "Hey, this is one of me!" I said in a voice an octave higher than I wanted it to be.

Sarah laughed. "Yep, that's my mom, always taking pictures of something."

I tried to imagine where Sarah's mom would have been when she took it. Sarah was gathering the things we would need. "Thirty-five-millimeter camera, check, standard lens, check, lens cover, check, film, check."

I cupped my hands around my mouth and said, Okay, pilot, you are cleared for takeoff."

She giggled and cupped her hands around her mouth. "You're a dork, check."

As we circled the railroad yard to get to my house, we approached the area where we had last seen Mr. Wilkerson. I was more than happy to go by quickly, but Sarah had something else in mind. She stopped at that section of fence and was taking the case off of the camera.

"Sarah," I whispered, "what are you doing?"

She waved for me to be quiet. Mr. Wilkerson was still there, and he was having an active conversation with himself, waving his arms and talking to the caboose. Sarah gave me a look that could have melted ice. I knew I had to be quiet. It seemed like forever before she finally pushed the button and the shutter clicked. It barely made a noise but Mr. Wilkerson turned around and stared right in our direction. I froze. I wasn't going to move an inch. I didn't want him to spot me, not after what happened in the library this morning. Sarah shot past me.

"Run!"

Had I known she was going to do it, I might have tried facing the right direction first. I glanced back into the old rail yard to see Mr. Wilkerson waving right at me and laughing. I was soon hot on the heels of Sarah running for home.

I had to sit when we got to my house. I wanted to crawl to the front porch, but I was not going to let Sarah see that, so I bit my lip and tried to ignore the cramp I had.

"Are you okay?"

"Mmm hmm," I said, not trusting my voice.

I would like to know where she got all her energy. She was hardly winded, and I was going to pass out. When I could finally speak without sounding like Mickey Mouse, I looked at Sarah. "The next time you want to go for a *run*, warn me first."

Sarah got in my face and said back,

"I gave you the hand signal, and I counted down from three."

She blushed.

"I 'm so sorry, Ben, I keep forgetting you have only lived here a few days." She held up her hand and whirled it in the air a few times. "This means run." She held up three fingers and counted. "And this means, on the count of three."

Chapter 22
Time Travel

♀ Ben opened the garage door and walked in ahead of me. He pulled the string to the bulb overhead and turned towards me. I stood staring at him for a brief moment as the yellow light shone on him, remembering the way he looked a few days ago when we met at this spot. He looked different to me now. I still couldn't believe he wanted to be my friend. Most kids wanted nothing to do with me when they found out I could see ghosts.

Ben must have been uncomfortable with my staring, because he used some of his own sign language. Sticking his thumbs in his ears, wiggling his fingers, and crossing his eyes, he danced around in the middle of the garage. He looked like a total idiot and I laughed.

I didn't laugh long. As Ben turned in circles, he tripped over a large crate and fell forward, hitting his head on a support beam. He landed on all fours and let out a groan. I rushed to his side as I tried to lift him to a sitting position.

"Ben, are you okay?"

He held his forehead with his hand and nodded. Pulling his hand away from his face, I found a small lump the size of a robin's egg.

It seemed to be growing.

"Geez, where did *that* come from?" he complained as I pulled the crate towards us. Inside were at least a half a dozen bottles, different sizes and colors with aging labels. Some had corks in them with a splash of dark liquid settling in the bottoms.

"Look at these." I uncorked one and took a sniff. The odor took my breath away and reminded me of Mr. Wilkerson.

Ben picked up a bottle and inspected it.

"These are old liquor bottles."

He explained to me what his dad had told him about their house being a speakeasy back in the 1920s. Ben had looked it up and learned it was the time of <u>Prohibition</u> which made selling, manufacturing, and transportation of alcohol illegal. A speakeasy was a place that sold alcohol and disguised its illegal activities with wild parties. The only way to get in, was to know the secret password.

Ben cleared off the workbench. I suggested making the area look more organized for the pictures. My mom always said the background was as important as the subject. You didn't want a cluttered background and things looking like they were growing out of your head. In one fell swoop, Ben pushed the junk into an empty cardboard box. He strategically placed the parts and a few rusty tools on the bench. I picked up his hat from the floor and placed it on his head backwards. I wanted to make sure I could see his face but also cover the knot in his forehead.

Posing him, I took pictures, the flash going off like a lightning storm. Making him hold a wrench or hammer, I told him one stupid joke after another. He smiled broadly as I clicked away. Eventually, I needed to change the <u>film</u>, so I pulled an extra roll from my pocket and switched them out. Ben looked at me with a funny look on his face and went pale. Before I knew what was happening, he was flat on his face on the floor.

♂ Every time the flash went off, I saw a second shadow, like someone was standing behind Sarah. At first, I thought it was just the flash playing tricks on my eyes, but the shadow changed places and shapes. It was when she was changing film, the real fun began. I was just standing there watching her, when I heard what sounded like a steam pipe leaking or air rushing. I looked over to see if she heard the same thing, but she was busy. Oh, please, not today and not in front of her. Sarah was looking at me funny. Before I knew it, the cement floor was rushing to meet my face.

I knew what had happened because it had happened before. The day was warm, I didn't drink enough water (again), I got dehydrated and I passed out. I guess I could be thankful I wasn't riding my bike when it happened. This time was different, though. I usually woke up right after falling, but this time, I got up, looked back, and saw myself still lying on the ground. It was like a TV show and the channel changed. One station faded out, and another faded in. I was still standing in the garage, but now it was nighttime. It looked different, cleaner and more like a carriage house with an old anvil and horse shoes hanging from pegs on the wall.

I saw Sarah over in the far-left corner of the garage kneeling, doing something in the cabinet. When she stood, I realized it wasn't Sarah – it was Elizabeth. She ran toward the tool bench and into the arms of some guy. They were talking, but I couldn't hear what was being said. I walked over to them, when the side door burst open and in walked Katrina. I recognized her from the picture we saw that morning in the library. She was acting cocky and making threatening gestures to Elizabeth.

I continued to walk closer to the three of them, in order to make out what they were saying. Elizabeth was pleading.

"Please, Katrina, don't tell Daddy. If he finds out I'm still seeing Henry he'll be mad, and I don't know what he'll do this time."

Katrina just laughed, and when she was done laughing she pointed at Elizabeth.

"Oh, this is going to be good. Poor little Elizabeth, got caught in the carriage house with her poor little boyfriend."
Elizabeth clung to Henry "What are we going to do?"

Katrina put her hand on the pearl necklace Elizabeth was wearing. "I like this necklace, sister. I sure wish I had one like it."
She tore the necklace from her neck, sending little round pearls rolling all over the floor.

Katrina laughed at the startled look on her sister's face and laughed even harder when she cried. "Oh yes, dearie, things are going to be different from here on out."

I guess Henry had had enough; he stood between the two of them.

"You better leave her alone, or I will…"

"Or you will do what, Henry?" Katrina said with a sneer on her face. "I will tell you what you will do, *nothing*." Katrina slapped him across the face.

I was so surprised by this. I took a step back and kicked over a bottle. Up to this point, I had just been watching this TV show, but now I seemed to be in it. Everyone looked over in my direction.

"Who are you and what are you doing here?" Katrina demanded.

Before I could move away, Katrina was standing right in front of me with her left hand tightened on my shirt. I saw her right hand too late to do anything. She slapped me hard across the face.

The left side of my face stung and when I blinked hard to clear my vision it wasn't Katrina, but Sarah looking at me. My shirt was wet in the front. My little brother was standing a few feet away with a Popsicle in his mouth. He slurped on it.

"See, I told you he was going to be okay. You didn't have to slap him."

"I didn't touch him." Sarah said, helping me to sit.

"Oh no?" Slurp. "I can see the handprint."

Chapter 23
Boastful Bauble

♀ As soon as Ben keeled over, my body thermometer dropped drastically. The air was frigid, like when you stand in front of the refrigerator with the door open. Ben was lying on his stomach with his face turned to one side. He was still breathing. I turned him over. His eyes were rolling around underneath his eyelids like he was dreaming. My skin crawled, as I grabbed Ben's cold hand. He squeezed it hard and refused to let go. I sat there on the floor of Ben's garage, holding his hand as the light overhead flickered and went out. A cupboard door opened and shut with no one visibly touching it. Muffled voices escalated in argument but I could not distinguish what they were saying. I rubbed my eyes with my free hand as three translucent shapes floated around the room.

A bright red hand mark appeared on Ben's cheek. When I saw it, I jumped back, in shock.

Mike was yelling Ben's name outside the garage.

"Mike! In here!"

The light bulb quickly rejuvenated its sickly yellow glow and Ben stirred. I placed both hands on his heaving chest and leaned in close to his face.

"Ben?"

I heard Mike making a slurping noise behind me.

"He did it again, didn't he?" Mike said as if it were no big deal. He had a Popsicle in one hand and a glass of water in the other. I grabbed the water and dumped it right on Ben's face. He jumped as the ice-cold water hit his skin and his hazel eyes flickered open.

After Mike skipped away and left us alone, I let out a relieved sigh and hugged Ben.

"I'm so glad you're okay."

He squirmed until he figured out I was stronger. His arms went limp.

"I give," he gasped as if I were squeezing the air out of him.

I kissed him on the cheek. When I realized what I had done, I let go and sat back on my knees. Ben turned a deep shade of red. Glancing around, confused, he grabbed his baseball cap and placed it on his head, covering the shrinking lump on his forehead. I heard footsteps approaching rapidly; it had to be his mom. If Mike was anything like my sister, he probably tattled and would be following close behind so he could enjoy watching his older sibling be humiliated. Mrs. Whiting walked into the garage with a concerned look on her face and a large glass of ice water in her hand.

"Ben, are you alright?" She moved quickly to his side.

Shaking her head, she handed Ben the water and he gulped the entire contents in three seconds.

"Thanks, Mom."

Standing behind his mom, Mike was making gestures, waving his finger at Ben and grinning with excitement.

"Mike! Stop teasing your brother," Mrs. Whiting said without even turning.

I giggled, reveling in the talent all moms possess, the amazing skill to see behind their backs. I flashed a quick grin to Mrs. Whiting as she looked in my direction.

"I hope Ben didn't scare you too much, Sarah. Are you okay? You look a little pale yourself."

I stood and brushed my pants off. "I'm fine, Ma'am."

She nodded and offered to fix us something to eat. Without giving us a chance to answer, she headed for the house.

"Give me ten minutes and meet me in the kitchen."

Luckily the red mark on Ben's face had blended in by the time his mom appeared. However, Ben must have felt the sting. He rubbed his cheek as he slowly stood.

"I'm sorry, Sarah. Are you okay?

He told me about the weird vision he had while he was passed out. He didn't get far into his story when he noticed I was staring at his shoes. Looking down, he stopped in mid-sentence. His facial expression changed from excitement to pure terror. Between his shoes was a single pearl.

♂ I couldn't get the dream out of my mind. I was still not convinced I was even awake. So, I said something I knew I would soon regret if I were awake.

"Sarah, pinch me."

She looked at me for a moment, reached out and gave my arm a good solid pinch.

"Ouch, not so hard," I said through gritted teeth.

"You said to pinch you. You didn't say softly."

I reached and picked up the small white pearl. It was warm, as if it had spent the day in the sun. Not wanting to touch the pearl any more than I had to, I dropped it in my shirt pocket.

"What does this mean?" I asked as we made our way out of the garage.

Sarah shrugged. "I'm not sure. Something happened in here. We have to find out what."

I closed the garage doors, when Sarah remembered her camera.

"Wait!"

She crouched and went back into the garage. She hadn't been gone for more than a few seconds when she called out.

"Ben, you had better get in here."

I lifted the garage door back up to see what she wanted. She was standing over by the boxes where she had left the camera. The camera's back was open, and the film had been pulled out in one long curly strand.

"Sarah, all of the pictures you took, they are ruined!"

Sarah picked up the camera and other equipment. My first guess was Mike had done this while Sarah's back was turned, but it didn't make any sense.

"Do you have enough film to take the pictures again?"

She turned with a smile and held up a plastic film case. She shook it with a rattle, meaning there was film in it.

"Remember? I had just changed the roll of film before you passed out. The pictures are in here." She was holding the plastic film case firmly in her hand, when we again left the garage.

We had just rounded the front of the garage when it hit me. I had been kissed! With everything else that had happened, I had forgotten one little detail. The more I thought about it, the slower I walked. The slower I walked, the further ahead Sarah got.

She looked back as she opened the door.

"Hey, are you okay? You're not going to pass out again, are you?" She let the door close and walked back towards me.

I chuckled.

"What is so funny?"

The question made me laugh harder.

"Nothing," I squeaked, my voice betraying me. This sent me into even a greater fit of laughter. Sarah was now standing in front of me.

"What is so funny?"

I composed myself long enough to say, "You kissed me!"

I guess she didn't see the humor in it.

"Boys," She rolled her eyes.
I quickly sobered up and went after her.

"Sarah, I'm sorry. I know it was only a kiss on the cheek but I have never been kissed before." I caught up to her as she walked the steps into the kitchen.

"Sarah, are you and Ben ready for something to eat?" my mom asked as she put the sandwiches out on the table.

"Yes, Ma'am."

"Okay, you two go wash up while I finish."

Putting the camera equipment on the table, Sarah and I walked through the hallway to the small washroom. I noticed halfway, I was instinctively keeping to the right side, away from the basement door. I turned and looked back at Sarah; she was doing the same thing.

She still hadn't said a thing as we took turns washing our hands but she flicked water in my face a couple times. I quickly washed my hands, dried them on the towel, and hurried back to the kitchen where I pulled the chair out for her. "Ben, that was very nice of you," Mom said.

I figured the brownie points I earned with my mom would be a plus, and if I earned any with Sarah it would be even better.

"Okay, I have peanut butter and grape jelly and I have peanut butter and honey," Mom said as she passed the tray to Sarah.
While we ate, my mom was talking on the phone with my dad.

"All right, I will tell him. No, I don't know why he would have that downstairs." There was a long pause while I tried to imagine what my dad was saying to my mom. I had an idea it was something for me to do. Mom hung up the phone and gave me a look. "Ben, your father was not happy with the job you did in the garage."

I took a drink of milk and tried to get as much peanut butter out of my mouth as possible.

"Mwhat?" I took another big drink of milk. "What do you mean? Sarah and I cleaned it yesterday."

"Well, your father said when he went to work this morning he looked into the garage. There were bottles all over the floor and the cabinet doors were open. He picked it up before he left for work."
I looked at Sarah and shrugged.

"Oh, one other thing, your father doesn't want you storing gas cans in the basement. We have a shed out back. You know storing cans of gas in the house is not safe."

Sarah and I exchanged looks and quickly finished our lunch.

"Thank you, Mrs. Whiting. That was a wonderful lunch," Sarah said.

My mom beamed from ear to ear. "Ben, I like your friend. She is so polite. You can learn a thing or two from her."

Sarah winked at me and gathered her camera equipment and handed it to me.

"Ben, would you be a gentleman and carry this for me?" she asked with a teasing smile as she headed for the door.

I looked back, to see my mom standing there, with her hands on her hips.

"I would be happy to."

Chapter 24
Mammoth Marcus

♀ Ben looped the camera strap over his head and stuck his arm through. I watched as he carefully tucked the camera close to his side, making sure the lens cover was on tight. My heart skipped a beat when he noticed I was staring again.

"What?" he asked as he raised an eyebrow and smirked.

I shrugged my shoulders. It seemed strange to me, I trusted him with Mom's camera. I couldn't remember ever trusting anyone as much as I did Ben. I guess when I pictured finding one true friend who would accept me the way I was, I didn't imagine it would be a boy. Yet, I never found a girl who understood my need for adventure as much as this awkward boy standing before me.

I nodded toward the street and walked ahead of Ben.

"Wait," he said. "I want to check the garage quick before my Dad gets home. We had better clean it up." When we left for lunch the liquor bottles were still out and strewn all over the place.

He slowly lifted the garage door. He seemed reluctant about looking in, and I didn't blame him. Just as the door lifted above his head and the daylight streamed into the garage, Mike jumped out from behind a box.

"Boo!"

We both practically jumped out of our shoes and the sharp pain in my tongue informed me I had just bitten it. Clutching his hand over his heart, Ben knelt and picked up a pebble, whipping it at his little brother. He hit Mike in the small of his back as he was turning to run.

"What are you doing in here, Creep?" Ben demanded.

Mike stopped in his tracks and rubbed the spot on his back where the pebble had hit him.

"I heard voices in the garage. I came to see if you and Sarah were making out again."

Ben's face turned a deep shade of crimson as he cornered Mike. But he put a hand on the camera and stepped back.

"You're lucky I'm not able to get my hands on you. Beat it!"

Not waiting for a second request, Mike took off out the door and yelled back to us, "I'm going for a ride on *my* bike!"

I could taste the metallic flavor of my own blood as I licked my lips. But I forgot about it when I saw the garage. It was as clean as a whistle. No crate, no bottles littering the floor and even the mysterious appearing gas can sit in its place in the corner.

Only one thing seemed out of place. Sitting on the windowsill, above the workbench was a single clear bottle. The sunlight was hitting it just right and it shone with an amplified glow. I walked to the sill, lifted the bottle, and turned it in the light, examining it. The bottle was clear with no label or writing on it, but the design embedded into the glass resembled an intricate spider web. At first glance, it looked as if a spider had taken up residence in the bottle and spun its silky web inside. But running my fingers over its surface, I confirmed it was pressed into the glass itself. A delicate spider was hidden in the design.

"Whoa!" Ben took the bottle from my hands. "This is cool!"

We agreed the bottle had not been there earlier. Ben put it in the camera case with the used film and headed to the door.

"Let's get out of here before something else happens."

The walk to my house was a quiet one. I liked the fact we didn't have to talk. We were okay with just walking together, so the silence wasn't awkward. I stuck my tongue out as I tried to see where I bit it.

Ben looked at me like I was nuts. "What are you doing?"

"I bwitmuay tongue!"

I asked him if he could see where it was bleeding.

Stopping in the middle of the sidewalk, Ben placed both hands on my shoulders, and leaned in close.

"You sure did, Sarah. It's bleeding!" He backed away with a grimace on his face as I turned to spit into the grass. He looked sick. "Maybe we can put an ice cube on it when we get to your house."

"What's wrong, Ben? You can't handle the sight of blood?" I teased.

"I'm a little squeamish sometimes. I'm a sympathy barfer too, especially with people I care about."

Giggling, I punched him on the arm. That's the precise moment I knew we would be best friends forever.

♂ Walking in silence gives you a chance to piece things together – the thing in the basement, old Mr. Wilkerson in the library, and the vision I had in the garage. They had to be connected but I couldn't figure out how. Looking at the ground, I neglected to watch where I was headed and walked into a wall of flesh called Marcus.

"Hey, dorks."

I looked up slowly, beginning at his size fourteen shoes, past his large gut, and eventually into his overly large face.

"Yeah, I am talking to you," he said with attitude.

The only thing I could do was smile. I glanced at Sarah. She was giving Marcus the evil eye.

"Just leave us alone," Sarah demanded.

"So, this is the new kid. And lookey here, he has a purse!"

I put my hand protectively on the camera bag, while my mind raced with the things I wanted to say. Most of them would have ended with me being pounded into the sidewalk.

"What, can't talk? Are you deaf and dumb like Casper's other loser friend?"

The last little comment loosened my tongue. I don't like it when my friends get picked on.

"Sorry, I was momentarily taken aback at the enormousness that stands before me."

I heard Sarah giggle.

Marcus's only response was, "Huh?"

I was on a roll so I continued.

"My friend Sarah was just telling me about you earlier this morning."

I watched as Marcus slowly swiveled his head and stared at Sarah.

"Oh yeah? What did little Miss Casper say about me?"

I stepped over in front of Marcus so I was between him and Sarah. His focus shifted back to me.

"Oh, it was nothing. We were discussing your sharp wit and intellect, and how your parents must be proud of all the years you have spent in grade school."

Sarah snorted. I reached behind me, grabbed her hand, and squeezed. I guessed he was still trying to determine if I had insulted him or not. I was praying he would take what I had said as a compliment and allow us to pass. Time seemed to stand still as we waited on the small section of sidewalk. I was almost ready to ask if we could go, when his hand shot out and grabbed the front of my shirt, lifting me so we were face to face. He belched.

"I don't like you. You use too many words."

I was surprised when Marcus just let me go and walked toward the street. Sarah and I watched in stunned silence as he crossed and continued down the road. We turned and looked at each other and laughed. Neither one of us could believe we had gotten off so easily. I took Sarah's hand and we ran just in case Marcus decided my little play on words was not a compliment. I couldn't run too fast because of the camera equipment, but soon we were standing in Sarah's front yard under the old shade tree. We both collapsed.

"Whew, that was close." I said as I carefully put the camera case on the grass.

Sarah giggled again. "I can't believe he didn't pound you, after you called him enormous."

I smiled and laughed again. "I don't think he even understood what I said, and when he does, I hope I'm nowhere near him."

Sarah got up and took the camera case off of the grass, pulled out the bottle we found in the garage, and handed it to me.

"Just stay there. I'm going to take this into the house. I will be right back."

While I waited for her to return, I looked at the spider design pressed into the glass. The glass had a bluish tint to it. On the bottom, it had a circle with "Mc" in the middle of it. There was still some yellowish colored glue stuck to one corner, possibly where it may have had a label at one time.

Chapter 25
Super Scout

♀ "Hey, lazy bones, get off the grass and come push me on the swing." I knew from the way Ben eyed the swing earlier, he was anxious to try it out. His face lit up like a Christmas tree, and he sprang to his feet as if weightless. He beat me to it and dove through the center of the large rubber tire.

"Beat you!" he yelled as his body balanced inside. With his arms out in front of him and his legs kicking behind him, he looked like Superman.

"Look! It's a bird, it's a plane, no it's..."

"Super Dork!" I chimed in.

I grabbed the knobby tread and spun him, round and round, faster and faster. I wanted to see what Ben was made of but was interrupted when Mom came out the back door and sat on the stoop. "Sarah, don't make Ben sick. "

I knew that tone. It wasn't a request. She tried to make it sound like she was being nice, but I knew better. I rolled my eyes and let go of the tire.

"Awwww, Maa, we were just having fun!"

The tire swing eventually slowed to a complete stop and Ben slid out on to the ground. Standing, he stumbled around in dizzy circles until he ended up collapsing near my mom's feet. She laughed and reached to give him a hand.

"You are certainly a comedian, Ben." She helped him up. He plopped himself on the step.

I climbed on top of the tire and clung to the thick frayed rope. Mom had taken her apron off, so I knew she was finished canning. Her face was pink and perspiring as she dabbed it with the handkerchief she had taken off of her head. I figured this would be the best time to ask for her help with developing our film and was going to ask when she read my mind.

"So, do you kids need help with your pictures?"

We talked and I told her about our little run-in with Marcus earlier, commenting on his lack of intelligence. Mom pointed out Marcus wasn't lucky enough to have two caring parents like we did. His dad had pretty much skipped town last summer. His mom had been struggling to pay the bills by working two jobs and leaving Marcus to fend for himself. Leave it to Mom to bust our bubble over the awesome sarcastic comments Ben had made in my defense. She asked us to think twice about pointing out people's flaws and judging them.

We mentioned the fact we were building a soapbox racer and Ben wanted to send the pictures we took into a Boy Scout magazine. A light went on in Mom's eyes.

"Ben, are you a Boy Scout?"

Ben nodded and gave her a large toothy smile.

"I'm surprised Sarah didn't tell you. I'm a <u>Merit Badge Counselor</u> for Photography."

The look on Ben's face was priceless. His mouth opened in shock then curled into a big grin. Not too many moms were as cool as mine. She put her arm around him and hugged him as she giggled like a little girl.

"It's okay, honey, I get that reaction all the time."

Mom always taught me girls could do anything boys could do. Even though her generation believed in the man working and the wife staying home to raise the kids, she always made sure to encourage me to push those limits. I asked her once why she didn't work. She said her dream job was to have kids and be the best mom she could be. It was her choice to stay home. Ben blushed, as she stood and messed up his mop of hair with her fingers. Turning to head back inside, she offered her services.

"How does tomorrow sound? I will help you earn your badge."

She instructed us to meet her in the basement at 10 a.m. sharp the next morning.

Once Ben and I were alone again, he regained the ability to speak.

"Your mom is, she's, well, you know…" He fumbled with his words.

"I know. She's cool."

He responded by pulling me back as far as he could and shoved the swing forward with his weight behind it. I flew into the lower boughs of the tree and hit my head on the leaves.

"Higher!" I yelled.

He continued pushing me until I lost my voice from screaming. Finally, tired, he climbed back into the center of the tire and sat below me so my legs dangled in his face. We floated together in silence. The breeze in my face, I closed my eyes until the swing slowed to a complete stop. Ben squirmed out from beneath me to the ground, and when I opened my eyes he was staring at me.

"What are you looking at?" I asked defensively.

His mouth wasn't smiling but his eyes were. He shook his head and looked down.

"You're up to something, I can tell." I said as I tried to get off the swing.

I could not move my fee. Ben laughed. Looking down, I saw he had tied my shoelaces together.

With a wink, Ben headed toward the driveway. He waved comically as I sat there, trying to figure out how I was getting out of this one.

♂ I was running down a long dark tunnel. The tunnel had loose dirt walls that crumbled if you touched them, roots dangled from the ceiling and old-fashioned light bulbs sent out a sickly, yellow, glow every twenty feet or so. I was running from something. I couldn't tell what it was. Heavy footfalls followed by coarse laughter chased me around each corner of the tunnel.

When I finally woke, I noticed I had kicked the blankets off my bed and the sheets were tangled around my legs. I just lay there and stared at the ceiling for several minutes trying to make sense of it. I had just swung my legs over the side of the bed when I noticed a large, black, shape with eight legs on the wall opposite of my window.

Ahhhhhhhhh!" I screamed and dove back under my sheets, pulling the pillow over my head.

Michael came running into the room to see what was going on.

"What're ya screaming for?"

I took a quick look out from under the sheets to point at the wall.

"Big black spider!"

I should have been brave and tried to save my little brother, but I was selfish in saving myself. I could hear him dying. He was making coughing and choking noises as if he were fighting for his life. After a minute or so of this, the dying noises sounded an awful lot like laughing. I peeked out from under the sheet. The spider was still there, and Michael was rolling on the floor with his face all red.

I looked again at the wall and noticed it wasn't a real spider but a shadow of one. Turning around slowly to look at the window, I saw the bottle with the spider design on it. I was pretty sure I had left it at Sarah's.

"Mike, did you put that there?"

He shook his head and pointed at the wall. In an imitation of me, he yelled, "Ahhhh! Spider!"

He launched into another bout of laughter until I hit him with my pillow.

After some intense pillow fighting, I looked at the clock. It was 8:30. I had to get a shower and get everything ready to go to Sarah's house to work on my photography merit badge for Boy Scouts. It was pretty cool Sarah's mom knew how to do stuff like that. She reminded me a lot of my mom. When I was in Cub Scouts, my mom was den leader and we did all sorts of crafts.

After I had showered and dressed in my Boy Scout uniform, I walked across the hall back to my room. Michael was talking to someone in his room, maybe his stuffed animals since I only heard his voice. I figured I could sneak to his door, throw it open and scare the little snot. As I tipped toed closer to his door, I heard little bits of what he was saying.

"Yes, I like this house." Silence. "My mom gave me my

stuffed dog when I was three. His name is Hunter."

Okay, so he wasn't talking to his stuffed animals. I was almost to his door when I heard him say, "My name is Michael Andrew Whiting, what is yours?" Silence again.

"I would love to be your friend, Elizabeth."

I almost fell. A cold chill ran up my back. I was dizzy. I was going to be sick. I was ready to run back to my room, when Mike opened his door and stood there looking at me.

"Who is Elizabeth?" I asked him.

Looking like he got his hand caught in a cookie jar, Mike put his finger to his lips. "Shhhhhhh, she is my managernery...friend. That is what Mom says it is, but her name is Elizabeth."

"You mean *imaginary* friend?"

Mike nodded and seemed embarrassed he couldn't say the word right.

I didn't dare look into Mike's room and see what was there. Instead, I hurried to my own room and closed the door firmly as I put on my shoes and gathered my Boy Scout book.

I got to the kitchen just as Mike was finishing off the last of the milk. It was going to be toast and juice again.

Mom was in the pantry. "Where are you going this morning, all dressed up?"

I liked it when she noticed my effort.

"I'm going to Sarah's house. Her mom is a merit badge counselor for photography, and we're going to work on it."

"Okay, but you have to take your little brother with you."

My face must have proclaimed I *did not* want my little brother going with me.

"Mom, can't he just stay here and play in the dirt or something?"

My fate was sealed. I got the look, and the speech: "Don't you *mom* me, young man. You will take your little brother with you. *understand*?"

I hung my head like it was a death sentence.

"Yes, Mom."

Feeding time at the zoo was done at the kitchen table.

"Let's go, twerp."

"Yay! We're going to Ben's girlfriend's house!" Mike said proudly.

It was going to be a long day.

Chapter 26
Static Sting

♀ Even with my eyes still closed, I knew it was morning. I could hear the faint melody of chirping birds outside the bedroom window and smell the strong aroma of cinnamon in the air. Mom must be making her famous French toast, I smiled sleepily. Deciding to keep my eyes shut a while longer, I listened for other signs of life. The house was quiet, with the exception of a distant bark in the backyard and the occasional cupboard door slamming shut in the kitchen. No one was talking, and the television wasn't on. I couldn't tell what time it was as I rolled over from my stomach to my side. As if on cue, the grandfather clock in the hall chimed. I waited for the slow but rhythmic song to end and counted ten bongs.

"Darn!"

By the time I got to the living room, Ben and Mike had already helped Mom push the coffee table off to the side and threw a large flowery blanket for a picnic-style breakfast on the floor. She disappeared to the kitchen briefly and returned with Steph in tow, carrying plates and maple syrup. Just as the four of us were sitting, the doorbell rang again. Mom rushed to the back door and I heard her laugh as it squeaked open. She yelled to us from the kitchen.

"Got room for one more?"

We looked at each other with curiosity. In walked Nate, with his camera and a clear plastic bag full of film cartridges. Mom explained how she had invited Nate, who was also a Boy Scout, to earn his merit badge along with Ben.

"Who taid your allowed to eat without me?"

I laughed as I patted the spot near to me on the floor. Nate threw his camera and bag on the floor, smiled shyly at Ben and Mike and waved hello. I introduced them as Nate fidgeted with his <u>hearing aid</u> and tapped on the box near his chest. Apparently, Nate had drained his battery again.

Poking Nate in the side, I signed for him to pay attention. A loud high-pitched squeal came from his hearing aid after he replaced the battery and he smiled.

"There! What did you tay?"

I introduced Ben again, and Nate leaned over to shake hands. The instant their hands touched, I heard the shock of static electricity and watched as they both recoiled in surprise.

"Oh yeah, I forgot to warn you. Nate has a weird electrical thing, shocks me every time."

Nate shrugged his shoulders and laughed. We all dug into our feast of a picnic.

♂ "How come you talk funny?" Mike just blurted it out.

Nate told my brother he was deaf and he had a hard time pronouncing certain letters.
Mike didn't miss a beat.

"That little box helps you hear then."
It sounded more like a statement. Leave it to Mike to have the guts to ask the tough questions. I was ready to tell him he was being annoying, when Nate looked at me.

"That okay. I am ut to it." He signed something quickly to Sarah and said to us,

"Don't worry. You will learn how to do tign language."

After finishing breakfast, we cleaned up and headed toward the kitchen with our dishes. Standing in the doorway, Sarah's mom was talking to someone on the phone.

"It's all right, Irene. I can reschedule and bring the girls with me to help."
Mrs. McNally hung up and turned to us apologetically.

"Kids, we are going to have to reschedule your merit badge class for tomorrow. I am so sorry."

I was disappointed but tried not to show it as we dragged our feet across the back porch to the driveway. Nate started his short walk across the street as Mike and I headed for home.

I wasn't ready to go home. As far as I was concerned, the next hour was free. The merit badge thing was cancelled, but the time was still open. Going home now would only throw away a good hour of explore. I stopped when we came to the south gate of the old train yard. I couldn't just go in; I had Mike with me. I had to wait for the right moment to ensure he wouldn't tattle on me: "Ben made me go in the train yard." I had to strategize.

"What are you looking at, Ben?"

I stood on my tiptoes and scanned the yard for another minute before I answered him with excitement.

"Oh, I can almost see the old steam engine from here."

He got on his tiptoes. "I can't see nothing."

I looked at him and sighed.

"Too bad, I wish I could take you there to see it."

Once again, he got on his tiptoes.

"You can show me, can't you?"

Yes, I said to myself. Out loud I said, "Okay, but we have to make sure Mr. Wilkerson is not in there first."

We walked down the sidewalk, a little further to where Sarah and I had seen the old caboose the day before. Looking through the fence, I didn't see any sign of the old man. Mike tugged on my shirt.

"What?" I said a little too forcefully.

Seeing the hurt look on his face, I ruffled his hair and in a little softer voice said, "What's up, twerp?"

It brought a smile to his face as he turned half way around and pointed down the street.

"Isn't that Mr. Wilkerson?"

I looked in the direction he was pointing. It was indeed the person of interest. He was headed in the direction of town. This was like a sign from heaven. The train yard guardian was going away, and we were going in.

"Ben is going to take me to see the trains," I heard Mike whisper beside me.

I fixed him with a glare.

"If you want me to take you in there, you can't be talking to any of your invisible little friends, got it?"

He nodded enthusiastically, and we walked back to the south gate, ducking into the train yard as quickly and as quietly as two kids could. There was only one train I wanted to see and it was right in the middle. I had spotted it my first time through with Sarah, and I wanted to see it again, for just a minute. It was a big black steam engine and coal car, a 2-8-0 Consolidation. We approached the old steam train as if it were on hallowed ground. Although the years of sitting in the bone yard had not been kind to the old steam engine, it was still a breathtaking site.

"Whoa," Mike said as we stood in front of it.

I echoed his sentiment. "Yeah, whoa."

"It's just like Dad's, isn't it?"

Yeah, it was just like Dad's model engine. We only ever saw the train during Christmas, but it was just as much a part of Christmas as the tree itself. My dad had gotten the electric train set when he was my age, and every year for as long as I could remember, it took the little people of the little village to places we as children only dreamed of.

"We're not going to stay long," Mike said to his invisible friend with some agitation. "You are going to get me in trouble. Now, shhhhhh!"

I only had to look at him, and he did the zip his lip move. I turned back to the old steam engine car. I loved trains, and this one was one of my favorites. This engine was a workhorse despite its size. It could pull loads twice as heavy as some of the others in service which was in the late 1800s. Consolidation 2-8-0's had been built for running freight in and round the western Pennsylvania area. They ranged in size from small, like this one, to ones that weighed more than 200,000 lbs. The wheel size on some of the larger models was sixty-three inches in diameter. I would have to ask my dad, but I believed this engine had been built and used in the Lehigh Valley area.

I helped Mike get into the engine and was climbing in myself, when we heard a loud crash. Mike and I jumped. Old Mr. Wilkerson was coming out of a maintenance shed, a hundred feet away from us. He was cussing up a blue streak and looking over his shoulder, saying words that would have surely gotten my mouth washed out with soap. Who was he talking to? The only thing to do was stay hidden. It was at this moment Mike announced he had to pee.

"You are going to have to hold it," I whispered.

When I was a little kid and had to pee, the only thing that seemed to stop it was doing the pee dance. Since we were crouched and hiding in the cab of an old locomotive, with a crazy old man nearby, the pee dance wasn't going to be an option.
"Ben, please, I got to go bad."

Looking heavenward, I said a silent little prayer Mike would be able to hold out just a few more minutes. Although, I was concerned about being caught, I was also bothered we had not heard the old man come back into the train yard. How did he get into the old shed? We could hear bits of the animated conversation he was having with himself. It was eerily similar to conversations I had heard Mike have with his invisible friend.

What we could hear sounded like "Just leave me alone," and "I will take care of it when it is time and not before." I guess prayers do get answered, because just as Mike was getting ready to explode, Wilkerson went back into the shed and slammed the door shut.

We waited another couple of minutes before climbing out of the cab and ran towards our home. When you are desperate, you can do miraculous things, and Mike was proving the old saying true. It took all I had to keep up with him. He no sooner got past the corner of the fence, before he ran behind one of the bushes and let nature take over.

Chapter 27
Wakeful Warning

♀ "Hey, girls, can you give me a hand with this?" Dad asked as he struggled with a large trunk. Dad had been volunteered to help Mom's friend, Irene, by moving various items for the church rummage sale and he had to empty his pickup truck.

Steph jumped off the tailgate and we both rushed to his side. Even with the three of us, the trunk was still too heavy to carry upstairs. Dad flipped the lid open.

"Hold on, let's empty this thing to make it lighter."

Emptying things was my favorite thing to do. It was where most of my treasures came from. Dressers, desks and cedar chests reaped many valuable knick-knacks to place upon my windowsill. But looking into the old trunk, I sighed. Besides the ugly green and blue striped wallpaper peeling off the inside, it seemed to be filled to the brim with fabric. Curtains, bedspreads, blankets, and a few balls of yarn were neatly tucked in place.

"Awww, man."

Dad pulled a metal garbage can from the corner and placed it near the trunk. We transferred its mildewed contents to the can until something fell from the folds of a blanket and hit my foot. Looking down, I saw what looked to be a pocketknife. Steph bent and picked it up, turning it in her hands as she inspected it.

"Where have I seen this before?" she asked with furrowed brows.

I snatched it from her fingers. "Dad, where did this trunk come from?"

He paused as if retracing his steps.

"I believe from Ben's house," he said, adding Mr. Whiting had found a few more things in the attic to get rid of.

The knife wasn't big. It had a brown plastic casing with deep grooves carved into it, resembling tree bark. Turning it over, I noticed a silver emblem. Sure enough, it was a Boy Scout emblem. This was Ben's knife.

"Giddy up, girls!" Dad said as he lifted the trunk again.

Shoving the knife in my pocket, I grabbed the other end. We carried the empty and much lighter trunk upstairs. Heading back, I couldn't imagine how Ben's knife ended up in an old trunk in his attic. Dad closed the barn doors as I walked through the yard toward the house.

Steph came up behind me. "Sarah, can I see the knife again?"

I pulled the knife from my pocket and handed it to her.

"Don't get any ideas. It's Ben's knife, ya know."

Steph wasn't smiling as she studied the knife and brought it close to her face. When she pulled out the blade, her eyes lit up for a moment, but she continued to scowl.

"What, Steph?"

Handing the knife back to me, she turned away and crossed her arms.

"It was just a dream I had. I don't want to talk about it."

She had been having more dreams than usual; Mom had mentioned Steph was talking in her sleep a lot lately. Nightmares, however, were rare for her.

"Come on, Steph, tell me." She shook her head stubbornly.

"Can you give me a hint?" I pleaded.

Turning to face me she nodded. "Okay, just one hint and no more questions."

Kicking the dirt beneath her feet, she stalled.

"*Steph!*"

"*Shut up, Sarah!*" she shouted. "*Just listen!*"

Frustrated beyond belief, I obeyed.

"Tell Ben to make sure he never goes anywhere without his knife," she instructed.

"Why?"

She looked me in the eyes and shook her head.

♂ Mike whispered something a few times but kept shrugging his shoulders and walking. When we reached our front yard, I turned him around.

"Okay, spill it. You have something to say, so say it."

A whole host of emotions swept across Mike's face as he stood there.

"I know I'm not supposed to talk about my managenary friend, but. . ."

Ever since he was born, Mike always carried on long and detailed conversations with no one. At first, everyone was kind of freaked out about it because we thought he was a little crazy. We took him to see a doctor. He said lots of kids go through this and Mike would eventually grow out of it. We were told not to encourage him or to give it a name and over time, things would become normal.

This was the most activity I had seen in a long time. And it didn't seem like a coincidence the friend was named Elizabeth.

"Okay, what is it about your imaginary friend has you so bothered?"

He drew in the dirt with his toe.

"Since we moved here, something has been different."

For Mike to want to talk about it, something big had to happen.

"What is different?"

I could tell he was still reluctant.

"Okay, I promise not to tell anyone."

I guess it was what he was waiting for.

"Ummmm, is it okay my friend is a girl?"

I was so not ready for this question. I had to repeat it back to him just to make sure I heard him correctly.

"Let me get this straight. You're worried cause she is a *Girl*?"

Mike nodded his head up and down.

I was going to ask another question, when I saw Mom standing in the front doorway.

"It's perfectly fine your friend is a girl. Just don't tell mom."

As we reached the front porch, Mom smiled at us. We smiled back, but neither one of us knew what we were smiling for.

Her smile broadened not unlike the Cheshire cat from Alice in Wonderland.

"So how was your photography class?"

Oh boy, this was not good. The mom network must have gone into action when we left Sarah's house.

"Sarah's mom had to cancel it. We ate breakfast and hung around for a bit."

Okay, so it was only partly true. With her arms crossed and the smile still firmly planted on her face, she continued.

"That's interesting. Sarah's mom called right after you left and apologized for having to cancel the class, and that was forty-five minutes ago."

Oh no. Mike and I looked at each other. I was trying to decide if I could outrun him, because I was not sure what was going through his mind. I decided to tell her the truth – or at least some of it.

"We went exploring a little."

My mom's body language was telling me, I wasn't out of the woods.

"Okay, so does exploring have to involve so much grease and dirt?"

Looking at my scout shirt, I noticed for the first time a big grease smear going across my chest. Mike's clothes didn't look much better.

"Sorry, Mom," we said in unison.

"I know you guys are just trying to get to know the neighborhood, please try to find a cleaner way of doing it."

We were promptly marched to the laundry room where we were taught the fine art of stain removal.

I didn't realize just how much hard work went into getting grease out of a scout shirt, until I had to do my own. Mike kept giving me dirty looks the whole time like it was my fault. Even he knew what trouble we would be in if we divulged where the grease came from.

Once we got done with the shirts, Mom had us change into "work clothes" and follow her upstairs to my room. When we reached my room, I was not prepared for what was there. Everything was covered in plastic, and the two walls that had wallpaper on them had long cuts in them. Turning around and facing us, she explained we were going to be helping her remove it.

"I have already started on this wall, and if we work together we can have this room done before your father gets home. I want to paint your room tomorrow."

She gave me a metal blade putty knife and told Mike to keep picking up the paper and putting it in the garbage can.

Mom was going around and spraying with a squirt bottle. Once she figured it had soaked in, we pulled. Starting at the top, she pulled it to where I could grab it and help pull it to the bottom. Most of the time this worked out well, but sometimes we would have to scrape the wallpaper off in smaller pieces. We worked for two hours straight with little breaks for water. It was a little after two when we stopped for something to eat.

While Mom was downstairs, I explored my room. Mike had gone to his room to play with his plastic army guys, so I was alone. I looked at the boards that made the walls in my room, when I noticed over by the window, the boards didn't look secure. I knocked on the ones under the sash. Three of them were loose. After several minutes of pushing and pulling them, I found they were interlocked from left to right. Once I had them out, I looked into the hole. My mind was racing with a hidden map showing the location of buried treasure, but all I saw was the outside siding.

I opened the bottom drawer of my dresser and retrieved my Boy Scout flashlight to look deeper into the hole. Shining the beam to the left,

I was disappointed to see nothing. I looked to the right and saw a wooden box, six inches wide by twelve inches long. I stuck my arm inside, to my elbow before reaching it. I sat back on my knees and was just about to open it...

"Whatcha doing?"

To say that I screamed was an understatement. I wanted to tie a bell around Mike's neck. Sliding the box under my bed, I hoped Mike had not seen it.

"Mom is going to be mad if she sees the hole," he said with attitude.

I put the boards back.

"This would be a good place to hide stuff," I said to Mike.

The rest of the day flew by as we prepped the room for paint. By the time I finished dinner, I was ready for bed. Unfortunately, sleep was not something that came easy that night. Downstairs on the pull-out couch, I tossed and turned, listening to noises. The couch bed had a huge lump right in the middle that was a pain in the butt. I kept obsessing over the box I had found hidden. I hadn't examined it much, but I noticed it was heavy and something inside slid from one end to the other when I moved it.

I took my little flashlight and pointed it in the direction of our old wall clock. The time was 2:59 am. It had always been a comfort to hear the old clock tick away the minutes of the day. Dad had turned off the chime, but you could still hear the hammer try to strike on the half hour and the hour. The noise reminded me of a necklace of beads being shuffled from one hand to another. "Shhhhhhlink, shhhhhlink, shhhhhlink."

3:00 a.m. the witching hour. I flopped back down on the couch and punched my pillows in frustration.

"Please let me go to sleep."

But my mind kept going back to the box. What was in it? Who did it belong to? Was it safe? Why would I be worried if it was safe or not? Nobody knew about it but me.

I finally decided, since I wasn't sleeping, I might as well just take a few minutes to get the box from under my bed. I wasn't doing anything else productive. As soon as my feet hit the cold hardwood floor, I wished I had worn slippers downstairs. I turned on my little flashlight and headed towards the hall.

As I reached the banister, I saw a flash of light shine out from under the basement door. Being extremely curious, I had to find out why.

Yeah, I know I don't like spiders and I'm jumpy when my little brother comes up behind me, but it doesn't mean I am a complete coward. I just have issues with spiders and sneaky little brothers.

The closer to the basement door I got, the colder the floor became. As I reached for the door handle, I heard Sarah.

"Ben, don't go in the basement alone!" Her voice was so loud in my head, it almost seemed as if she was there with me. I withdrew my hand from the door and backed away. I re-thought my plan to explore.

As I headed up the carpeted stairs, holding on to the banister, I didn't look back. I was afraid my curiosity might override my friend's warning. Instead, I concentrated on placing each foot with great care so as to not wake anyone. I had learned over the last few days, I had to walk down the hall in a certain way, to avoid the squeaky boards that would announce my presence.

I was making good progress when I heard the squeak of a hinge from my room. I had heard that sound before. It was my closet door. I put my hand over the front of my flashlight and shined it at my feet while I checked to see if the door to my parents' room was closed. It was. I reached out to open my door and heard the squeak again. Turning the handle slowly, I pushed it open.

The dusk to dawn light my dad had installed on our garage, cast strange shadows as it poured into my room. With everything covered in plastic, my furniture looked like ghosts. We opened my windows earlier to let the place air out. The light breeze blew the plastic and made swishing sounds as it blew back and forth across the floor. I shined my flashlight in the direction of the closet; it was shut tight. As

I went around my bed to the side where I had put the box, I came to a sudden stop. There, where I had put back the boards, stood a gaping black hole. The boards were placed carefully against the wall. I whirled, dropped to my knees, looked under my bed – and let out a sigh of relief. The box was still where I had hidden it.

As I reached under the bed, I glanced towards the closet. The door was now slightly opened where it had been closed before. I grabbed the box and stood. I shined the light at the closet, which was once again closed. Most likely it was just the breeze, I told myself. I would talk to my dad about it tomorrow if he had time.

I had just stepped out of my bedroom when a loud bang came from downstairs. Throwing stealth and curiosity out the window, I ran through the hallway to my little brother's room. Pushing his door open, I crossed the room in two large steps to land on his bed. He sat and rubbed the sleep from his eyes.

"Is it morning yet?"

"No... it isn't time to get up yet."

Mike rolled over and went back to sleep. I guessed he wasn't surprised I was there. I had been asked earlier if I wanted to sleep in his bed and I had turned it down; I was practically a grown up. But now, sleeping in the security of my little brother's room, seemed like a good idea. Reaching below, I slid the box under his bed.

Chapter 28
Puzzle Paradox

♀ Dad was standing with his back leaned against the sink, eating a piece of burnt toast. Plugging my nose, I squeezed by him and grabbed a glass and the milk jug.

"Aww, come on, Sarah. Burnt toast is good for you, it puts hair on your chest," he said as crumbs fell out of his mouth on to the floor. So that was where my manners came from.

"I'll remember that the next time I want to braid my chest hair," I said, poking him in the side.

As I took a sip of milk, I noticed the open jar of peanut butter had tiny black specks inside and there was a puddle of milk on the counter.

"Mom is going to flip. You got crumbs in the peanut butter again." I commented as he wiped his hands on the front of his pants. "No, she won't."

He put the lid back on the jar and shoved it to the back of the cupboard. Taking a new jar from a bag next to the toaster, he placed it in front of the cans of tuna fish. Finger to his lips, he whispered, "Our little secret, okay?"

I giggled and hugged him tightly.

"Gotta run." he said as he walked out the back door. "Going to an auction today. Steph is in the car waiting."

No sooner had they pulled out of the driveway when I raced to Steph's room. Steph had a diary, a little red book with a gold lock. If there was anywhere to find her secrets – how she knew about Ben and the knife – it was there.

Each time I entered Steph's room, I had the overwhelming urge to dirty it a little. It was way too perfect. Her bed was always neatly made with at least a dozen stuffed animals perched on top of her pillow. You never saw clothes on the floor or dresser drawers hanging open. Each little knick-knack had its own place on her dresser, and the books on her shelves were always arranged in alphabetical order. Not only did it make me sick, but I had to be careful when I was snooping.

I went directly to the bed where I gingerly lifted each stuffed animal and looked beneath it. Kneeling, I lifted the bed skirt and peered under the bed. Not even a dust bunny. I lifted my head too quickly and banged it on the bed frame. "Ouch!" I rubbed the back of my head.

Sitting on the floor, I scanned the room and tried to put myself into a nine-year-old girl's head.

"Where in the world would she hide it?" I mumbled.

The animals on the bed were staring at me. "What are you lookin' at?"

My gaze settled on the closet across the room – the mother lode.

I jumped to my feet and opened the two louvered doors quietly. Steph's closet had always been the place to find anything and everything I could possibly want. It housed not only her clothes and shoes, but boxes and shelves of everything under the sun. This floor to ceiling, awesome, organized, modern day treasure chest had to be where she hid it. I teased my sister about keeping things, calling her Grandma Steph because our grandmother was the queen of recycling. Grandma not only kept paper grocery bags but also bread ties, takeout containers, and every color, shape, and size button ever made.

I pushed the clothes to the side so the light above would reach the floor. It was covered with shoes neatly lined in rows. I reached overhead and pulled two boxes down, only to find doll clothes and school projects. As I pushed the clothes further aside, I noticed one of the coats had something square in its pocket. Reaching in, I hit the jackpot. I pulled the red-bound diary from its hiding place, triumphant. Now, I just needed to get the lock open without breaking it.

I rushed to Steph's dresser and opened her jewelry box. I found an old Christmas pin shaped like a penguin, perfect for the job of lock picking. Sticking the pin into the lock, I jiggled it around feeling for some type of release.

Footsteps were coming up the hall. Oh no! I wasn't going to get kicked out of developing class over my sister's diary. Throwing down the pin, I rushed to the closet and back to the dresser again. Running in circles, I couldn't decide what to do first. Did I put the pin back? Did I close the closet door? Which coat was the diary in again? Once I realized I couldn't get out of the room without Mom seeing me, I dove into the closet.

Leaving the pin where it sat, I closed the doors and pulled the clothes in front of me. Mom was humming as she came into the room. I heard her plop something on the floor and the sounds of her opening the drawers on Steph's dresser, putting away clean clothes. Mom had been doing laundry to get it out of the way of the dark room.

I realized I was still holding the diary and quickly stuck it back in a coat pocket to get rid of the evidence. When it was safe and Mom had left the room, I exhaled. I was shocked when the closet doors flew open.

I shrunk against the wall again. Mom hung the robe on a hook to the left and reached out to straighten the hanging clothes. Just as I was about to be found, the doorbell rang. Ever heard the expression "saved by the bell?"

Mom froze in place and yelled, "Be right there!" She closed the closet doors and headed downstairs.

Moving quickly, I left the closet, returned the pin to its proper place, and got out of there. My lock picking would have to be saved for a later date.

♂ As I stood on Sarah's front porch holding the mysterious box, I smiled anxiously at Mike. It was killing him that I refused to answer the numerous questions he had asked about it on the walk over.

The box was beautifully crafted with little inlaid roses in each corner. I used my sleeve to brush away some of the dirt and dust caked on it. The wood looked like <u>birds eye maple</u>. It had swirls in the grain and must have been polished to a glass-like finish at one time. The roses were inlaid with reddish purple wood. A brass strip, one quarter of an inch-wide, cut right across the center of the box from right to left. There were two sets of tiny brass hinges, a pair in the front and a pair in the back. How did you open it?

Mike frowned at me while he knocked on the screen door. Sarah's mom came to the door, looking frazzled.

"Why don't you boys go into the backyard and hang out for a few minutes while I finish getting things ready and we wait for Nate? I will send Sarah out."

We sat on the steps to the back porch. Sarah bounced out the door almost instantly and threw herself next to me.

"What is that?"

I handed it to her as I relayed the story of where I found it and what had happened the night before. As I talked, she twisted and turned it, looking at it from one angle or another, while she blew strands of hair out of her eyes.

"I can't see how it opens," I admitted.
She smiled like she knew a secret.

"This is an old puzzle box. My dad has collected a couple of these over the years. They made boxes like these to keep valuables safe. It is kind of like the locks on a diary."
Spinning it one more time, she was now looking at the bottom.

"Gotcha!"

Flipping the box back over so she was now looking at the top, we both heard a faint click.

The brass piece that ran down the center of the lid popped up. Slowly, she removed the brass strip, revealing the lid was two pieces that opened from the middle. She placed it on the steps between us and opened the lids. Her hand was in the way of seeing what was in the box, but I heard Mike's surprised reaction.

Inside, was a man's huge gold ring. I slapped Mike's hand away as I picked it up. I couldn't believe how heavy it was. As I turned it so we could see the face of it, we let out a gasp. The face of the ring was a small spider and looked like it was made of crystal.

"Those are diamonds." Sarah said.

I wasn't going to argue with her. I looked closer at the ring and recognized the spider. It was the same spider stamped on the bottle we had found in the garage.

I handed the ring to Mike, who was fidgeting with excitement. One by one, we unloaded a treasure trove of miscellaneous items – dried flowers that looked like they had once been roses, a hand carved wooden horse, several letters, along with a fat envelope at the bottom of the box. Sarah took one of the smaller envelopes and opened it while I took the fat one.

I wouldn't make a good archeologist because I didn't open the envelope with much care. The old brown paper tore easily enough. When I shook out the contents, the first things to hit my hand were round, silver coins. I almost yelled jackpot while the rest of the envelope's contents - old bills - fluttered to the steps. Mike jumped up to gather them while I unfolded the last thing in the envelope, a note. I read it aloud.

My Dearest Elizabeth,
  This is all I have saved for the day that I can provide for you a home of our own. Please keep this safe, I do not trust those I bunk with, I have found them more than once going through my personal belongings. I look forward to the day we can both leave this place and start a life of our own. You are in my dreams at night and my thoughts during the day. Always know I love you.
Yours forever,
Henry
  Ps. I am so sorry about last night in your daddy's garage, had I known

your little sister was going to show up I would have chosen another place to meet. I will replace your pearl necklace someday.
Our love is eternal.

Chapter 29
Progress Perfected

♀ Mike froze in place, with his hands full of money and the ring on his thumb.

"Did that letter say Elizabeth?" he asked with wide eyes.

Ben handed the letter to Mike who was stuffing the money back into the box. Mike looked at the letter, and then at his big brother with urgency and desperation.

Ben nodded at Mike. "It's okay. You can trust Sarah."

There was a brief moment of silence as Mike looked at me and back to Ben again. "Even if you told me not to talk about it, *ever*?" he asked.

Ben nodded again and smiled with uncertainty, almost as if he was afraid of what his brother was going to say.

"Elizabeth is my minaginary friend," Mike blurted out.

I looked at Ben's face and could tell it was profound in some way, but I was lost. Before I could complain I was being left out, Nate came around the back corner of the house.

"Hey!"

Ben grabbed the letter from Mike's hand and shoved it back into the box along with the ring before I had a chance to even say hello. By the time Nate reached out and gave me a shock on the shoulder, Ben already had the box tucked under his arm.

Mom stuck her head out the back door to let us know she was ready for class to begin. We headed for the basement.

Mom had one of her puzzles set up on the kitchen table, ready and waiting for Mike, and bribed him in with the promise of cookies and milk. As Nate headed toward the stairs, I pulled Ben aside to reassure him.

"Nate is cool. I know we can count on him to keep quiet."

He attempted to smile, and I could tell he was still worried about the box. Taking it from under his arm, I carried it to the bottom of the basement stairs and slid it under the bottom two steps. We would have to continue this later. For now, we had film to develop.

Mom had cleared two areas for the boys to work in, each far enough away from the other so as to give them enough space. At each station were supplies, a bottle opener, an old film canister, scissors, a pitcher of clear liquid, a silver cylinder resembling a thermos, and what looked like an oversized spool for thread. Next to the supplies were two of her old kitchen aprons and two red bandana handkerchiefs.

Nate gave Ben a funny look as he held the yellow flowered apron in front of him and posed like a model. Ben smiled and mimicked the same with his checkered red and white apron with "Bless this Mess" on the front. As they flipped their make-believe long hair and fluttered their eyelashes, I shook my head and glanced at my mom who was oblivious of the silent comedy team behind her back. By the time she turned to face us, they were dressed and behaving.

I pulled up a stool as she explained the steps they were going to practice with junk film that had no photos on it. <u>Film</u> looked like long strands of transparent grey plastic. Segmented squares ran down the length where each photo was etched into the surface. Nate stared intently at her lips and nodded as she spoke. They would go through the steps to developing practice film three times with the lights on, twice with the blindfold and finish by developing their own roll of film for real with the lights off. Film had to be developed in the dark because you ruined it if you exposed it to natural light.

I watched as they went through the process for the first time. Removing the end cap off of the film canister with the bottle opener, they pulled out the tightly wound film. Taking the scissors, they trimmed the end of the film straight across to get rid of the tape and uneven edges. They wound the film around the spool and put it inside of the silver film tank, making sure the lid was on tight.

It seemed simple enough and I could tell the boys were confident. They grinned at each other and gave the thumbs up sign. Mom had them repeat the process two more times, making sure to give Nate some individual instructions and stressing the importance of putting everything back in the same exact spot. This was mostly for Nate's benefit since when the lights were out, he wouldn't be able to get instructions by reading her lips or by me signing. Once they had memorized their work areas, she put them to the test by putting their blindfolds on.

It reminded me of playing pin the tail on the donkey except we didn't spin them in circles to make them dizzy. They were uncoordinated enough without the spinning. I sat back and enjoyed it as they stumbled, knocked things to the floor, and laughed uproariously. Nate dropped his film canister four times and eventually got turned around and confused. I stepped in and led him back to his station as Ben swung his arms stiffly out in front of him like Frankenstein and knocked the pitcher over. A flood of solution ran onto the floor near his feet. Before we could warn him, he slipped and fell hard on his backside.

Mom covered her mouth to hide her giggles and declared a time out to clean up the mess. I pulled Nate's blindfold off and pointed to Ben who was still sitting on the floor. Nate laughed as he pulled off Ben's blindfold and offered his hand. Ben acted embarrassed and reached to take Nate's hand. Hesitating, he wrapped his hand in his apron and accepted the help.

Once everything was straightened, mopped, and back in order, we began again. This time we used the "cement technique." Mom had the boys imagine their feet were stuck in cement to prevent too much jumping around. It seemed to work magnificently as they moved together like synchronized swimmers. After the final practice run with lights on, the mood shifted to a more serious one as the boys retrieved their own film.

Mom assigned me to stand behind Nate as she stood near Ben. She counted down from three on her fingers and switched the overhead light off. I always hated this part. I didn't like having my eyes wide open only to see complete blackness. I reached out and held on to Nate's belt loops on the back of his blue jeans as he moved quickly. As I closed my eyes, the sounds seemed amplified in the dark – the faint clinking of metal against plastic, the quick snip of the scissors, and the rattling sound as lids were tightened.

I heard Ben say, "Done." Nate had already finished first

because he was standing still.

Mom walked past us to the light switch. "Everyone ready?"

"Ready, Freddy!" I called out. The lights flickered back on.

Our eyes adjusted to the brightness of the room while Mom brought two new pitchers of developing solution to the counter. I caught Ben rubbing his backside. When I saw a huge wet spot on the back of his pants, I smiled sympathetically. The boys took turns filling their film tank through a small hole in the lid and swirled it gently in their hands. After a few more minutes, they drained their canisters and repeated the process two more times with different solutions until it came time to rinse the film. They moved to the large double cement sink, opened their tanks, rinsed the film or <u>negatives</u> thoroughly, and attached clips to both ends to hang them for drying.

Mom complimented them on a job well done and instructed us to head outside for a couple hours until the film dried.

♂ Sarah and I raced for the stairs, grabbed the hidden box, and headed outside. Nate came running after us, followed closely by Mike and Steph. "Hey, wait up!"

I looked at Sarah and it was like some agreement passed between us. Sarah grabbed a blanket and spread it on the grass. All five of us formed a circle on the plaid fabric, with the box in the middle. Like it or not, what had started out as just a ghost story, had turned into a mystery that went far beyond what I or anyone else could ever have imagined. We sat for another few minutes as if waiting for the box to do something on its own.

"Okay umm. Before we look in the box again we need to let Nate, Steph and Mike in on everything that has happened so far since we moved here,"

I looked at each person in the circle to see I had his or her attention. Once I was sure they understood and were listening to me, I continued.

"Before we do this, I want to make sure everyone here understands what is said here will not go anywhere else." Looking directly at Mike, I emphasized, "We won't tell anyone, will we?"

Just as I was getting ready to continue, Mike blurted out, "Ben, is it okay if I told Steph what I saw in the box?"

I reassured him while Sarah put her hand into the center of the circle with her little pinky extended.

"Pinky swear."

I was second with my little pinky, then Nate, Steph, and finally Mike. It was a good thing Sarah had long fingers.

"Repeat after me, I, state your name."

The group followed by saying, "I, state your name." After the giggles and an explanation, we started again, each of us substituting our names. "I, Ben-Sarah-Nate-Steph-Mike, will not tell anyone about what is said here."

A whirlwind swept into the backyard picking clean the dandelion fluff and swirling it around our group. I was lightheaded. Sarah was rubbing her arms like she was cold.

Mike broke the silence by whispering in the direction of the tree.

"Mike, what are you doing?"

The smile on his face couldn't have been bigger.

"Ben, my maginary friend wants me to tell you something."

I lifted one eyebrow.

"Elizabeth says, 'Thank you.'"

For some reason I was not surprised. I sat for a minute before deciding where to begin. It was like we were sitting around a campfire telling ghost stories minus the campfire, of course, and in this case, the story was true.

I told everyone what I had witnessed so far since we had moved into the house. What had happened to Sarah and me in the basement. I told them of the little dreams or visions I had had. Sarah and I talked about the train yard and the library, old man Wilkerson, and the strange noises in the basement of our house. Sarah filled in the spots I missed.

Mike spoke up.

"Do you think seeing ghosts is like seeing manginary friends?"

I didn't know what to say. I mean, he did have a point.

Steph was next. "I have dreams, too, Ben, but they aren't like the dreams you had."

We could tell this was hard for her to say, so we remained quiet while she searched for the words.

"My dreams sometimes show me things that might happen, but

I don't always understand them until later." Her eyes got serious. "I had one just yesterday and you were in it." She looked at Sarah. "I told Sarah about it because we found your pocket knife in the old trunk. Remember, Sarah?"

Sarah reached into her back pocket and pulled out my lost Boy Scout pocketknife. She turned it over and over in her hand before slowly handing it to me.

Steph continued. "I saw it and knew you needed it" She looked at her hands as if embarrassed.

"I'm sorry, Ben. Sometimes my dreams don't always make sense. But I do know you have to have that knife with you."

Once the stories stopped, we were frozen in place until Sarah reached for the box. She turned it over so we could see the back. In the sunlight, I could see two places, shiny from repeated handling. As Sarah applied pressure on these two spots, they pushed in. The brass bar fell to the blanket, followed by the contents of the box. As the letters, ring, and money appeared, a low whistle came from Nate. Steph gasped.

"I found this box in my room behind my wall," I announced.

Possessive of the box and its contents, I wanted to let everyone know it was mine. This was not like me, but it was important the contents remained with the box. I quickly gathered the paper money and the silver dollars and placed them back into it.

Nate asked if he could look at the large gold and diamond ring, which was glittering in the sunlight. I handed it to him.

Sarah was opening another one of the letters, taking care not to tear the envelope the way I did with the large envelope earlier. Steph and Mike were looking at the hand-carved horse figure when Sarah gasped. She sniffed and tried to control her voice. "You guys have to listen to this."

My Dearest Elizabeth,

My heart broke seeing you standing by your parents' grave by yourself. How I wish I could have held you in my arms to comfort you. I blame myself for their deaths. I know you don't feel the same, but it was my fault. Had I been more patient and waited, they would still be alive today. Someday, I will be able to stand by you without anyone judging us. I will wait for you for as long as it takes. Soon Katrina will not need you as her guardian, and we will be together. Never forget I

love you, you are in my heart always.
Love,
 Henry

    I wouldn't admit this to anyone, but I was a little teary-eyed when Sarah finished reading the letter.
Nate broke the silence. "I have teen this ring before."
 He was holding the ring in the light.
    "The guy the library was named after, Mr. Robinson. His picture is in the library, over the entrance door. He is wearing a ring like that."
    Sarah and I were in the process of gathering the stuff and placing it carefully in the box, when Sarah's mom called us back in.
    "Hey, Scouts, are you ready to see how good you are at taking pictures?"
Nate and I high-fived each other as we both shouted, "*Yes!*"

Chapter 30
Necromancer Nate

    ♀ Steph and Mike took off in the direction of the barn. I bent and picked up the blanket to fold it. Ben flashed me a smile and held up the knife to thank me for finding it. I nodded and smiled back. Taking the box, Nate reached the bottom of the basement stairs first and stood waiting for us. Ben took the box with ritualistic ceremony and placed it beneath the stairs. I could picture them saluting each other. Instead, they grinned at each other and high fived. Ben recoiled after the zap of static. Nate laughed.
    "Don't worry, you get ute to it."
    The darkroom looked different after the break. While we were making our secret pact on the back lawn, Mom had been doing some major rearranging. On one side of the table sat a large machine resembling an overhead projector. This contraption, though oddly shaped, was fairly simple and easy to use. The negatives went into a slot right below a white light bulb, which reflected the image on to

special paper near the bottom. On the other side of the table was an ordinary kitchen timer and four trays, each filled with clear liquid. Mom had already trimmed the long strands of negatives to shorter pieces, put them in sleeves, and labeled them according to whom they belonged to. I looked at the reddish colored bulb above our heads that replaced the normal one from earlier and got excited. This was my favorite part, when the magic began.

The second half of class went much smoother. The safelight gave the room an odd orange hue, and although the room was still relatively dark, the boys could see enough to navigate. They were amazed at how only seconds under the enlargement machine light, could turn a blank piece of paper into a photograph. They dropped each and every white piece of paper into the first tray and watched as the picture slowly appeared. We gushed over the images as they formed an assembly line, set the timer, dipped them into each tray, and eventually hung them to dry on the clothesline. Occasionally, I would see a faint spark of light as their hands touched.

"Not again!" Ben said as they burst into a fit of laughter.

I asked Mom, who seemed to be entertained, if the spark would do anything to the photos. She said the source of light was so small it wouldn't make a difference.

Just as the last print went into the third tray, we heard a popping sound. The safelight above our heads dimmed and went dark. I froze in place.

"Hey! Who turned out the lights?" Ben shouted.

"No one move," Mom said. "I think our bulb blew out."

The timer went off to signal it was time to transfer the final photo into the last tray. I heard the swish of liquid as Ben fished around for the paper and plopped it into the last rinsing tray. I saw a brief zap of light as he touched hands with Nate who was reaching out in the darkness. As I listened to the sounds of my mom shuffling her feet in the direction of the door, the temperature dropped and the hair on my arms stood up. As if on cue, Ben said, "I don't feel too good." I heard a thud on the floor across from me.

Nate was still wandering around nearby, unable to hear what was going on, and I assumed he was slightly panicked. He kept asking, "Anyone there?"

Mom apparently reached the door. I heard the jiggling of the doorknob, but for some reason she wasn't opening it.

"Mom! Open the door!" I yelled.

Mom replied with frustration in her voice, "I'm trying, honey, the door is stuck."

My legs crumpled beneath me as I sat on the floor shaking.

"Ben! Ben? Are you okay?" I yelled as I looked blindly in his direction.

There was no answer.

Just as I crawled toward Ben, the safelight flickered back on. I looked up and noticed Nate standing with his hand on the bulb. At the same precise moment, Mom managed to push open the door, letting in enough light to reveal Ben lying on the floor in a heap.

Mom rushed to Ben's side as I mustered up enough strength to reach the regular light bulb on the shelf near to me and hand it to Nate. Nate replaced the safelight bulb with the other one, which brought the room back to full light again. Ben had opened his eyes and looked around confused. Mom had her hand under his head.

"Are you okay, Ben?"

He nodded and asked for a drink of water. Mom rushed upstairs while I crawled over to him. I didn't hear Nate calling my name. It wasn't until he raised his voice that I snapped out of it and looked at him.

He was standing under the clothesline. The photos that had been hanging on it were scattered around his feet. In his hand, he held the safelight bulb – and it was still glowing.

♂ Just like the other day in the garage, I was light headed. I could hear the same loud noise and remember calling out. It was as though I was falling.

I found myself in Sarah's basement, but the boxes and dark room equipment were gone. It was empty save for an old wringer washer and a washbasin sitting next to it. A man followed a woman down the stairs. The man looked a lot like Sarah's dad.

They stopped in front of the washer, where the lady put the

empty basket and turned to the man.

"Charles, I don't understand why we shouldn't warn Henry to be careful."

Charles touched the woman's arm.

"Rebecca, while we don't approve of what Hilliard is doing, Henry was hired on as a mechanic's helper. As far as I know, that is *all* he is doing."

Rebecca pulled away from him.

"He is a nice boy. I don't want to see him get hurt, and you know he will if he gets involved in that other... business."

Charles held his hands up in surrender.

"I will talk to him tonight before he goes to bed. Speaking of beds, we have room for another boarder in the loft. James must have left last week. Funny, he didn't take his belongings."

I came to with Mrs. McNally's hand under my head and Sarah peering at me. I was still trying to clear out the cobwebs in my head, but I kept hearing Sarah's name over and over again, each time getting louder. For a moment, I thought I was the only one hearing this until Sarah looked over in the direction of the repeating voice and gasped.

When I looked over, there was Nate, doing the most peculiar thing, a magic trick – the one where the magician holds the light bulb in his hand, and it lights up. I laughed at the look on his face. It was like he was surprised the trick had worked. Startled, he dropped the light bulb, and it shattered on the floor. I couldn't figure out was why he was doing magic at a time like this.

I was soon sipping water from a paper cup and my head was much clearer. This was the second time this week I had had a dizzy, passing-out episode. Every time it happened, I experienced some sort of vision. Before now, they had only happened at home in my – let's face it – haunted house. But Sarah's house wasn't haunted, was it? Why here? Why now? Why not anywhere? What if I passed out when I was riding my bike? Heaven forbid what if I was at school?

When I was well enough to stand, I made my way over to Nate. I hadn't noticed before but scattered in a circle at his feet were the pictures we had just developed. Being careful of the broken glass from the safety light, Sarah and I helped Nate pick up the images. The three of us were unnaturally quiet. Sarah's mom walked over and saw the broken glass on the floor.

"Okay you guys, why don't you let me get the rest of this? I don't want anyone getting cut." She checked each of our hands, making sure we didn't have any glass stuck to them. "We have had enough excitement for one day. What do you think?"

We nodded our heads in unison. Fishing the balance of the pictures from off the floor and checking them for glass, Sarah's mom handed them to her.

"Why don't you take these upstairs? We will look at them in the living room."

Like zombies, we followed Sarah up the stairs. When we were at the top and walking down the hallway, she turned around and smacked my arm.
"Ouch! What did you do that for?"
I must have looked dumbfounded.

"It's for laughing at Nate." Sarah not only looked mad; she also looked scared. I was missing something here.

Nate had gone into the living room, so it was just Sarah and I in the hallway. "Before you hit me again, can I explain why I was laughing?"

She folded her arms across her chest and scrunched her eye brows together. "Go ahead, I am listening."

I took a half step back just to be on the safe side and described what I had witnessed in my vision. I got to the part about the light bulb. "Honest, I thought he had performed some kind of magic trick. I didn't realize he was scared. It looked more like he was surprised."

"You would be surprised too if the light bulb you were holding was glowing after you took it out of the socket."

I followed Sarah into the living room, where Nate was sitting in the middle of the couch. I told him why I laughed and apologized.

"That okay, I undertand."
Sarah sat on one side of Nate and I sat on the other.

"Let tee the picture." Nate reached for the stack and laid the pictures out before us like playing cards. I picked through them. The first one I pulled out was when I displayed the soapbox racer parts. It was good. Sarah had a talent for this. You could tell she had been paying attention to what her mom had shown her. The rest of the pictures had me acting like a complete dork, eyes crossed, fingers in ears. I was kind of embarrassed to see these pictures, but Sarah liked them, and Nate even chuckled.

Mrs. McNally came down the hall. She pulled up a chair and sat across from us on the other side of the coffee table. She had brought Nate's pictures and set them on the end of the table.

"Let's see what you have here, Ben."
She smiled at Sarah and me as she flipped through them.

"These look good, you two. I like the way you have framed in the work bench and the parts to your racer."

I knew she made her way to the end of the stack when she covered her mouth and laughed out loud. My face burned with embarrassment. However, on the last two pictures, she stopped commenting and carefully looked at each one.

"Sarah, did you make any changes to the settings before you took these two pictures?"

She showed them to us. They were almost like the previous ones except they had dark shadows in the corners that looked a little like silhouettes. A cold chill run up my arms as I sat looking at them. These were taken close to the time when I passed out in the garage. Sarah insisted she had done nothing different. Her mom mumbled something about taking the camera in to have it checked.

"Old cameras can do weird things if they are not regularly maintained," she explained.

The last image was the one Sarah had taken on our way to my house. It was the picture she had taken of old man Wilkerson when he was talking to himself. This picture was perfect in every detail except for a dark silhouette right in front of him. I wasn't going to say anything to anyone, but the silhouette looked to have lots of curly hair.

Chapter 31
Aggressive Ambush

♀ As we huddled around the coffee table, I couldn't shake the feeling we were being watched. I was warm enough and Ben showed no signs of lightheadedness so it couldn't have been a ghost. Did he make any connection between his passing out and our ghostly encounters?

Out of the corner of my eye, I saw movement outside the front window. Shifting only my eyes while keeping my head still, I glanced in that direction. At the bottom of the sash a pair of eyes under a blue baseball cap peeked in. Ben gathered his pile of photos and set them aside as Mom fanned out Nate's on the coffee table. While keeping my eyes glued on our spy, I listened as Mom commented on the "beautiful candid shots" of Nate's family on their last vacation. Mom mentioned a second class to work on some basics and their final project and left the room in search of her planner.

"Pssssst. Don't look now but we have a visitor," I whispered as I repeatedly moved my eyes in the direction of the window.

Ben caught on right away, but my whisper was too faint for Nate to hear. Ben elbowed Nate in the side, stood quickly and walked around the other side of the coffee table so his back was to the window. I tried hard not to laugh as Ben overly exaggerated the movements of his mouth while no sound escaped his lips. Nodding, Nate stacked his photos in a pile, glancing at the window at the same time.

I gave the countdown hand signals as nonchalantly as possible, "3 ... 2 ... 1!" On one, we all ran quickly in the direction of the front door in an effort to ambush our uninvited guest. We came face to face with Marcus on the front porch.

He didn't seem so scary when we first rounded the corner. Trapped like a rat in a maze, Marcus was hunched over with a panicked look on his face. When he stood from his kneeling position beside the window and crossed his arms across his chest, I was almost surprised to see how unusually large he was. My confidence shriveled when he smiled his crooked looking grin and laughed.

"Well, well, well. If it isn't Sara scare'ya and her deaf and dumb friends."

I took one brave step forward.

"What are you doing on my porch, Marcus?"

Marcus uncrossed his arms, shoved his hands in his pockets, and spit a large wad of tobacco near Ben's foot. Nate wrinkled his nose at the sight and moved slightly in front of me, while Ben stepped over the disgusting brown heap in defiance.

Appearing surprised by our bravery, Marcus poked Ben in the center of his chest with his chubby pointer finger. I heard a hollow thud and exhale but Ben stood his ground.

"I took a short cut today and my palm started to itch." Marcus said as he held out his hand palm up.

"What you trying to tay?" Nate asked.

Marcus mimicked Nate's speech and wiggled his fingers. "Come on, hand it over."

Ben pushed in front of Nate and knocked Marcus's hand away. "What are you talking about?"

Shaking his head, Marcus grabbed both Ben and Nate by their shirts and shoved them aside, clearing his way to me. In two steps, he was way too close for comfort. His strength was apparent as he took my arm and twisted it.

"The money, where is it?"

I realized Marcus had been spying on us. He must have been watching us when we were on the blanket. I saw the look in Ben's eyes as he silently pleaded with me to keep quiet. Playing stupid at this moment would not have been a good idea considering the pain I was in. I caved.

"In a safe place, where *you* will never find it!"

He twisted my arm again as I cringed and gritted my teeth.

"You're gonna break her arm!' Ben yelled with a worried look on his face.

The tears formed and trickled down my cheeks.

"Okay, stop." Ben demanded, "I'll give you the money. Just let her go."

Marcus let up on the twisting while he ordered Ben to get the box.

"No funny business. You say a word to the parents and I break your girlfriend's little arm."

Nate followed Ben into the house until Marcus held his free hand up to stop him. While we waited, I vaguely remembered my dad mentioning Marcus had a part-time job at the lumberyard for the summer to help his mom pay the bills. Despite his death grip on my arm, I felt sorry for him. He shuffled his enormous feet.

"What are ya lookin' at, freak?"

"Not much," I replied with a sarcastic smile.

Ben returned with the box in hand and ordered Marcus to let me go. Instead of opening it and taking the money out, he offered it to him. I was curious why Ben would give it to him when he was so protective of it earlier. Before I could figure out what he had in mind, Marcus reached out with his meaty hands and grabbed the box. In one smooth movement, Ben yanked it back, raised his knee and aimed for Marcus's groin.

Everything moved in slow motion. I watched as Ben's knee shot upward and hit Marcus in the thigh. Guess he didn't figure in the height difference when he came up with this bright idea. Marcus reacted with shock more than pain as Ben yelled, "Ruuuuun!"

We all took off in different directions, Nate into the house, I ran toward the oak tree, and Ben toward the driveway to the street. Marcus barely hesitated and made a mad dash down the driveway after Ben. Unfortunately, he caught up quickly and tackled him to the ground as the box flew through the air and bounced on its corner. The lid sprang open and the contents scattered. Instead of beating Ben to a pulp, Marcus got busy collecting the money strewn over the driveway. Once his mitts were full of cash, he took off down the street. I could hear his distant laughter when I reached Ben, who was still lying on his stomach.

Nate apparently saw everything from inside the house and came running to meet us. Ben rolled over and pulled himself to a sitting position in the grass. I bent and picked up the box, which seemed to have only some slight damage on its one corner. Nate collected the rest of the contents. As Ben picked pebbles out of his knees, I pointed out that nothing seemed to be missing except for the money.

"You okay?" Nate asked as he sat next to Ben.

"Uh huh," he mumbled.

Handing the box back to Ben, I smiled. "Well, we learned one important lesson for today."

Ben and Nate looked at me while they tried to figure it out. Bending over, I leaned in close to Ben's face and continued,

"The next time you get a bright idea, make sure you pick the fastest runner."

♂ My knees hurt. When I looked down, I saw my jeans had torn and I had bits of dirt and small rocks ground into my knees. I just wanted to go home – not to my new home, but to my old one. There I didn't have enemies like Marcus looking through windows or hiding behind bushes.

I stood and headed for home when I heard the screen door close and Mrs. McNally call out. "Ben, don't forget your little brother."
Mike had a Popsicle in his mouth. I waved at him to hurry.

"Are you going to be okay?" Sarah asked.

At that point, I didn't know. I just shrugged my shoulders. "I guess I will see you guys tomorrow. I have to get home. My dad wants my help today."

I turned and felt Sarah's hand on my arm. I guess my tough act didn't fool her.

"Are you sure you're going to be okay?"
I dropped the tough guy mask.

"I'm trying to be," I said as I attempted a smile and turned towards home.

Mike and I walked most of the way in silence, which was only broken by Mike slurping on his Popsicle. After the last of it was gone, Mike stopped walking. He had his head cocked to one side, like he was listening to something. Nodding his head once or twice he whispered, "Okay," and walked again.
When he had caught up, I asked him, "Was it Elizabeth?"
He looked at me with a little smile on his face.
"Yep, and she wants you to know Marcus isn't all bad"
I shrugged my shoulders and kept walking.

"Don't worry, big brother, we'll be okay here," Mike said as he took my hand.

At home Dad was unloading an old push mower from the back of his truck and pushing it towards the garage. It looked like he had picked up a stray and brought it home. I had never known my dad to buy a new one; he always found used ones. He knew a secret about them: most people who sold their old ones only got rid of them because they didn't know how to take care of them. Our two or three-year-old lawn mowers were as good as new once they were cleaned up. All we did with them was scrape the old grass out from underneath, sharpen the blade, put in a new spark plug, clean the carburetor, and put in new gas. If it looked like it needed more, dad wouldn't bring it home.

My spirits lifted and I forgot about my skinned knee when my dad waved at us. I loved working with him. Uninterested in machines, Mike went into the house. In the garage, I inspected the new find.

"This one will be yours when we get it fixed," he said as he got out his toolbox.

"I am sure you noticed how many lawns there are in our neighborhood, right?" He pulled out a wrench. "When I was your age and lived just a few blocks away from here, I used to make a lot of money during the summer."

He was right. This area would be a great place to start a little lawn mowing business. Seeing I was catching on, he continued. "I talked to some old friends I grew up with and they would like you to stop by and talk to them about maybe taking care of the yards this summer."

He ruffled my hair as he finished his last sentence, got up and headed to the back of the truck while I removed the spark plug. When he returned, he had something wrapped in a blanket.

"While I was out last night, I saw something else you may like."

He laid the blanket-covered object on the work bench. He waited for me to unwrap it. I removed the blanket and stared.

"Ben, I know I have been kind of grumpy over the past few weeks and we haven't had a lot of time to spend together," he said as I ran my hands across the best gift he ever gave me.

"I know you are building a soap box racer and, well, you are going to need something to steer it with."

I gave him a big hug. Dad had given me a steering wheel and

shaft from an old go-cart. It was a little rusty and needed some work, but it wasn't the gift that meant a lot. It was the fact my Dad got it for me.

Chapter 32
Pieces - Pieces

♀ Nate and I stood at the end of the driveway watching Ben and Mike disappear in to the distance. I couldn't help feeling bad for Ben. He did save me from extreme pain, but he also lost the money and a big piece of his pride in the process.

With his hands in his pockets, Nate remained quiet. One thing about having a hearing-impaired friend is he never got uncomfortable with silence. I have known Nate most of my life, since we were five, and he has always known how I was feeling by just looking at my face.

"I feel the 'tame way, Tarah," he said, looking me in the eye.

We rounded the corner in the back by the garage and found Steph sitting on the ground by the sidewalk. She was busy drawing with a piece of chalk. From the looks of it, Steph and Mike had devoted their time during the second half of class to creating masterpieces. The walk stretched at least ten feet from the back door to the garage door, and every section was crammed full. It was obvious which drawings belonged to Steph. They were mostly flowers, butterflies and rainbows, while Mike's consisted of dump trucks, tractors, and turtles, all in green and yellow.

Nate and I slowly walked from section to section. Every once in a while, we cocked our heads, and acted like art collectors.

"I just love the way the blue in the sky accents the stark white of the clouds," I said with a snobby tone.
Nate chimed in, "We have to buy it and hang it over our 'tofa."
Steph rolled her eyes.

When we got to the last section of the cement we stopped short. The drawing at our feet was different from the others. The lines seemed stronger and less childlike. There was only one color used; it was red.

The scene had a train, railroad tracks, and what appeared to be a smashed-up car. Beside the car on the ground were two stick figures, both with x's for eyes.

"Who drew this one?" I asked Steph as she attempted to wipe the chalk from her pants.

"I dunno."

"Did Mike draw it?" Nate questioned her again.

"I don't think so. The only colors I gave him were green and yellow," Steph pointed to the other drawings.

Nate gave me a puzzled look.

"Did you draw the *whole* time we were in the basement?" I asked as I searched for the missing red chalk without success.

"We took a break to get a Popsicle." She stuck out her blue tinted tongue as proof.

I nodded in the direction of the barn. Nate could barely contain himself as he jumped in front of me and walked backwards.

"Tarah, this is extiting!" His brown eyes looked enormous, and his mouth seemed to move in fast-forward. In one deep breath, his questions came at warp speed. "Whodidthedrawing... whatabouthtelightbulb... Whatdowedonow?"

I raised my eyebrows. "Breathe, Nate, Breathe."

We entered the back door to the barn where Dad's workshop was. I knew from the smell it was staining day. The long fluorescent bulbs overhead lit the cramped area. Along the back wall were metal shelving and an extremely large compressor tank. The rest of the room had various dismantled projects: a wagon wheel missing a spoke, a dresser with no drawers, and a lime green rocking chair with half of its paint stripped off. In the center of it, was my dad, his partially bald head barely visible above the mess.

"Hey, Dad!" I shouted as Nate and I walked through the maze of furniture.

The floor was littered with sandpaper, sawdust, and dirty staining rags, making it look like a tornado had gone through recently. I didn't understand how he could work in such a mess, but he seemed to know where everything was.

Just when I believed we had found our way, we rounded the corner and hit a dead end.

"I feel like a mout' looking for cheese." Nate remarked, wrinkling his nose and sticking his front teeth out.

Dad stuck his head up. "Turn left at the table top and right at the barrel."

We finally made it to the center where Dad was straddling a chair with three legs, a can of stain between his feet. Dipping a brush into the dark liquid, he slapped it carelessly onto the seat of a long deacon's bench. I picked up a rag and wiped the excess stain that pooled on the surface of the wood while Nate pulled over a wooden crate and sat.

The intense smell reminded me of a cross between gasoline and nail polish remover. I knew this smell well, as Dad often reeked of it even after washing. The tint seemed to be always under his fingernails.

Dad continued to slap the brush on the bench seat, sending drops of spray onto Nate's shoes.

"Might want to back up if you don't want brown shoes." he said loudly without even looking at us.

Nate laughed. "No biggie."

Even though the process of staining was messy, the end product always turned out beautiful. Dad's talent for rebuilding and matching old furniture was an art.

"Dad, did our relatives always own our house?" I asked as I continued to wipe the bench.

"Uh huh, why?"

"Just curious. Someone told me our barn was used for boarders."

Dad paused and looked up. "Yes, it was, when your great-grandpa owned it. Our house has been owned by the McNally side of the family all the way back to the early 1800's."

Dad filled me in on some family history. Great Grandpa Milton had worked as a "boomer" for the railroad. Boomer was slang for a drifter who went from one railroad job to another, staying for a short time on each job. They had a variety of skills and went wherever needed. Grandpa worked from the time he was sixteen until he was in his early twenties. He traveled across the country until a <u>handcar</u> ran over his leg and left him partially disabled. He retired at a young age and bought our property cheap with the railroad pension money. He took a part-time job as a mechanic's apprentice and boarded vagrants and railroad workers, giving them a safe, clean place to stay. He met Grandma after he repaired her parents' car.

"Your great-grandpa was a good man," Dad said respectfully.

The people Ben saw *were* my relatives. Nate and I exchanged an excited look.

"When your grandpa died, your mom and I moved in to take care of Grandma," Dad continued. "We inherited the house when Grandma passed.

I stood and motioned to Nate.

"Thanks, Dad. Gotta run."

Dad mumbled as he pried the lid off another can with a screwdriver. When we were half way through the maze, Dad called out.

"Oh, Sarah, there is a box of things in the barn loft that was left from when Grandma lived here. I remember being told some of it belonged to boarders."

My heart skipped a beat. "Really, what does it look like?"

"It's not too big. It's in the rafters toward the back. It has a name on the side."

Nate and I took off running. Before we knew it, we were taking the steps into the loft two at a time. Once we reached the back of the barn, I gazed upwards into the rafters. Nate pushed a cedar chest from the aisle to the back wall and stood on top of it, his head barely over the rafters.

"Do you see it?" I yelled. Nate didn't answer so I pulled on his pant leg.

"I tee it!" he screamed.

Nate got down from his perch and pushed the chest four feet to the right. We both climbed on top, pushing our heads between the rafters. Cleaning away the cobwebs, we saw a box with black lettering on the side. It looked to be wooden, no bigger than a shoebox, and extremely dirty. Since it was out of our reach, I grabbed a brass floor lamp and used it to try and push the box to the floor. It only moved slightly due to the fact it was wedged against an old bicycle.

I came up with the bright idea of climbing onto Nate's shoulders to gain more height. I could see the worry in Nate's eyes, but he reluctantly agreed. Holding on to the rafter, I hung with my feet dangling just above the lid of the chest. Nate positioned himself beneath me as he stood from a squatting position, raising me higher. I let go and held the lamp like a tightrope walker until Nate regained his balance.

My mother would have had a heart attack. As we balanced on top of the cedar chest, I extended the lamp and poked the box. Dust flew into the air and floated downward, but the box stayed put. Just as I was ready to poke it one more time, Nate yelled, "Oh, oh!"

His body swayed as he teetered on the edge of the lid. Falling forward, I hit the box, which fell to the floor as Nate slipped off the edge. I flailed and grabbed the rafter where I dangled by one arm like a chimpanzee at the zoo. Nate landed on his feet and thinking quickly, pushed an old Victorian loveseat under me to break my fall. I landed on the velvet surface of the cushion in a cloud of dust.

No sooner had the dust cleared before we were racing for the box. Nate turned it over and wiped the grime from the side with his hand. The name was printed in bold black letters, PROPERTY OF E. ROBINSON.

♂ The rest of the afternoon, Dad and I worked hard to get the old lawn mower running. We tested the spark, set and reset the settings on the carburetor. When we got it running, we mowed the lawn behind the garage together, each with our own machine. I tried to keep up with his long strides and did pretty good for the most part. Once we were done mowing and raking, it was pretty close to suppertime.

We stood side by side and watched the long shadows created by the house. The subtle patterns the lawn mowers had made in the lawn look like a green patchwork quilt.

"Looks good, doesn't it, Ben?" he asked as he put his hand on my shoulder.

Yeah, it did look good – and I felt good, too.
Dad ruffled my hair as we walked back towards the house.

"Let's get washed and ready for supper. Afterward, we will take a look at what you are building."

As we neared the house, the fine hairs on the back of my neck stood on end. I stopped and turned around to scan the back yard. I was sure we were being watched. Did I see a shadowy figure at the back of the yard fade into the darkness? Had my eyesight been a little better, I might have been sure.

"What are you looking for?" My dad asked from the bottom step of the back porch.

I turned around to follow him. "Nothin"

I don't remember supper. It had shape and flavor, but all I could think about was getting back out to the garage and working with my dad on the soap box racer. Once supper was finished, it was a mad dash to get the dishes done. Mom soon dismissed me from the kitchen because in fast wash mode, I was getting water around the sink and on the floor.

"Get going, before I have to mop the floor." she said, shaking her head.

I guess Dad was just as anxious as I was to work out in the garage because he was right behind me. "Let's see what you got here."

I showed him the parts I had gathered together and pulled off the wall the set of plans I had drawn up. "This is what I want to make." I was embarrassed by my drawing.

"I didn't have any graph paper, so the lines aren't straight."

"Don't worry about it. Let's see what parts you have, and where we can go from there."

We started building. I watched as he cut the boards on the table saw and helped by holding them as he pushed them past the spinning blade. We had to make some design changes to make it safe and so we could use the steering system from the go-cart. When we had the parts for the basic frame ready, we took a short break and sat on a couple of old five-gallon paint buckets. This was my opportunity to ask Dad some questions.

"Dad, Sarah was saying our house is, well..."

He had a big grin like he knew what I was talking about. "I see your new friends have told you of the ghost, huh?"

I nodded.

"Let's see, is it the story about the hanging man, or about a body buried in the basement?"

I hadn't heard of the hanging man.

"The basement."

"Hmmmm, the body in the basement."

He pulled the rag out of his pocket and blew his nose.

"That was always my favorite one. If I remember the story, it went like this. There was an older couple living in the house, a grumpy older guy and his timid little wife. They were always fighting and one day, she disappeared and he was seen dragging something from the garage to the basement. Sometimes they see the old guy at the hardware store buying cement or carrying bags of cement to the basement. Am I right so far?

"I guess you and your friends have looked in the basement for a newer looking patch of cement?" He patted my shoulder, leaned in and kind of whispered. I nodded and smiled sheepishly.

Dad admitted with a wink, "I'm pretty sure it's part of the reason our contractors kept quitting."

We got up from our buckets and headed back over to where we had the racer's parts laid out on the floor. I still had some questions I wanted to ask about the house.

"Who were the first owners?"

He looked up from the racer and raised an eyebrow.

"Why all the interest in the place? You don't still believe the house is haunted, do you?"

I coughed. "No, just interested in the history."

"Well, Hilliard was the original owner of the place. He had two daughters. I can't remember the names of the girls."

I almost blurted out Elizabeth and Katrina.

Wiping his hands on his pants, he looked into the rafters.

"There was an old story about the Hilliard family. The parents died when the girls were in their teens. One of them was old enough to take care of the younger one. Anyway, the parents were killed in a train accident." I inhaled sharply.

Dad didn't notice as he continued. "The weird part is no one knows what happened to the girls. They lived in the house for a little while, and one day, they just vanished. Some people assume they went out west, others say they went south. No one ever heard from them again."

Dad looked at the old clock above the workbench. It was getting close to nine o'clock.

"Hey, we need to get this cleaned up. It's getting to be that time."

Grabbing a broom and a dustpan, I made short work of the saw dust on the floor. We moved the racer parts to one side of the garage, and Dad pulled his truck into the other side for the night.

"Thanks Dad." I said as he got out of the cab.
He put his hand on my shoulder. "You're welcome."

Then he said something he didn't say often, but when he did, you knew he meant it. "Proud of you Ben."

Chapter 33
Taboo Talk

♀ Nate and I sat on the plank floor of the barn attic together and flipped the wooden box upright. When I compared the wooden rectangle to a shoebox, I couldn't have been more accurate.

On the top, an outline of what looked to be a man's shoe was barely visible. The wood had darkened with age, along with the black painted footprint that adorned its surface. A latch centered on one end made it obvious the top served as a lid. What we had found was a shoeshine box.

My dad had told me shoe shining was a common job in the early 1900s for young boys. Sometimes, children had to work to help support their poverty-stricken families. They walked the streets or set up on a busy corner and yelled loudly to attract potential customers.

Inside the box was usually a tin of shoe polish, a stiff-bristled brush, and a soft rag. The shoe outline on the top was where the customers put their feet.

Nate flipped the latch open and carefully lifted the lid. The inside smelled similar to the stain dad used on furniture. I figured it was old shoe polish.

The contents reminded me of the junk drawer in our kitchen which was full of miscellaneous, unrelated objects. We shoved everything into the shallow drawer; closing it had become a feat of extreme determination.

It amazed me with all the stuff inside the shoeshine box, the lid was closeable. I imagined someone sat on the lid much like an overstuffed suitcase to latch it. Nate and I both reached our hands inside simultaneously and bumped knuckles. A loud zap and a barely visible flash of light caused us both to giggle.

"Lady firt." Nate said with a game show hostess's wave of his hand.

I reached into the center of the jumbled mess with my pointer finger and thumb and plucked the end of a gold chain. Lifting it into the air, I pulled until a <u>pocket watch</u> appeared on the end. The silver round casing spun in circles. After a few seconds, it came to a complete stop, its black and white face finally in focus.

Nate reached out and put his palm under the suspended watch and pulled it closer. There was no cover and it looked as if the glass had shattered a long time ago. The white enamel face was worn on the edges and it only had one hand, the minute hand. Nate set the watch off to the side as he took his turn.

His hands shook with excitement as he pulled out a box of playing cards with a folded-up yellowed piece of paper stuck to it. Upon closer inspection, an old grey-tinted piece of gum seemed to be the glue holding the paper in place. The paper was folded in three long sections. When Nate opened it, it displayed a handmade advertisement for some Italian restaurant called "Angelina's." A section at the bottom was circled in pencil.

I read it out loud. "Jobs- Kitchen help wanted. Apply in person."

Tossing the flyer aside, I dug deep into the box and pulled out two books. The covers were plain and worn, the pages curled and torn. Inside the cover, a name penned in large black letters.

"Ernesto Robinson," I said as I flipped through the pages.

They seemed to be ordinary math and English books at an elementary level. There were notes in the blank areas above and below the text in some kind of foreign language. While I flipped the pages, a photograph fell out of them to the floor. It was a faded black-and-white picture of a handsome man in military uniform. He was smiling beneath a large metal hat that resembled an upside-down bowl with a strap under his chin. On the back was one word – Papa.

History being my worst subject, I asked Nate if he knew

anything about wars.

He shook his head. "I 'tink at hitory, Tarah."

We agreed to add a history lesson at the library to our list of things to do Monday. The remaining items in the box were a half empty tin of shoe polish, a crushed pack of Lucky Strike cigarettes, leather work gloves, a bulging can of unopened sardines that looked like it was going to explode, and a <u>Saturday Evening Post Magazine</u>.

As we were filling the box, Nate noticed a tiny rectangular piece of paper pressed firmly against the wood side. With his fingernail, he pried it gingerly away from its hiding spot. Huddling our heads together, we inspected what looked to be a train ticket from 1930. It didn't seem to be used because it wasn't torn or have holes punched into it. The print was so faded at the top it was not legible. We couldn't tell what the destination was. Towards the bottom, though, was a familiar name, but different.

"Elizabeth Hilliard-Robinson?" Nate furrowed his brows, "I thought tee loved Henry."

Confused, I nodded. "Me too, I don't remember anything about Elizabeth getting married."

We sat thinking of the possibilities and agreed on one thing. Since the ticket was never used, something must have happened to Elizabeth before she could use it.

The air in the loft was thick with humidity and seemed to be getting worse. Nate wiped a bead of sweat from his forehead with a quick swipe from the back of his hand. He gently placed the ticket back inside of the box, closed the lid, making sure it latched. It was time to get back downstairs and cool off. At the top of the stairs, I noticed Dad's favorite flashlight sitting on the ledge by some old lanterns. I picked it up.

"Hey, my dad has been looking for this for the past two weeks."

With the box still under one arm and his free hand fidgeting with his hearing aid, he stood in the middle of the aisle.

"You're draining another one?" I screamed loudly.

Tapping on the battery pack near his chest, he nodded. I grabbed the shoeshine box from under his arm and waited while he played with the wiring and checked his connections. He shook his head and shrugged his shoulders.

"Torry, have maybe five-minute left on thit battery."

That was twice this week already. I could tell he was getting a little frustrated. I juggled the weight of the box and rested it against my hip. It was heavier than it looked. As I shifted the box to my other hand, the flashlight slipped from my fingers and hit the floor. Its light flickered on and shined brightly across the dusty planks. Nate retrieved it, and placed the light directly beneath his chin, laughing like an evil villain, "Bru ha ha ha…"

He barely finished the last "ha" before the light dwindled and went out.

"Torry, I tink battery don't like me."

I nodded toward the stairs while giving him a roll of my eyes.

As we left the barn, a cool breeze hit me in the face, smelling of freshly cut grass. I paused, closed my eyes, and lifted my face to the sun. I loved summer; the only thing I didn't like was it went way too fast. Like they say, time flies when you're having fun. When I opened my eyes, Nate was staring at me, grinning from ear to ear.

Shaking his head, he reached out with one hand and took the shoeshine box from me.

"You look different." He said a little too loudly.

I wrinkled my nose and frowned. "Whatcha mean, *different?*" I signed. Nate acted nervous and hesitated before speaking.

"Um, we were little before. Now you're grown up and ... well, pretty."

I burst out laughing and punched him in the arm. "Shut up, Nate!"

I turned and headed for the back porch. I hadn't realized it had been that long since Nate and I hung out together. I opened the back-porch door, held it for him, and pointed to the spot beneath the wicker table. He placed the box down, rubbed his arm where I had hit it, and turned to me with an apologetic look. I hoped I hadn't hit him too hard. I didn't want the day to end with him thinking I was mad.

"I'm sorry," I signed with a smile.

He handed me the flashlight and put both hands in his pockets. "Tee you tomorrow?"

I nodded and held up nine fingers. Before I knew it, he was out the door running down the driveway.

I plopped myself on the weathered, white wicker chair and picked at the cracked paint. I enjoyed seeing the different colors the chair used to be. I remembered my dad stripping thick yellow paint off of a large desk. We found every color of the rainbow before getting to the actual wood, where there was an intricate inlaid design of ivory.

Little pieces of white paint fell into my lap and formed a pile. I was startled when Dad opened the porch door and walked in.

"Hey, sweet pea,' he said as I tried to put my hand over the pile of paint chips on my lap.

"Hi, Dad, are you done staining?"

Dad stopped in front of me and looked at my hands.

"Better get rid of that before Mom sees," he said, raising his eyebrows.

Sitting on the bench across from me, he took a handkerchief out of his pocket and blew his nose loudly.

"How is the ghost hunting going?"

Smiling, I mentioned we had found the box and pointed to where it rested under the table. He looked at the name.

"E. Robinson," he said with a hint of uneasiness in his voice.

"You know who he was?" I asked as I sat up from my slumped position.

Dad rubbed his chin nervously. He stood and paced.

"Mr. Robinson was someone we were never allowed to talk about in our house."

"Why? What did he do?"

Dad explained how kind-hearted his grandparents were and how they not only took in railroad workers, but anyone who was in need of a warm place to stay. Ernesto Robinson had been one of them. Grandpa had not only given him a place to stay but taught him English. Many years after, when Ernesto became a wealthy business owner, he tried to buy Grandpa's property and our house for an extremely large amount of money and Grandpa refused.

"Grandpa used to say he chose morals over money and would die an honest man," Dad said as he ended the story.

I sighed with frustration. "But why was Mr. Robinson so bad?"

Dad shrugged his shoulders. "I don't know, Honey. Grandpa refused to talk about it."

The rest of the day flew by. I wandered around in a stupor trying to figure everything out in my head. I made a list of things we needed to look into at the library on Monday. Dad cooked hamburgers on the charcoal grill, and Mom put a checkered tablecloth on the picnic table so we could eat outside. Steph was busy playing with her stuffed animals in the back yard, setting them in a circle on a blanket.

The sun faded quickly, and the night brought a million stars to the dark and endless sky. I climbed the oak tree and perched on the lower branch with my back against the trunk. There was an opening in the leaves, which gave me a clear view. Did Elizabeth ever gaze at the night sky looking for a shooting star? Whose love did she wish for? Was it Henry's or Mr. Robinson's?

It wasn't until Mom called from the back door I knew it was way past my bedtime. "Sarah? Are you out there?"
"Yeah, Mom!"
"Time for bed. Steph's been asleep for an hour."

I swung my legs over the edge of the limb and hopped to the ground with a thud. Mom was busy folding laundry while Dad was in his recliner watching the news. I walked silently past them and headed for my room.

As I passed Steph's room, I could hear her mumbling in her sleep. I only paused a second, but it was long enough to hear she was dreaming.

♂ I didn't feel much of the shower that night, just got wet and went through the motions. My mind was still on the day's events. I was reminded of my recent failure every time I washed my left knee. I had so wanted this place to be a new start without bullies.

I turned off the shower at the insistent pounding on the door.
"Ben, hurry up, I gotta go!"

Why was it little brothers always had to pee when you were in the shower?
"Go use the downstairs one," I yelled through the door.
"Dad's down there right now."

Oh, that was a problem. It was best to let the bathroom air out before any one used it.

"Okay, I'm hurrying."

I toweled off and dressed, leaving my skin mostly wet, but in this humid environment I never got dry anyway. As soon as I unlocked the door, Mike brushed past me, unzipping as he went by.

"Hey, let me get out of here first!" I complained as I shut the bathroom door behind me.

Slipping between the cool sheets of my bed and finding the cold side of my pillow was my first order of business. The cold side always helped me sleep better. The second was to read for a few minutes from the latest edition of Popular Mechanics. I loved this stuff. Build your own gyro-copter or submersible. I soon fell asleep with dreams of adventure and finding buried treasure on my mind.

I had only been asleep for just a short time. My dreams of flying machines were just taking flight. I felt a cold hand on my left shoulder and fingers being traced lightly down my arm, coming to a stop at my hand.

I sat straight up in my bed and grabbed my left arm, trying to rub warmth back into it. The echo of a fading dream but whispers of reality were still with me in my room. Over the sounds of the night, I concentrated on the words that echoed in my room.

"The box.."

What the heck did it mean? *The box!* Oh, my goodness, I had left it in the garage. How could I have been so stupid? In all the excitement of working with my dad I had forgotten about it.

I climbed out of bed, pulled on a sweatshirt, and slipped into a pair of sneakers. Creeping across the floor so as not to wake my parents, I slowly opened the door. *"Squeeeak."*

I made myself a mental note to get WD-40 for the hinges as I walked down the hall. I heard a noise coming from Mike's room.
"Bout time you woke up."
I spun around and was hit in the face with the beam of a flashlight.
"What are you doing up?

In his doorway, Mike shrugged his shoulders as if it were no big deal.
"Waiting for you."

"What do you mean waiting for me?" I asked, confused. I had just figured out I needed to go somewhere and he was waiting for me?

"You're going to go get the box, so I am going with you."

By the tone in his voice I could almost hear him rolling his eyes. This was just too weird.

"How did you know that?"

He let out a small sigh of frustration. "Are you sure you want to know?"

I did, but not right now.

With Mike and his flashlight in the lead, we headed down the stairs to the kitchen. Mike hesitated before the door leading to the outside. "This is where you have to go first."

By the reflected light of his little flashlight, I could see he was just as scared as I was. Swallowing a couple of times, I looked from him to the door and back to Mike again. He nodded me forward. I reached out and opened the door to the darkness beyond.

I wasn't sure what I expected to find waiting for the two of us, but all that jumped out of the darkness at us was a baby toad. We walked across the driveway to the garage. It was a quiet, dark night so I was glad for Mike's flashlight. We were about ten feet away when I heard something moving around in there. We stopped, looking at each other. My mind was telling me to go back and get Dad, but my feet moved forward. I stopped at the door as Mike pressed the flashlight into my hand. I turned it in the direction of the windows and peeked inside. Dad's truck was parked on the far side in front of the bench. As I panned the light across the floor I saw something.

"What is it Ben?" Mike whispered.

"Someone has been in there."

Not wasting any more time, I pushed open the door.

In the middle of the floor was the little treasure box, broken to pieces. The lids were in one place, the bottom in another, and the contents scattered on the floor. I quickly looked around with the flashlight to see if Marcus had come back to take the rest of our treasure. As I whirled the light around the room, Mike did the sensible thing and turned on the overhead lights. The lights bothered my eyes; I closed them for a brief moment before continuing my search.

We were the only people there, so what would account for the noises we heard? Mike helped me pick up the scattered contents and take inventory. The little carved figurine was missing but the ring and letters were there.

I noticed the inside of the box looked crooked. I turned it over and looked at the bottom.

"What ya looking at?" Mike asked.

"I don't know." I grabbed a flat bladed screwdriver off the wall. I pried the inside bottom of the box. At first nothing happened. With a little snap, it gave way.

Inside the hidden place were several pieces of official looking documents with "shares" written across them in raised letters. I lifted them out carefully. Stuck to the real bottom of the box was a folded piece of paper. I had to pry carefully at the edges, but finally it came away. As we unfolded it, we saw a hand-drawn map. It appeared to be a map of the town we lived in. Our house was there and marked with a handwritten X. Sarah's house was labeled "McNally's" and the train yard, library, and other places in town were clearly marked. Connecting one place to the next was a series of dotted lines.

"It's a treasure map," Mike said, echoing what I was thinking.

A series of loud bangs from the direction of the storage cabinets made us both jump and cry out. The cabinet door in the corner was opening and closing.

"Ben, it looks like the cabinet is breathing."

I wished Mike hadn't said that. Gathering the treasure trove of stuff, we sprinted out the side door without stopping to close it behind us. We didn't stop running until we were safely inside our own house. I stowed the map under my mattress and slid the box back under my bed. Two hours later, I finally fell asleep.

It seemed like my head had just hit the pillow when Mike shook me awake.

"Ben, wake up, hurry! There is a police car in our driveway!"
Once I was able to focus with both eyes, I looked at Mike. "Huh, that's nice." I rolled over to go back to sleep.

"Ben, get up!"
I poked Mike hard in the ribs.
"Ouch," he squealed.

Mike punched me in the arm. Clearly, he wasn't going to let me go back to sleep. I sat up in bed and tried to clear the cobwebs out of my head. Mike grabbed my hand and pulled me towards my door. "

Wait a minute, let me get some slippers on."

I shook him loose and put on my slippers. When he grabbed my hand again, I lifted my hands in mock surrender.
"I know how to get outside. I don't need your help."

I led the way down the back stairs to the kitchen. The smell of pancakes and eggs greeted us.

"Hi, Mom, why is there a cop car in our driveway?" I asked casually.

"Someone broke into the garage last night and messed things up."

Mike and I looked at each other and raced to the side door. In some distant part of our brains we heard Mom say, "Boys, get back in here and get dressed first."

In my honest opinion, pajamas could be worn all day on Sunday. We hit the side door at the same time and almost tumbled out onto the sidewalk.

There was a black and white cop car sitting in our driveway. I was a little disappointed the lights were not on. What good is having a cop car at your house if you aren't going to have a siren or the lights working?

At the garage door, we froze in our tracks. I remembered the way we had left it the night before. What greeted us was not it.

The half-gallon paint cans dad had on the shelves looked as though they had exploded. The parts to my racer were scattered all over the floor. Dad had pulled his truck out of the garage and was standing by the police car talking with the officer. As we walked over to them, we overheard the officer say, "I would get a steel door without a window and a dead bolt for the side entrance."
My dad ran his hands through his hair. "What about my truck?"

Mike and I turned at the same time to look. Scratched down to bare metal on the driver's side of the truck was the word *"LEAVE."*

Chapter 34
<u>Crooked Capture</u>

♀ I was riding my bike down the hill on Avon Drive with my hair flying loose from my ponytail. Just as I let go of the handlebars, ready to scream, I felt a cool sensation on my face…

Steph was standing above me with her squirt gun aimed directly at my face. "Geez, I had to check to see if you were alive," she said as she squirted me again.

I complained as I rolled over to my stomach.

"Do you mind? Some people like to sleep in, ya know."

Steph continued to pester me by flicking my arm.

"Nate is here. He said he saw a police car at Ben's house!"

I practically sprung from bed as if catapulted by my mattress. Standing and disoriented, my heart raced.

"Where, when, what happened?" I asked while I slipped on some shorts and a t-shirt.

Steph didn't answer. Her expression was relaxed, and she didn't seem upset in the least.

"What's the matter with you? Aren't you worried?"

She shook her head and smiled knowingly.

Tripping across the floor full of clothes, I grabbed my sneakers and shoved one of them on my left foot without even untying it and pulled my hair into a ponytail. The entire time I raced around my room, Steph stood still and watched. When I hit my big toe on the corner of my dresser and hopped around the room on one leg, she laughed. "You don't have to rush. Nobody's hurt."

I glared at her with a look that could kill. With one smooth move, I whipped my right shoe at her but missed her head by a mile. She squirted me right between the eyes.

By the time we both made it to the kitchen, Nate had already consumed a piece of peanut butter toast and a large glass of milk. A frothy milk moustache covering his top lip, he waved.

Mom was refilling his glass.

"I couldn't let your friend starve while he waited."

I shook my head and headed towards the door.
"Freeze!"

I stopped with my hand on the doorknob and turned my head in Mom's direction.

Hands on her hips, she gave me a look of concern. "Sarah, I realize you want to get to Ben's as quickly as possible, but there is no excuse for the way you look."

My clothes were a little dirty and my one shoe was still untied. I shrugged.

"March back upstairs right now, young lady, and take a quick shower. I will get you some fresh clothes out of the dryer and some toast to go."

I let out a long sigh and rolled my eyes. "Yes Mom."

As I ran up the stairs, Mom yelled from the kitchen. "Don't forget to brush your hair, too!"

Steph and Nate were waiting anxiously at the back door. I set the world's record for the quickest shower and dressed in clean clothes. Nate held a piece of toast meant for me. The three of us headed out the back door and raced to the end of the driveway. I took a bite of my toast and threw the remainder to Sandy who had been trotting behind us with a stick in his mouth.

We headed through the gates of the old train yard without a second thought. Sprinting past the old locomotives, we flew like the speed of light. We would have made it to Ben's with record time, if it were not for one speed bump.

Nate and I were neck and neck as we reached the far entrance near the gate. Steph had been six feet behind us. But when we rounded the corner, I glanced back and didn't see her.
"Hold up!" I hollered.

Nate continued to run until he noticed he had no competition and skidded breathlessly to a stop.

Steph just disappeared. The path was straight from one end of the train yard to the other. The only way we would not see her was if she had veered off somewhere.

"Steph!" I yelled in a panic. No answer. Nate gave me a troubled look as he pushed in front of me and led the way back.
 We both yelled, "Steph, where are you?"

Slowly we walked back through the yard, looking down each row of rusty train cars. When we got near the middle, I heard a faint, muffled voice saying, "In here!"

I grabbed Nate's shirt and pulled him with me in the direction of the sound. We followed the voice to the old metal shed where a large wooden railroad tie was wedged against the door.

"Steph are you in there?" I yelled as I pounded on the door.

"I'm here!" she cried.

Nate and I pulled the railroad tie with all our might but it didn't budge. Steph's crying got louder.

"Hold on, Steph, we'll get you out!"

We scanned the area for something we could wedge between the shed and the extremely heavy piece of wood.

"I tee tomething!' Nate said as he reached underneath a nearby train car.

It looked to be the handle to a shovel, missing the end. Quickly, Nate wedged the broken end of the shovel between the railroad tie and the door and we both pulled on the handle. It took four times of "Heave Ho" before the wood slid far enough away from the door to open it.

Steph was barely able to squeeze through the opening. Sobbing, she ran into my arms.

"How did you get in there? Are you all right?" I asked.

Steph's face was covered in coal dust. Her tears had left little trails down her cheeks. The back collar of her shirt was torn and she was bleeding from a scrape on her right elbow. Steph shook her head and ran in the direction of Ben's house.

"Let's get out of here."

Once outside the gate and down a block, she slowed to a walk. Nate put his arm around her shoulder and tried to comfort her.

"It otay, 'Teph, tell us what happened."

Though she was still crying, she was able to give us every detail of her frightening experience.

Half way through the train yard, she ran right into Mr. Wilkerson, who dragged her by the back of her shirt to the shed where he locked her in. She had tried to scream, but he put his hand over her mouth.

"The whole time he was talking, but he wasn't talking to me."

"What did he say?" Nate and I asked in unison.
She swallowed hard and spoke with a shaky voice.

"He said, 'Don't worry, Katrina! I've got it handled, but I hate you for making me do this!'

♂ Mike and I exchanged glances when we read the message carved into the paint of the truck door. Who would want us to leave? Mr. Wilkerson, Katrina, Marcus? We hadn't been here a week yet, and already we were being asked to leave.

Dad interrupted me. "Boys, get on some work clothes. You two are going to help me clean this."

Sunday was not going to be a day of rest.

In the house, Mike and I were greeted by two little stacks of pancakes on the kitchen table.

"Hurry up and eat first. I have laid out some clothes you can mess up with paint," Mom said as she placed a large container of OJ in the middle of the table.

Mike was pacing me as I ate, so we finished eating at the same time. I noticed more and more he was copying me. Mom said it was because he wanted to be like me. What would he think if he knew how badly I wanted to be like him some days?

By the time we had gotten back outside, Sarah, Steph, and Nate were all excitedly talking to the police officer.

"Okay, tell me one more time what happened, and the rest of you be quiet this time." The officer said. "Go ahead, Stephanie."

Steph looked from Sarah to Nate, and back to Sarah again. "We were running through the train yard... "

The officer held up his hand. "Okay, stop. You mean you were trespassing through the train yard?"

He looked directly at Sarah when he said it. She looked at the ground.

"Yes, Sir, we were trespassing, but we were trying to hurry and get here because…"

He held up his hand again. "That is no excuse for breaking the law."

Her shoulders slumped. "No, Sir."

Flipping a page in his little notebook, the officer looked back at Steph. "Now continue, Stephanie."

"Ummmm, we were *trespassing* through the train yard and I was trying to keep up with Sarah and Nate when I bumped into Mr. Wilkerson. He came out of nowhere and I couldn't stop. He grabbed me by my shirt." She showed her torn shirt collar and the scrape on her elbow. "He dragged me into the shed, and I couldn't get out." Steph cried as she finished the story. I looked at the officer and caught the name on his tag: Officer Mundy.

Officer Mundy flipped the page and turned to Sarah and Nate. "Okay, before I begin with your story I want to make it clear. You may not like Mr. Wilkerson, but he was put in charge of the train yard a long time ago to keep out trespassers." Looking at each of us, he made sure we understood what he was saying. "Now tell me what happened."

Sarah and Nate took turns relaying their part of the story, how they back tracked to the shed and found the heavy railroad tie wedged against the door. When they were done, the officer put his pencil away, took his hat off, and ran his fingers through his hair.

"I will admit this is a little extreme, even for Mr. Wilkerson. I will bring him in for questioning and tell him he can't take the law into his own hands." He looked at us. "Now, Sarah, I have had this talk with your dad before. It looks like I am going to have to do it again. *Stay out of the railroad yard!*" It wasn't like he was yelling, but it had the same affect.

The officer turned towards my dad. "Mr. Whiting, I will file this report. If you have any further instances of vandalism, please let me know immediately."

They shook hands. Officer Mundy got into his car and drove off down the street towards the entrance to the train yard.

"Ben, Mike…" I knew that tone of voice. "I am only going to tell you this one time and I want you to listen. Stay away from the train yard." He got into his truck. Before he drove off, he rolled down the window. "Tell your mother I'm going to the hardware store to see about getting a steel door for the garage. Before you can play with your friends, get a bucket of warm water and start cleaning the paint. There are some rags under the bench."

No one said a word as we gathered an armful of rags. We

turned and walked towards the paint mess. It was a kaleidoscope of colors. Half-gallon cans of blues, greens, dark reds and bright yellows were mixed in a spray of color that fanned out from the shelf. I headed to get a bucket of water when Nate's hand stopped me.
"What wrong with thit picture?"
He looked at each of us and pointed.
"If someone made thit mett, where are the footprint?"

Chapter 35
Tortured Triangle

♀ Nate was right. It looked as if someone came into the garage in a tantrum of rage, grabbed the cans of paint off of the shelves, and hurled them to the floor. How did they get out without leaving footprints? Practically every inch of the floor was covered and most of the paint was still wet. With the exception of Mr. Whiting's footprints from moving his truck and the clean spot where his truck had sat, the floor was covered. The paint was thicker near the center of the garage, where the shelves were, and lighter near the front door. The splatters resembled the sun with its center the darkest. Longer, thinner lines radiated outward like rays. The dented cans were scattered, their lids laying face up. Weirdly, the racer parts lay on top of the paint and were still pretty clean. Equally strange was the lack of footprints. The only way anyone could have made such a mess without walking back through it to get out of the garage, was if they had the ability to fly.

Ben appeared with a bucket and two scrub brushes. He sighed loudly, "I don't know who did this, but I know it's my fault."

Mike objected. "If the cupboard didn't breathe last night, we would have closed the door."

Nate and I exchanged looks as we both giggled.

"Don't laugh at him, Sarah." Steph piped up.

"He's telling the truth, guys," Ben said. "It did look like it was breathing."

After he explained what had happened in the middle of the night, I headed towards the back of the garage, my sneakers slipping around in the puddles of thick paint. Like an inexperienced ice skater, my legs were spreading too far apart to balance. If it were not for the same support post Ben had knocked his head on, I would have ended up on my backside.

Clinging to the post, I regained my balance and slid across the back section to a dry spot near the cupboards. I reached and opened the bottom corner one. "Is this the one you saw breathing?"
Mike answered, "Yes, how did you know that?"
"This is the one I saw open and close when Ben was passed out."
"And the one I saw Elizabeth open in my dream," Ben said.

Everyone slid through the slippery paint to the cupboard. Kneeling, I opened the door as far as it would go. We tried to stick our heads inside at once and ended up knocking heads. It was empty except for a few nails and seemed solid. Ben reached in and pounded on the sides to listen for hollow spots and came up with nothing. As we sat around the open door, Mrs. Whiting appeared with the garden hose. "I hope none of you have good clothes or shoes on. This is going to be a messy one."
I caught a sparkle in Ben's eyes and laughed.

Cleaning is not one of my favorite things to do, but this time was an exception. The paint was luckily latex, which made it possible to clean it with soap and water plus a little scrubbing. Once we wiped the bulk of the puddles with rags, the real fun began. After a brief battle over the hose, we let Nate spray the floor. Steph swept the water out the front door into the gravel with a large push broom. Ben and I picked up the racer parts and checked them for damage while wiping them clean.

Mike disappeared and came back with both scrub brushes tied to his sneakers with old shoelaces.

"Ta da!" he announced loudly. I almost passed out from laughing when he made his grand entrance.

With his arms outstretched and the arms of a red jacket tied around his neck, Mike dragged his feet across the garage floor and actually made a difference. The swirls of color scrubbed away as Nate sprayed near his feet. Steph tried to talk Mike into switching jobs, but he was racing around and giggling too much to even hear her. Eventually, Mike's weight on the bristles flattened them out so they looked like an extremely worn toothbrush. Bristles bent in every direction with a tint of color on the ends. I didn't mind being soaking wet. The day was a humid one, and the cool water from the hose was refreshing. Once the paint was cleaned, we sat on the wet floor in a circle.

Despite what happened to Steph, this day was going well. I realized I didn't feel lonely or different anymore. Looking at each person − my sister, her new best friend, my old best friend and my new one − I'm positive I would never be lonely again.

♂ The water had formed a little puddle in the middle of the circle. I could see the reflected faces of Sarah and Nate who sat across from me. I looked at Sarah's reflection in the water and caught her staring at me. When I glanced into her eyes, she reddened a little and stuck her tongue out and giggled.

When I looked back at the puddle, I caught sight of movement behind her. Looking around, I saw nothing out of the ordinary, just the back of the garage. I squinted my eyes, as I peered into the water and saw the reflection of the cabinet. The cabinet door was slowly opening. But when I looked directly at it, the door was closed. I backed away from the small pool of water but I could clearly see the door to the cabinet was open and Katrina was standing next to it. I tried to tell everyone we needed to leave, but I could only point to the back of the garage and mumble.

I barely had time to lie back before the roaring noise of wind carried me away. I can't say I was getting used to this, but I knew what was coming. When my vision cleared, I was once again lying on the garage floor. It was nighttime. I sat up. Standing in front of the cabinet were Henry and Katrina.
"Katrina, where is Elizabeth? I have to talk to her."

Katrina, with her arms folded across her chest, just pouted and said nothing.
"Please, Katrina, tell Elizabeth I have to talk to her."

The scowl on her face made it even more pinched. It looked like it would only be a matter of time before her whole face just sucked itself in and disappeared.

"Elizabeth is no longer interested in you, Henry. She is going to marry Ernesto Robinson." Katrina stepped in closer to Henry and ran her hand up his arm to his shoulder.

"Katrina, I told you before, I don't love you. It's Elizabeth I love!"

Katrina moved her hand behind Henry's head and pulled him in for a kiss. "You will learn to love me."

Just then, the door to the garage opened and Elizabeth rushed in. "Katrina, have you seen my cameo?"

She just stood there, as if time had suddenly stopped.

Acting shocked, Katrina pushed Henry away. "Henry, I told you I only want to be friends, nothing more."

In shocked silence, Henry just stood there saying nothing.

Elizabeth looked as if she had just been slapped.

"Henry?" She darted from the garage, crying.

"Why did you do that?" shouted Henry. "I came to stop her from going through with this… this so-called marriage."

With a smug smile on her face, Katrina spoke confidently, "I told you, you will learn."

Running past, Henry called out into the night. "Elizabeth!"

Chapter 36
Spider Signs

♀ When Ben pointed, we all turned to look at the back of the garage. Steph asked, "What are we looking at?"

Nate said, "I don't know."

I was the only one seeing it. Three misty figures mingled and floated above the damp cement floor. A sudden surge of emotions left me sad and depressed. Mike was shaking his head and frowning.

As I spun back to Ben, he was pulling himself up to a sitting position. He looked extremely pale, his eyes clouded with confusion.

"You passed out again, didn't you?" He rubbed his forehead and forced a small smile. "I knew it! I knew it! You're our early

warning system!"
Everyone nodded in agreement.
"Early what?" Mike asked.

"I have noticed right before a ghost shows up, Ben gets light headed or passes out. It happened in the garage the first day I met him, again in the basement during class, and now this time."

Ben stared at me. "You're right, Sarah. I was afraid you wouldn't believe me.
Nate asked, "Did you see anything?"

Ben pushed himself to his knees as his eyes widened. *"Yes,* I saw everything."

As Ben relayed the information to the rest of us, I mentioned what I had seen in the back of the garage. He continued with the description of the vision. "…and when Elizabeth walked in on Katrina and Henry… "

Mike chimed in. "She thought Henry was a jerk and told the old guy she would marry him."

Ben raised his eyebrows. "Did your imaginary friend tell you this?"

Mike looked at the ground like he was embarrassed. Steph slid herself closer to him and gave him a high five, which brought an instant smile to his face.
"Steph, tell them about your dream."

My little sister did not seem to want to share. She punched Mike in the arm. "That was our secret!"
They argued back and forth until Mike insisted, "It might help.'

A look of seriousness and concern replaced Steph's smile. She seemed to be struggling with finding the right words.

"The guy Elizabeth was supposed to marry was mean and scary," she said in a rush. "And don't ask me how I know, I just know."

The excitement had us worked into a frenzy. Each one of us had offered a piece of the puzzle, with the exception of Nate who sat quietly. I looked at Ben and nodded towards Nate as Mike and Steph jumped around doing another set of high fives. Ben flicked some water on to Nate's face. "Hey, you okay?"
Nate shoved both hands into his front pockets.

"Uh huh, jut a little left out. You 'till want me part of the team?" he questioned.

I put my arm around his shoulders. "You are a part of the team no matter what."

Ben mentioned his recent find inside the broken box and ran to his room to get it. He laid the map on the workbench and took a piece of graph paper from the Scout magazine near the racer parts. He laid the graph paper on top of the map and taped it to the back window of the garage. "We better make a good copy of this just in case we lose it."

Nate pulled a pencil from the tin can near the shelves. It wasn't sharpened, so Ben took his knife from his pocket, whittled off the end, and gave Steph a quick wink as he put it back into his pocket. She beamed with approval.

The sun shined through the window and the two pieces of paper as Ben traced the lines. He slowly and carefully started in the middle of the map by connecting the dotted lines, working outwards. When he had filled in the center part, he paused.

"What up?" Nate asked.

Ben backed away from the paper still taped to the window. Although he had not completed it, the pattern we saw was one that took us by complete surprise. In the center of the paper was the library, the largest of the buildings and the dotted lines that stretched out in every direction resembled the legs of a spider.

♂ I could feel the hair standing on the back of my neck.
Nate moved towards the window to get a closer look. As he did, he passed under the lone light bulb. It glowed brighter.
"Nate, Stop!"
He did.
"Okay, now back up a little bit."
As he backed up, the light bulb went back to normal.
"Now walk toward me again."
The light bulb glowed brighter.
"Okay, stop. Now reach up and touch it."

Everyone was watching intently as he reached to touch the bulb. The glow increased until it was almost too bright to look at. Just before his hand reached it, we heard a small "pop" and the light went out.

"Dat was trange," Nate whispered.

"Hey, guys, if I am reading this map right…" Sarah grabbed the pencil from my hand and drew on the map. "This is Ben's house."
She placed an "X" on the map.

"And this is my house." She placed another X on the map. "Now let's see, this could be my Uncle Dave's house," she said as she placed an "X" next to it.

"The first place we should look is Uncle Dave's House, and find out why the dotted lines go there."

Steph looked up from talking in whispers to Mike. "Uh, Sarah, Uncle Dave is on vacation."
Sara looked back at Steph with a smile on her face. "Exactly!"

I watched as Sarah filled in a few more details on the map tracing. She carefully removed the tape from the corners, put the copy of the map on the workbench, folded the original back up, and handed it to me. "Okay, who is up for a little adventure?"

It was clear from everyone's face, no one wanted to be left behind.

Mike broke the silence. "We need to take a flashlight." He ran out of the garage in the direction of the house.

While we waited for Mike to return, I showed Nate my plans for the soapbox racer. I pointed out the steering column my Dad had brought home.
"Can I ride it when it done?" he asked. He smiled when I nodded.

Now I just needed to finish building it. One adventure at a time, I reminded myself.

Mike ran back into the garage, skidding to a halt. "You guys ready?"

We followed Sarah out of the garage single file. Sarah, with her long hair tied in a ponytail, was followed closely by Steph, who was mimicking Sarah's every movement. Mike marched behind Steph like a little tin soldier, talking to no one in particular. I followed him and Nate brought up the rear, stepping on the back of my shoes, which when done just right pulled my foot out of my shoe. It was called giving someone a flat, and I was positive he was doing it on purpose. But every time I looked back, he smiled and apologized.

Before long, we were standing in front of Sarah's uncle's house.

It was the same size as Sarah's place, but instead of a barn, her uncle had a garage much the same as ours, only a little smaller.

"Okay, where do we go first?" I asked Sarah.

"Well, the dotted line leads to the garage. I guess we start there."

The old-style doors had been replaced with newer slide-up ones. The windows looked dark. Sarah was looking at me, trying to gauge my reaction to the place. I whispered to her. "I'm not going to pass out."

I was the first to reach the side door. I grasped the doorknob. Gulping, I looked back at the group.

"Hurry up!" Mike whispered.

I turned the handle, but the door was locked.

"Wait," Sarah muttered as she stepped past me. "I know he keeps a key here somewhere." Moving a plastic frog, she uncovered a hiding place for a little silver key. "Here, try this."

The key fit and I turned the handle. The door opened with only a little squeak. With the door standing open before us, we stood and waited for something to happen. I could feel everyone's eyes looking at me.

"I'm not going to pass out!"

I walked into the darkened room. My eyes soon adjusted to the darkness. The garage was a lot like our garage; same cupboards on the back wall, same cement floor, and so on.

I turned. My brave friends were still outside looking at me.

Chapter 37
Dead End Dilemma

♀ Pushing past Ben, I squeezed between the garage door and my uncle's classic car, being careful not to scratch the paint. At the front corner, I reached behind the large red toolbox and flipped the switch for the overhead lights. The fluorescent fixtures flickered above our heads and flooded the area with light.

My uncle's garage was much cleaner than ours. As a matter of fact, clean wasn't the word for it. Mom always teased we could eat off the floor. The shiny painted cement was light gray with no hint of dirt or dust. The back wall was lined with cupboards much like Ben's, only Uncle Dave covered the area above them with pegboard. His tools hung carefully with a magic marker outline around them to make sure they were returned to the right spot. The side walls were plastered with various racing posters and an occasional calendar with a girl in a bikini on it.

Mike spoke first. "Whoa! Will you look at this place?"

Nate nodded in agreement as Steph quickly ran to the car and bragged. "Uncle Dave is fixing this car by himself and he even put a new tatter top on it."

Ben giggled and Nate put his hand over his mouth to hold back his laughter.

"You mean rag top?" I asked.

Steph stomped her foot and gave me a dirty look. "That's what I said!"

Mike walked over to stand beside her and slowly reached to touch the white convertible top. Steph smacked his hand away. "Do not touch!" she said with a frown.

Ben was checking out the partially dismantled engine in the back corner while Nate seemed mesmerized by Miss July on one of the calendars.

"Your uncle married?" Ben asked.

"Nope, not yet. He hasn't found Miss Right," I remarked.

Nate giggled and pointed to the calendar. "Tee look like Mit Right!"

I walked to the back of the garage, swatting Nate in the back of the head when I passed him. "Quit drooling and let's get to searching, Boys.

I made it clear anything we touched had to go back exactly the way we found it. My uncle would have flipped out if he found his cupboards had been rifled through. We each chose a cupboard and knelt on the cold floor. We searched through organized shelves of motor oil, parts, tools, and car magazines, but found nothing.

Ben, however, was intently studying a label on the inside of his cupboard door. "These cabinets are made by the same company as the ones in our garage."

Mike pulled his head out from behind his door. "They are the same ones, just a different color."

Ben emptied the stacks of magazines from the shelf and pulled the entire shelf out.

"I wouldn't do that if I were you. Steph warned.

He leaned into the opening until all we could see was his bottom half. "Mike, bring me your flashlight."

Mike stood at attention. "Flashlight! Check!"

Ben took the flashlight and pulled his Boy Scout knife from his pocket. He pried the bottom panel loose to reveal a hollow bottom. The five of us joined Ben as we crammed our heads inside. I expected to see some kind of hidden treasure, but only saw cement. Sitting back on his heels, Ben rubbed his head.

"You okay?" I asked.

"You're not going to patt out?" Nate chimed in jokingly.

Ben, obviously frustrated, snapped back, "Quit asking me that question! *I am not going to pass out!*"

Steph made an interesting suggestion as she stood. "Maybe we should have a code word he can use for when he's gonna pass out."

Mike giggled. "I know. We can yell *timber!*"

We laughed and joked while Ben still continued to stare at the cement. "Let's get this cleaned and figure out our next stop. I have a hunch I hope I can prove."

♂ With the blade of my pocketknife closed, I tapped the cement floor in front of the cabinet. It made a solid sound and you could hear the metal of the knife ring. I did the same thing inside of the cabinet but this time the sound was different, more of a dull thud.

I felt Sarah's hand on my arm. "What are you looking for?" she whispered.

"I'm not sure yet."

Once we had everything put back where it belonged, we left the garage. Sarah was the last one out the door. She locked it and put the

key back in its hiding place.
"Sarah, can we see your uncle's basement?" I asked.
"Okay, but we have to be quick."

We followed her to the side door of the house, where she reached under the potted plant to remove the key.

"You guys stay here. I don't want you to track any dirt into the house," she said as she unlocked the door and led me inside. "Take off your shoes."

I did as I was instructed and followed her down a short flight of stairs to the basement. When Sarah turned on the lights, I was disappointed. The basement was finished and carpeted from wall to wall. It was a large family room including a sectional couch and a large console TV and stereo. What I had been looking for was a basement similar to mine.
"It's not here,"
I turned around and went back up the stairs.
"Ben, what are you looking for?"
I sat at the top of the stairs to put my shoes on. "I don't know yet."

Once we got back outside, I pulled out the copy of the map we had made earlier. With a pencil from my pocket, I made a list of places the dotted lines went to.

"Okay, this is my house, and this is Sarah's Uncle's house." I paused to trace some of the other lines. Since I didn't recognize the other landmarks, I figured maybe we should start at the center and work out.
Sarah said exactly what I was thinking.
"Let's go to the library. It seems to be where all the lines lead."
You could feel the excitement of our little group begin to build.

With Sarah in the lead and the rest of us following behind like tin soldiers, we soon found ourselves standing in front of the large doors of the majestic building.

"Maybe the dotted lines on the map were for people who had overdue library books." We turned to look back at Mike, but it was Steph who laughed first. Maybe I was going about this wrong. Maybe there was a simple explanation.

"Uh, look, the library is closed today." Nate pointed at the sign hanging on the door. "Closed Sundays."

I took charge.

"Well, let's just take a look around the library. Maybe we can come up with something."

I ruffled Mike's hair.

"I don't believe the dotted lines were for late library books. Good idea, though."

Mike grinned.

"Let's split into two groups," I said. "Nate, you and Sarah go left. Mike, Steph and I will go to the right. We will meet around the back of the building."

I pulled out my little notebook and tore off a few pages of paper. "Here, take this and make notes of anything strange you see on or around the library. I'm not sure what we are looking for, just look for something out of place or different."

I watched as Sarah and Nate went off, and kind of wished I could have been in her group. I guess Sarah sensed something because she turned around and caught me looking at her. I quickly turned and squeaked out, "Let's go, guys."

My mind was racing back through the books I had read over the past few months. Trap doors, buried treasure, hidden clues – and all I could think of was Sarah. The three of us had just come around the side of the building and had yet to find anything out of the ordinary, when Mike said, "What are we looking for again?"

"Look for anything out of the ordinary, weird markings on the building, maybe a loose brick."

The back of the building was covered in thick vines. "Oh great. How are we going to find anything in this mess?" Steph said.

I was ready to give up when Mike pointed out a hole in the vines. "Hey Ben, what is that?"

On closer inspection, it wasn't a hole as much as it was an open window to the basement of the library. While I was on my hands and knees looking through it, Nate and Sarah came around from their side of the building. "Hey, what are you looking at?" Sarah asked.

I stood grinning from ear to ear. "You guys want to explore the library?"

I looked at each person to see if they were with me. Mike shook his head. Steph said no. Nate shrugged his shoulders. Sarah smiled and said yes.

"You guys will get into trouble," Nate said.

"You can keep guard. I am going through the window into the basement. There are shelves just under the window I can climb on."

Checking to see if I had enough paper and a sharp pencil to take notes with, I was ready to descend into the library's basement. I only needed one more thing. "Mike, give me your flashlight."

Chapter 38
Reckless Rummage

♀ Ben slid his feet through the basement window, slowly lowered his body into the darkness, and disappeared. It wasn't until I saw his fingers waving wildly, barely visible above the sill, that I felt relieved.

Nate grabbed my arm with a zap of static and shook his head in disapproval. "Tarah, don't."

To tell the truth, I had a bad feeling about it, too. Steph and Mike seemed to be whispering to themselves while looking around suspiciously and keeping guard.

I signed to Nate, "I will be okay, I promise." I knelt and poked my head through the vines and into the window. It was not as dark as it looked from the outside. I could see a light off to one corner.

Ben was standing with his arms up as if ready to catch me. "Come on, Sarah.'

The opening was pretty narrow. A rusty metal frame held a single piece of glass that hung by hinges at the top. I couldn't tell what exactly was holding it open. Sitting on the ground, I stuck my feet in first. If I did this correctly, I would lower myself to a sitting position on the shelf and jump to the basement floor.

Unfortunately, just as I turned to Nate and gave him the thumbs up, Mike yelled, "Someone's coming!"

I slid through the opening, bounced off the shelf and fell to the floor. It was a lot further down than it looked. Fortunately for me, Ben cushioned my fall by serving as a pillow. I'm sure Ben expected a little more time to prepare and a lot more grace involved. Instead, he got the air knocked out of him.

I rolled off of him just in time to see the window slam shut, hear the glass shatter and watch three pairs of feet run by. Before I had a chance to say a word, Ben threw a tarp from the floor over our heads, pushed me against the wall, and covered my mouth with his hand. I was going to bite his fingers when I heard voices.

"Hey, Hal! It looks like those kids were up to no good. The window is busted!"

My heart raced as I listened to Ben's rapid breathing in my ear. His hand slowly moved from my mouth to my waist as we huddled together in hiding. Another man's voice reached our ears.

"Stewart, you go grab a piece of board from the supply room and I'll get my tool belt from the truck. We'll have this boarded in no time."

When the footsteps faded, Ben threw off the tarp and crawled. "Follow me," he whispered.

The first thing I noticed was the smell. The strong odor of bleach tickled my nose hairs, making it hard to inhale. I noticed a large white container and a spray bottle on the floor as I crawled toward the corner. Ben headed for a large desk and squeezed his lanky body into the tiny square hole where the chair was supposed to be. He motioned with his hand for me to join him. I protested.

"If you think I'm gonna fit in there…"

The men were unlocking a door. They had returned to board up our only means of escape. Ben did his best impression of a human pretzel as I forced my way under the desk. I hadn't ever been that close to a boy, *ever!* His knees folded to his chin. Facing the drawers, I wedged myself against the back of the desk while sitting on his feet. To say we were cramped was an understatement. As sounds of hammering began, I noticed the smell of bleach had grown stronger. Pinching my nose, I looked at my partner in crime. I could only see his eyes above his dirty, knobby knees but sweat was rolling down his forehead and he was gasping. Awkwardly, he managed to pull a handkerchief from his pocket and place it over my mouth and nose as he held his breath for what seemed to be thirty seconds at a time. It seemed like we sat under there for an eternity. Finally, the hammering stopped, and the men went back out through the door and locked it. When the basement grew silent except for fading, muffled voices, we crawled out of our hiding spot.

Ben sighed loudly and stood, painfully unfolding his body with creaks and groans. Walking over to the spray bottle, he lifted it to his nose and coughed. Pointing to the black speckled surface of the wall under the window, he said, "They're treating for mold."

I fanned myself with the handkerchief. My eyes were watering. "That explains why the window was left open." My heart sank when I looked at the window. There was no way we were getting back out that way. When I turned back to Ben, he was gone.

"Ben, where are you?" I asked hesitantly.

"Over here."

The basement looked dusty. At one time, it was most likely used as part of the library. There were still shelves lining the walls, although there were no books on them. The stacks of boxes and miscellaneous furniture told me the basement was used for storage now.

I followed Ben's voice around the corner to a large open area. He was scanning across the vast rows of boxes with Mike's flashlight. Something tickled my face. I reached up expecting to brush away a cobweb but found a string instead. I noticed a large lighting fixture with one long bulb in it.

"Lookey here!' I said as I pulled the string.

The light came alive and cast a bluish tint, revealing the perimeters of the room. I gasped at the sight before us. The room was larger than my dad's loft and a hundred times more cluttered. Ben's eyes were wide with excitement. "Where do you want to go first?"

A chill spread to the back of my neck as a dark shadow crossed the room behind him.

"Sarah?" he said with panic in his voice. I reached Ben's side just in time to catch him in my arms.

♂ I barely had time to call out Sarah's name before everything turned white.

When things cleared, I was sitting just below the window. The room was filled with large crates and barrels, each branded with the spider image. I heard voices arguing off to my left. I made my way in that direction.

Henry was struggling to bring a large barrel into the room. A large person with his back towards me was standing in his way.

"Henry, I told you to stay away from Elizabeth," the man in the doorway said.

Henry didn't say a word as he continued to struggle with the barrel.

"I guess you didn't hear me, so let me make this clear," he said again. The man in the doorway drew back his fist and hit Henry right in the nose, knocking him down. Henry didn't see it coming until it was too late.

"Now, I am only going to tell you one more time. *Stay away from Elizabeth!* Do you understand me?"

Henry picked himself up off the floor, wiped the blood from his nose, and nodded.

The large person said, "I can't hear you."

Henry replied, "Yes, Sir."

The man in the doorway apparently didn't like that answer.

"Yes, Sir, *what?*"

Henry bowed his head. "Yes Sir, Mr. Robinson."

I watched as Mr. Robinson counted the barrels Henry had brought in and made a notation in a tablet. "Once you are done with this, there is another shipment due in at midnight. Make sure it is unloaded and stored before sunrise."

In the distance, I could hear the rushing of wind. "Ben, wake up, please wake up," Sarah was saying over and over again.

Remembering where I was, I sat up.

"I'm sorry, Sarah. I wish I had more control over this." I had been lying on the cold cement floor with my head nestled in Sarah's lap. "How long was I out this time?"

Sarah looked at her watch. "About five minutes."

Something was out of place. Standing, I walked back to the boarded-up window. In my vision, the door Henry was in was on my left. Now the only door I could see was the one the workers had used, and it was straight in front of me. I tried the door and found it was securely locked.

"What's wrong?"

I jumped. I hadn't heard Sarah behind me. "The door is locked, the window is boarded, and I have no idea how to get out of here."

"Tell me what you saw in your vision."

I related the whole thing to her and explained my confusion about where I had seen the door. Sarah asked me to repeat it several times before she jumped and ran to the side of the room where I had seen Henry and Mr. Robinson. "Ben, bring me your flashlight."

I pulled the flashlight out of my pocket and walked over to her.

She was pulling boxes and other stuff off of the shelves that ran along the back of the wall. Each shelf section was four feet wide and went from floor to ceiling. As she finished clearing off the shelf in front of her, she motioned for me to hand her the flashlight. She shined the light back and forth. With a little squeal, she jumped up and down. "Take a look!"

I carefully peered into the area she had just cleared. On the left-hand side was an ornately carved door handle with a spider design embossed into it. I grinned. "Okay, let's see if we can finish unloading this shelf and move it out of the way."

We soon had it unloaded. Someone had bridged the opening to cover the door. I pulled on the bottom shelf. Nothing happened, so I tapped on it from underneath until it came loose. Soon, we had the door uncovered.

Sarah tried the knob; it was locked.

Taking the flashlight, I examined the lock closely. It was an old-fashioned skeleton key type, just like on my Grandma's old house. It looked like something was stuck in it from the other side. I dug out my pocketknife and cleaned out some of the cobwebs. It looked like someone had locked the door from the other side and left the key in the lock. I had read someplace about how to get a key in this situation. I dropped to my knees and looked at the bottom of the door. The gap between the door and the floor was a little over an inch.

"Sarah, I need your help. Go get a piece of the tarp we hid under." I said as I handed her my knife.

Sarah returned with a section of tarp. "Is this going to be big enough?" I pushed the tarp under the door until only a tiny section remained on our side. I hoped enough was on the other side to do what I had planned.

"Ben, what are you doing?"

I kept forgetting I was part of a team.

"If this works, we will be able to open the door and get out of here. Hand me my knife,"

I slid the thin blade into the lock. Pushing in gently, I felt the key slide out the other side. I wanted to keep even pressure so the key didn't turn. My patience and steady hand were rewarded when the key popped free and landed softly on the tarp. Dropping back to the floor, I delicately pulled the tarp toward me. At one point, it was like it was being pulled away from me. When I peered under the door with the flashlight, all I could see were four little furry feet scampering away. I continued to pull on the tarp again and soon the top of the key became visible. I gently dropped my hand and picked up my prize.

"Ta da!" I pushed the key into the slot. "Let's see what is behind Door Number One!"

It didn't budge at first, and I feared the lock was frozen. I jiggled it a little bit. With a loud snap, the door unlocked. Grabbing the flashlight, I pointed it in front of me as I pushed the door open. The room beyond was blanketed in a thick coat of dust. As far as the ray from our little flashlight traveled, we could see huge webs full of scurrying spiders.

"Spiders?"

I heard Sarah gulp as she plastered herself against my back and looked around my shoulders.

"I don't like spiders."

With a shrug, I let out a nervous laugh. "I guess this was the reason why the group chose the spider for their symbol. Let's just be thankful they didn't choose *rats!*"

Chapter 39
<u>Creepy Crawlers</u>

♀ I could feel my skin crawling. Not sure if he realized my intense fear of them, I repeated myself.

"Ben, *I don't like spiders!"*

He turned to me with a serious look on his face, flexed the muscle in his right arm, and proudly announced, "Have no fear! Super Ben is here!"

I didn't laugh at his silly display. Instead, I pinched him to make my point. "Snap out of it! I am not going in there!"

Rubbing his skin, he said nothing, but I could see the gears moving in his head as he paced back and forth in front of the door, rubbing his fingers through his hair. His cheeks were turning bright red, and so were the tips of his ears. Instead of blowing up at me, he handed me the flashlight and stormed off in the direction of the boarded window while mumbling.

Standing at the doorway, I shuddered. The webs were strung from every corner and seemed to weave together in the middle. It reminded me of a huge ground web with a tunnel down the center. There must have been a draft coming from the basement because the webs seemed to be moving; sucked into the darkness and back out again.

"Ben, the webs are breathing!"

Ben came around the corner, frowning, with what looked to be a coat rack. He charged into the room, wielding the coat rack like a sword, clearing away the webs. In less than a minute, there were no more webs and the end of the rack had a large wad of something that looked like cotton candy. Standing in the middle, Ben beckoned with his pointer finger. Shaking my head, I refused. With a huff, he grabbed my hand and dragged me in. He shined the flashlight around us. "Look Sarah, no spider webs mean no spiders!"

It looked like an ordinary storage room now with a few crates and a lot of dust. Letting go of Ben's hand, I reached for the flashlight. He pulled his hand away and put the flashlight behind his back. "No, I am keeping it, and you will quit being so ... so ... *stubborn!"*

My heart skipped a beat. I had never seen him take charge like this before. For once, I didn't have to be the tough girl, and I kind of liked it.

"Okay, I'll try."

Ben shined the flashlight into my face and plucked a piece of ivy from my hair. "Must have been from when you fell through the window," he said.

"Uh huh," was all I could say as I looked through loose strands of hair dangling in front of my eyes.

Ben dropped the ivy and pushed the hair away, his hand lingering near my face. He was going to kiss me!

Ben leaned in slowly, his eyes locked with mine. His hand frozen in mid-air next to my ear, awkwardly fell to my shoulder. I followed his lead as he closed his eyes and puckered up.

Just as our lips were about to touch, the door behind us slammed shut with such force, the ground shook. I screamed out in pain as Ben stepped on my toe and dropped the flashlight. Kneeling, I grabbed my foot and rubbed my big toe. He bent to pick up the flashlight just as I stood back up, resulting in a collision of our heads. Needless to say, I concluded, this first kiss thing was a lot more complicated than I expected.

Once the stars cleared from my vision, I stood upright. Ben shined the flashlight at my face.

"Are you okay?"

I started to answer when a large, furry spider on an invisible thread lowered itself an inch from my nose.

♂ From the moment Sarah opened her mouth to scream, I realized this day was not going like I had planned. I put my hands over my ears, but still the scream was loud enough to shatter glass. Sarah spun around and ran for the door, leaving me to deal with the little spider. I carefully grabbed the silken thread and took my little spider yo-yo over to join his friends on the coat rack.

"Ben, the door is locked!" Sarah screamed.

Dropping the large Q-tip, I walked to the door. I wasn't worried; I would just do what I did the last time and push the key out, drop it down on my shirt and unlock the door. But as I reached the door and looked into the keyhole, my hopes of an easy fix were dashed. The key was not in the lock.

"Ben, you do have the key, right?"

Looking back at the door, I got on my hands and knees and peered underneath. My eyes caught sight of the key on the other side of the door. I stammered out a reluctant "Uh oh." The key looked like it was six inches away.

"If I could just squeeze my hand under the door.."

Sarah whispered in my ear. "Ben, please tell me you have the key."

"The key is on the floor and I can... almost... reach... it."

I was within inches of reaching it when I spotted a grayish brown rat approaching the key. If I had not seen it with my own two eyes, I would never have believed it. Almost as if trained to do so, the rat picked up the key in his mouth. As it ran away, I swear it turned to me and smiled.

"*Noooooooooo!*"

"Ben, are you okay?"

I shined the flashlight in Sarah's direction.

"No, I'm not okay. I just want to get out of here, and I am not sure where here is."

With my back against the door, I drew my knees to my chest. Sarah slid down the door to sit by me. After a few minutes of silence, she pinched my arm.

"Hey, quit acting like a baby. We can do this together."

I looked closely at the room we were in. Old wooden beams spread across the ceiling. The walls were made of closely fit stone, and the floor was hard packed dirt. Right in the middle, heading toward the door, was a deep set of lines. I got up to examine the lines and discovered they were iron rails. I blew the dust off the top of one of them. "Sarah, take a look at this."

"Doesn't this look like a miniature set of rail road tracks?"

I had seen tracks similar to this every year at the mall around Christmas. After standing in line for hours to have our picture taken

with Santa, we enjoyed a brief ride on his miniature train.
"We can get out of here if we follow these tracks."

I grabbed the coat rack. "Remember when you said the spider webs looked like they were breathing?"
Sarah nodded.

"That means there is air flowing from somewhere, and that somewhere is our way out."

I handed Sarah the flashlight and walked towards the far wall. "You shine the light and I will knock down the spider webs," I said as I followed the little train tracks out of the room.

We hadn't gone more than a few feet before the floor sloped down and a tunnel appeared. There were so many webs we had not seen it before. We were gradually going deeper into the earth. The tunnel was the same type of construction as the little room we just came from, but it was only four feet wide. The walls were made with tight fitting stones, and the ceiling was held up with large wooden beams. Old light bulbs ran down the center of the ceiling about every twenty feet or so. Webs were everywhere, and I had to be careful not to break one of the bulbs.

We were making good progress, when the tunnel opened into a large chamber. I stopped at the entrance.

"What's wrong?" Sarah whispered from behind me as she peered around my shoulder with the flashlight.

The chamber appeared to be roughly circular in shape with tunnels branching off at different angles. The first thing I noticed in this room was the lack of spider webs. The tunnel we had just come from was loaded with the little dust-collecting webs, and yet this room had just a few here and there.

"Shine your light around," I said with excitement.

As she panned the beam outward, I counted eight side tunnels, including the one we had come from, that branched out from this large cavern-like area. From each of the tunnels came a little set of train tracks. They all met in the middle.

"Ben, look at the center of the room."

My eyes followed the flashlight's beam to the center of the room. At first, I was not sure what I was looking at. We slowly made our way to the middle where there was a round steel plate with two sections of curved railroad track. A few feet away, there was a steel bar with a turning wheel the size of a truck tire at the top. It looked like whatever rode on these tracks could be directed toward another tunnel with the turntable. "Wow, this is pretty cool."

I walked over to the handle and couldn't resist giving it a turn. Nothing happened, so I grabbed with both hands and tried again.
"Be careful, you don't know what it will do."

I didn't need anyone telling me to be careful. I already had this thing figured out. Just when I was ready to give up, the wheel turned.
"*Yes!!*" I said triumphantly.
A loud screeching noise filled the air.
"Ben, watch out!"
The steel turntable I had been standing on continued to spin. I let go of the handle but it continued to spin faster and faster and more out of control. I grabbed Sarah's hand and we backed away slowly. The screeching noise grew louder and louder. We both had our hands over our ears. It did little to block out the noise. As Sarah pulled my hand in the direction of the tunnel we had come through, the spinning stopped abruptly.

"Okay, no more touching things!" I announced.
"I told you so." she whispered.
"Which way do we go?"

Sarah played the flashlight over each one of the branching tunnel ways.
"Hmmm... let's see." She stopped on the second tunnel to the right. "That way."

I looked at her with curiosity. "How do you know we should go that way?"

With a smug smile on her face she explained, "Well, if you look at the spider webs in the corner, they are blowing towards us, so it means air is coming in from that direction."

Chapter 40
Tunnel Tour

♀ Ben charged ahead with his trusty coat rack. Glancing at the end of the rack, I shuddered. The ball of webs at the tip was growing large and beginning to resemble a round fish bowl full of spiders. I would have been less squeamish, if there had been glass holding the spiders in. Every time I looked, there seemed to be hundreds of them scrambling to find a way out. I prayed we would see daylight before the mangled nest became even larger.

"Don't look at them," I whispered to myself.

Ben stopped in his tracks so fast I ran right into him, narrowly avoiding the mass of spiders. He tipped his head sideways. "Do you hear that?"

"Sorry, I was just talking to myself and ..."

Ben interrupted me when he spun around and put a finger to his lips. "Shhhh, listen."

I paused for a second but heard nothing. Excitedly, he took the flashlight from my hand and replaced it with the coat rack. I squealed and threw it behind me into the darkness. Shining the beam up at the dangling bulbs, I could see movement. They swayed back and forth as I felt a tremble above.

"There's something up there and I know what it is."

Ben took off running ahead, leaving me alone in the dark. He got fifty feet before he stopped, turned around and shined the light back into my face.

"Sorry."

I walked hesitantly toward him.

"What about your spider sword?"

He laughed. "It's not much farther now."

Ahead, I could see a slight curve in the tunnel and only a few webs near the ceiling. I let out a sigh of relief.

"Whew, how do you know we're almost there?"

Ben shined the flashlight on his own face and grinned. "Trust me. I remembered something from the map."

Grabbing my hand, he practically dragged me behind him. As we approached the bend, a slight breeze blew across my face. It was warm and smelled faintly of fried food. The tunnel walls were now red brick, and the floor was no longer dirt, but cement. Once around the corner, he was obviously surprised.

"Oh no." he whined.

In front of us, the tunnel had caved in. Amongst the dirt, rock, and brick piled before us, several barrels branded with the spider symbol lay half buried. The tracks disappeared under the debris.

Yet, I could still feel a slight breeze. Taking the flashlight, I shined it to the ceiling of the tunnel. Just before the cave-in, I spotted an iron grate. There was no light coming from it, so I assumed it didn't lead to the outside.

"Look, that's where the air is coming from."

Centering himself directly below it, he took a deep breath in.

"It smells like Chinese food. Is there a Chinese restaurant in town?"

"I think so. I've never been in there, because they have dead chickens in the window."

Ben quickly turned and dug around one of the barrels.

"Help me dig this out. If we put it under the grate, we should be able to stand on it."

Propping the flashlight up on the pile of dirt next to the barrel, I started digging. Before long we had the barrel uncovered. Thankfully, it was empty, which made rolling it much easier. Pushing the barrel onto its end, we centered it below the grate, and Ben climbed on top. The ceilings were only seven feet high at the most, so he had to hunch over when he stood. I watched as he pushed on the grate with all the strength he had. It didn't budge. Ben's face turned bright red as he put his shoulder against it and shoved hard. The rusty metal shifted as he groaned and strained against its weight. Finally, the grate popped free as Ben shoved it aside and stuck his head into the hole.

"Where are we?"

"It looks like the basement of a Chinese restaurant," he answered as he raised himself through the opening.

I climbed on top of the barrel. Ben reached down and pulled me up. We lay on the basement floor, exhausted. I looked over at him and wasn't surprised that he was covered head to toe in webs. His face, still a bright red, was dirty around his mouth, making him look like he had a beard. The cool cement against my back was refreshing but the hot air coming from an exhaust fan above us was unbearable.

"Let's get out of here and find the rest of the gang. They're probably worried sick." I stood and approached the stairs.

Ben sprung to his feet with newly found energy and raced me to the top.

Opening the door quietly, we peeked into the kitchen. Although it was little, a lot of people were crammed into it. A cook, with black hair encased in a hair net, was adding rice to a large steaming pot, while a petite older woman stood at the sink loading dirty dishes on to a conveyor belt. Three others, who looked to be our age, were cutting up vegetables on a butcher block across from the stove. A large man carried two dead plucked chickens by the neck to the back corner. I cringed as I heard the loud chopping noise and tried not to imagine the poor headless bird becoming someone's lunch. Ben nudged me and nodded in the direction of the back door. We had a clear path as long as everyone stayed put. I started the countdown. "One, two..."

Just as we were ready to race out, the large man with a cleaver in his hand opened the basement door. His expression showed his total surprise at finding two filthy, scared kids right in front of him. I saw the cleaver, the way the sharp edge caught the light in such a way it made my knees weak.

"Ruuuuuuuun!" I heard myself yell at the top of my lungs.

We both took off. Ben dropped to the floor and crawled in between the man's legs and out the other side, heading for the back door. I had no choice but to push past the arm not holding a sharp object and made a detour toward the front counter. I didn't look back, but I could hear the man screaming something I didn't understand and the slam of the back door as Ben ran out into the alley. The faces of the customers were only a blur as I flew through the dining room and out the front. The last thing I heard was the urgent ringing of the bell attached to the front door.

⬅➡

♂ I didn't have to be told twice to run. One look at the meat cleaver was the inspiration I needed. I never felt so alive as I slammed open the back door and ran into the alley.
"Sarah, we made it," I said, turning back.
I was alone. My heart almost stopped.
"Sarah? *Oh no!*"
I sprang to the back door only to find it locked.

She hadn't made it past the crazed cook with the meat cleaver. In less than a week, I had found my best friend and gotten her killed by some cook who right now was trying to decide how best to serve her to the lunch crowd.

Okay, I was being overly dramatic. I was old enough to know Sarah was not being murdered in the kitchen of a Chinese restaurant, but I couldn't help envisioning the possible trouble she was in. My dad called it my overactive imagination.

With my head bowed, I walked towards the main street. The closer I got to the street, the more my adventurous brain took over and the madder I got.

"Nobody is going to chop up my best friend for any lunch menu." I mumbled to myself.

"Hold on, Sarah!" I yelled as I ran around to the front of the building.

The alley was a blur as I gained speed. I was so intent on rescuing my friend. I didn't notice I had run right past her.

"Ben!"

"Can't talk now!" I shouted back as I headed for the front door. When my brain finally caught up with my legs, I realized it was Sarah who had called my name. She was standing on the corner looking at me with a big grin on her face.
"You were coming to rescue me, weren't you?"
My face turned bright red.
"Ummm, yeah."
"That is so cute."

She fell into a fit of giggling. Taking me by the hand, Sarah pulled me back towards the library.

"Let's go find the rest of the group before they call the police or something."

By this time, Mike was probably panicked. It seemed like we had been in the tunnel for hours, but according to the clock on the bank, it was less than forty-five minutes. Just as I was getting used to holding Sarah's hand, I heard Nate's voice coming from the direction of the Post Office. I could hear the panic in his voice.

"We have to get your parent. They could be tuck down there until tomorrow!"

Sarah let go of my hand and ran towards our friends. She snuck up behind Nate and messed his hair.

Steph was the happiest to see everyone. Jumping from the stone steps of the Post Office, she gave her sister a big hug. It seemed to surprise Sarah.
"What's wrong, Steph?"

Steph just shook her head and gave Sarah one last squeeze before sitting back on the steps.

"Where were you guys?" Nate asked once the shock of arrival had worn off.

I sat beside Steph. Shaking off the dirt and the spider webs, we told them of our adventure, about being locked in the room, of the hidden door and the tunnels. I had the map out while we talked. I pointed to the dotted lines going from building to building.
"These lines represent tunnels."

Sarah stood. "We need to find out more about the town before we go off on any more underground adventures. Someone in this town has to know what was going on back then."

She turned full circle with the map in her hand. "I will ask my mom tonight about someone we can talk to. I'm sure she will know."

Sarah handed the map back to me. I carefully folded it and put it away.
"Hey, Ben, what is that stuck to your foot?"
Mike pointed to my right shoe.

I looked on the bottom of my shoe; a scrap of paper was stuck to it. It looked like a label of some type. It was extremely old. Pulling on it carefully, I was able to remove it. When I turned it over, I saw the little spider emblem in the right-hand corner and the following words in big bold print: "Rosalina's Rice Wine Vinegar." I carefully folded it and placed it in my pocket with the map.

"Okay, group, we still have a lot of daylight left. Where do we want to go next?"

I was ready to suggest we head back to my place, when Mike spoke up.

"Where does Brutus work?"

We turned to look at him.

"Who is Brutus?" Steph asked.

Turning his head to his right, he held up his hand.

"Shhhhhhhh, I can't hear what she is saying." Within just a few minutes, he giggled. "I meant to say where does Marcus work?"

After we had stopped laughing, Sarah asked, "Why do you want to know where Marcus works?"

Mike looked at the ground. "I have to do something there. I can't tell you what, but it is important we do it today."

Sarah pointed down the road. "He works at the lumber yard, loading and unloading trucks. He might be there today. It's only six blocks away, across the railroad tracks."

Once again, we marched in line with Sarah in the lead. When we got to the Chinese restaurant, Sarah slowed and casually walked by, trying to appear nonchalant. As we passed by the little park, I remembered sitting on the bench spitting my bubble gum out of my mouth while trying to blow a bubble. A lot had happened in the last week.

Our little troop was soon passing a grand, beautiful house with a well-kept hedge. It was a two-story home with a covered porch that wrapped around the whole front of the house. In each top corner of the deck were fancy scrollwork woodcarvings. My dad called these homes "<u>Ginger Bread Cottages</u>" because of all the fancy woodwork they had.

As we passed the iron gate, I could hear singing. Peering into the yard, I saw a lady in an old-fashioned sun hat. She was on her hands and knees pulling weeds out of her flower garden.

Sarah was motioning me to hurry.

When I got past the gate and up to her, she whispered, "I didn't want you to make eye contact. If you do, she will want to talk to you and you will be stuck there forever."

I rolled my eyes.
"Forever?"
She nodded.
"Yeah, forever."

    The rise in the road and the railroad crossing signs were just ahead. The lumberyard was open, because we could see trucks pulling into and out of it. We were close enough to hear a familiar laugh. It was Marcus.

    Mike crossed the tracks, trotting down the hill on the other side, and hid behind some tall shrubs. Once we caught up with him, we saw where the laughter was coming from. Marcus and several other big guys were standing around a <u>Datsun pickup truck</u>. He was loading the truck while the older guys bossed him around. Marcus shook his head and smiled even as he turned beat red.

    When he was done loading it, he went to the back and grabbed the little truck's bumper. You could see the strain on his face as he tried to lift the back end off the ground. At first, nothing happened. Eventually, the rear wheels slowly lifted off the ground. The older men cheered and slapped each other on the backs. One of the men clearly hadn't believed Marcus could do it and was handing the bigger guy some money. After this little display was complete, the men broke up and went back to work.

    Mike shoved his hands in his pockets and headed back across the railroad tracks towards home.

"Mike," I whispered, "Did you have to do something here?"

He shrugged. "This is what we had to do. Now we can go home."

Chapter 41
Recheck & Recharge

♀ "That's it?" I yelled. "We walked all this way for that?"

    Mike looked at me with a smirk. "It's only six blocks and over the railroad tracks, Sarah."

The warmth crept up my neck and into my cheeks.

Steph interrupted. "It's okay Mike, she's just hungry. Sarah gets grumpy when she's hungry."

I shot a dirty look in her direction as Nate clutched his stomach.

"I'm tarving too." he said as he staggered around until he keeled over, playing dead.

Ben kicked Nate's shoe. "Put your tongue back in your mouth. We are *all* hungry."

"I can't make it back to Ben's house with an empty tank." Steph whined.

Nate jumped to his feet and pulled my ponytail.

"You tinking what I'm tinking, Tarah?"

Nate's mom worked part-time during the summer at the local Red Barn restaurant. She only worked on Sundays and never past six o'clock. My mom said it was to give her a break from the kids and allow her the chance for grown-up conversation. If you asked me, I would have said she wanted the extra money for her hair styling appointments and hairspray. She had high, poufy hair that never moved.

"Follow me, it on the way." Nate said as he took the lead.

By the time we reached the restaurant, my poor feet had blisters and my head reeled from hunger. The building was shaped exactly like a barn and painted a bright red with white trim. Peering through the plate glass window, I saw the counter was busy. Nate knocked on the glass and waved to a pretty woman standing by the deep fryer. She smiled brightly and signed something to Nate and disappeared into the back. Nate nodded and motioned for us to follow him.

A high fence surrounded a yard at the back of the building. Inside, a picnic table painted red with a white stripe down the middle, sat off to one side balanced by a large dumpster on the other side. There was a faint smell of rotting food, but at this point, you could have placed garbage in front of me and I would have eaten it. Nate knocked a series of codes on the back door and the metal door swung open. His mom gave him a big hug.

"Well hello, kids. Why Sarah, it's been way too long!" She hugged me tightly and pushed me out to an arm's length as she looked me over. "My, have you grown into a lovely young lady."

Steph pushed herself in front of Ben and smiled sweetly.

"Hi, Mrs. Blair."

Nate's mom tweaked Steph's nose. "Stephanie, my heavens, is that you?" Steph twirled in a circle as if she was a princess in sneakers. "Such a beauty you are." Mrs. Blair fussed.

Nate introduced Ben and Mike. He signed quickly and rubbed his stomach. Mrs. Blair disappeared through the back door and returned with a red plastic tray. Heaped on top were five hamburgers and a huge pile of fries. We sat at the picnic table as we took in the aroma of the hot, fried food. She placed five large drinks in front of us with a handful of straws. With our mouths shoved full of food, we nodded and mumbled a thank you as she went back to work, waving at us and smiling at Nate.

"See you at dinner tonight, honey."

Fifteen minutes later, we sat quietly at the picnic table, cluttered with wrappers, empty cups, and ketchup packets. It looked as if a pack of wild dogs had been let loose and gobbled up the food.

"That hit the spot." Mike groaned. "I ate too many French fries."

Steph and I cleared the table as the boys lifted the lid to the dumpster for us. With a large belch, Nate bent to tie his shoe. Mike pulled on Ben's sleeve and whispered something to him. Ben looked around, discreetly took him around the back corner of the fence and reappeared a couple minutes later with Mike pulling up his zipper.

"Had to see a man about a horse." he said imitating a cowboy in a movie western.

We laughed. Where else would you see a horse but at a Red Barn?

♂ If I had been back home on a Sunday, I would have been ready for naptime after a big lunch. One of those family traditions growing up was to have the family over for lunch, watch whatever sports team was playing or take a nap. Right now, my body was saying nap, and I was doing my best to not yawn.

"Hey guys, what do we want to do next?" Sarah asked as she finished putting the last of the trash in the garbage can.

We sat around looking at each other when Nate finally spoke up.

"Let's tee if we can find the tunnel at your house."

The dotted lines on the map did go in that direction. As we walked toward home, we abandoned our single file formation. Now with full stomachs, we were bunched up, pushing each other off the side walk and doing other silly things.

I must have been sleepy or daydreaming.

Sarah was snapping her fingers in front of my face. "Earth to Ben, come in, Ben."

We were standing in front of my driveway and everyone was looking at me.

"He gets that way when he's thinking about something," Mike said. "He just kind of zones out."

My face grew hot with everyone staring at me.

"Shows over, nothing to see," Sarah said as she came to my rescue.

Taking the map out of my pocket, I looked at how the lines crawled across the page. Each place they touched played a part in this mystery, but how and what did it mean?

"Guys, I want to go over to the train yard before we look around my house."

"Are you sure you want to do that?" Steph asked apprehensively.

"Don't worry; I don't want to go in. I just want to look at where the shed is and if the lines on the map go to it."

We crossed the street and came face to face with the wall of vines. After a few minutes of careful searching, we finally found a spot where we could see the utility shed in the train yard.

Maybe I shouldn't have been surprised, but Sarah rubbed her arms like she was cold; Mike said something to his imaginary friend, and I got light headed. Before I could fall, I gripped the chain link fence and locked my knees. Anticipating what was going to happen next, I closed my eyes and fought the sensation of falling and waited. When the feeling of being light headed stopped, I opened my eyes – or at least in my vision I opened them.

I was standing in the train yard. It was dark, but the area in front of the utility shed was lit with an overhead light. A big boxcar sat on the short section of track in front of the shed. Someone was unloading barrels from the car and putting cardboard boxes back into it. "Henry, get your butt over here and hurry, I haven't got all day."

Standing not more than five or six feet away from me was Mr. Robinson. He was a hefty man, and he was smoking a large cigar. Each time he puffed on it, the glow from it lit up a little bit of his face. I had seen the face before; a much older version hung above the door in the library.

"Yes, Mr. Robinson." Henry loaded another barrel onto a wheeled cart and took it into the shed.

Mr. Robinson's hand came up to his mouth. I saw a gold ring, similar to the one I found hidden in the box with the letters from Henry. When I opened my eyes, Sarah was pulling on my arms.

"Ben! Let go!"

I tried to figure out what was wrong with her. She kept looking back through the fence. There was Mr. Wilkerson on the other side. He was mad, his face was beat red, and he was yelling. "I told you kids to stay away from here! Now git!"

How long had I been out this time? My hands were locked tight onto the fence. I had to concentrate to get them to release it.

Sarah led me across the street back to safety. Once there, the rest of the group surrounded me.

"What happened? Why did you just stand there?" Sarah asked.

While I was in the vision, the old man had come out of the shed and saw us standing there. He yelled for us to get away or he would call the cops. Nate made the sign of moose horns on his head and taunted him. "Nah nah nah nah nah." It got him mad.

He picked up a stick and approached the fence. Everyone took off running back across the street, except me. When they turned around, I was still standing there. He must have assumed I was being defiant as he yelled and swung the stick back and forth. Sarah ran back across the street to get me.

I related what had happened to me as we walked back to my garage. When we reached it, no one was sure what to do.
Sarah said, "Let's take a look in the basement first."

It had been a while since Sarah and I had been down there. We decided to use the exterior cellar door. The staircase was not as haunting as it had been at night, and with this large of a group, I wasn't as frightened. In single file, we walked the short flight of stairs and through the basement door. I turned on the lights. My dad had been doing some more work. A pile of two by fours lay in one corner, near chalk lines that were drawn on the floor. It looked like he was going to put in some walls in the near future. I was looking at the lines on the floor when I heard Sarah let out a scream. She had her hand covering her mouth and was pointing over into the corner where the old shelves were. Standing in the corner was the coat rack we had used to clear out the spider webs.

Chapter 42
Diligently Driven

♀ Everyone looked back at me with confused looks, except Ben. His face went pale. Nate walked over to the coat rack and poked at the nest of spiders wrapped around the top.
"I never taw 'piders make a web like that before."
Mike and Steph both ran to take a look without getting too close.
"It looks like there are thousands of them in there." Steph scratched her arms and shuddered.
"Makes my skin crawl."
Mike poked Ben in the side with his finger, startling him out of his trance.
"What's wrong?"
"You taw this before?" Nate asked.
Ben nodded. "I found it in the library right before Sarah and I almost ki…" He stopped himself; he had almost given away his feeble attempt for a kiss.
"You almost what?" Steph asked with her hands on her hips.
His cheeks flushed a bright red, and he avoided looking in my direction.
"Well…we…uh…um," he stammered nervously.
"We almost kicked a *huge rat!*" I shouted as I came to his rescue.

Mike's eyes grew large as he looked at Ben with awe. "Was it bigger than the ones back home in the <u>irrigation canals</u>?"

Ben nodded and held out his hands like a fisherman showing the size of the one that got away. After a few minutes, we decided to blame the appearance of the mysterious coat rack on Katrina. We moved forward with the search for the tunnel.

Ben mouthed the words "Thank you" as the others set off in search of a secret doorway.

We each took a corner of the room, with the exception of Mike and Steph who seemed inseparable. I didn't pay attention to what everyone else was doing.

Why did Ben try to kiss me in the first place? Having him as my new best friend was exciting, and the last week had proved to be the beginning of the most adventurous summer yet. Even though having my first kiss was something I looked forward to, I was not sure I was ready for it so soon. I made up my mind if Ben tried to kiss me again in the near future, I would set him straight."

"Eureka!" Ben shouted. He moved some boxes away from the brick wall.

We came running to his side as he ran his fingers over the old brick wall near the back of the basement.

"I don't know why I never noticed this before," he said excitedly.

Mike stuck his face close to the brick. "I don't see nuthin."

I stared at an unevenly spaced red brick with mortar missing in between, but I didn't see anything, either. Ben seemed awfully proud of himself as he stuck out his arm like a magician about to perform a trick.

"Look like a brick wall to me," Nate admitted.

"Look closer."

Ben moved aside while the four of us crammed close together with our noses almost touching it. Steph was the first to notice.

"I see it! There is a letter "E" on the corner of the brick!"

Jumping up and down, Ben laughed like a lunatic.

The red colored brick looked to have been scratched with something sharp in the corner.

"But what does it mean exactly?" I asked.

Ben stopped his little celebration dance and looked at me with one of those "I can't believe you don't get it" looks. "Sarah, where is the cameo? I'm pretty sure the numbers we found inside of it have something to do with this wall."

I instinctively reached for my front pocket, but the cameo had not been there for days. "I put it in the box the day Marcus took the money."

Ben's eyes lit up just before he sprinted for the stairs. Moments later he reappeared with the cameo in hand and sweat running down his forehead.

"We are so close, I can feel it!"

He tried to pry open the back of the cameo but he was having problems. Standing with my arms crossed across my chest, I waited for him to ask for help. It wasn't until I tapped my foot that he looked over at me.

"Okay, okay. You do it."

With the lightest touch of my finger, I triggered the hidden latch and popped open the back.

"Some things girls just do better than boys," Steph announced.

Ben greedily snatched the cameo from my hand and held it to the light. "E.V.H. 12S, 16E, 4N." He looked closely at the wall until he found a barely legible letter "V" in the lower left corner of another brick. It looked like it had been scratched into the surface as well. "Help me find the "H". It has to be here somewhere."

We split up and looked closely at each brick, moving boxes out of the way as we went. Nate found the "H" in the far-right corner near the floor.

"Now what do we do?" Mike asked.

Ben put his hand on the brick with the "E" on it. "We go south on this one," he announced and counted down 12 bricks. He pushed on the twelfth brick.

The brick slowly moved almost three inches into the wall.

"Hurry, Mike, count 16 bricks to the right of the "V" brick and push in!"

Mike was eager to help. He counted to the sixteenth brick.

"We went east, didn't we, Ben?" Ben nodded as Mike pushed his brick in.

"North!" I shouted, counting up four from the "H" brick. Nate pushed in the fourth brick.

We stood silently waiting for something to open. At first there was nothing. Just as I let out a sigh of disappointment, a loud thud came from behind us.

♂ We wheeled around towards the sound. It had come from the corner of the basement over by the old storage shelves. Racing each other to that spot, we waited. Two minutes went by, then five.

"What are you kids doing?" my mom said from just behind us.
I yelped. "Mom, why do you always sneak up on me like that?"

My mom just stood there with one arm on her hip and the other arm wrapped around a basket of clothes she was bringing down to throw into the washer.

"I didn't sneak up on you. I came down the stairs to do some laundry and found all five of you staring at the wall."
It must have looked pretty silly.

"Why don't you guys go play outside? It is such a nice day. You don't need to be in some stuffy old basement."

I wanted to argue, but Sarah nudged my arm and gestured towards the basement door. We dragged our feet in disappointment and gathered on the front porch.

"What are we missing? I know there is a secret door in the basement. We heard the sounds." I settled into my thinking mode, knees drawn to my chest and resting my head on my knees. "We are so close, I know it!"

Mike sat on the steps beside me. "Ben, don't worry, we will figure it out. We are a team, remember?"
I ruffled his hair. "Yeah, we're a team."

After a short silence, Steph spoke up. "We need to talk to someone who knows what happened a long time ago in town, someone who was alive back then."
Nate raised his hand like he was in school.
"Go ahead, Nate," Sarah said.
"We tould talk to Mr. Wilkerson."
A visible shudder ran through the group.
"Okay, bad idea."

It was Mike who had the best idea for the day. He suggested we talk to the old lady we had seen outside gardening earlier in the day. "She looked older than dirt."
Sarah was the first to voice her opinion. "No, they are just creepy."
"What do you mean 'they'?" I asked.
Sarah seemed to have a bad taste in her mouth.

"They are the town twins. They're ancient and have lived here for forever."

Okay, so they were old ladies who might be perfect for what we needed to know. "Ummmm, do 'they' have a name?" I prompted.

"You don't want to go and visit them. One of them will try to feed you herbs she grows in her garden, and the other one will want to feed you candy."

"And their name is?" I asked again. When Sarah didn't answer, I lost a little patience. "Sarah, what are their names?"

"Ben, you don't understand. They are the town gossips, they are weird, they know things, and their house smells like soap and old people."
"So, what is the big deal?"

Sarah didn't want to talk about it anymore. I asked Steph what their names were, but the look Sarah gave her sister made it clear this was a subject not to be discussed. All it did for me was to make me want to know even more. "Sarah what is going on?"

Sarah got off the porch. "Ben, I don't want to talk about it. It's time for me and Steph to go home."
She grabbed Steph's hand and walked briskly toward her house.

I looked over at Nate. It was apparent by the look on his face and the way he shrugged his shoulders he didn't know what was going on, either.

"I guess I had better get home, too." With a mock salute, he headed towards his house.

Dad pulled his truck out of the garage and rolled down the window.

"Hey, you two, want to go with me to get some ice cream?" I didn't have to be asked twice and neither did Mike.

Chapter 43
Forgive & Forget

♀ Steph struggled to keep in stride with me, but my long legs and purposeful gait were too much for her.

"Sarahhhhh, wait for me!" she whined, lagging behind.

I paid no attention. I was too busy trying to hold back the dam that was ready to break. The mere mention of the twins brought back so many wonderful memories – and disappointments.

I had spent many hours with Opal and Odelle Knickerbocker when I was little. When I was three, my mom was pregnant with Steph and was put on bed rest. My dad, busy running the antique shop, was unable to take care of me. He asked the sisters if they would look after me during the day. Every day, Opal walked me to their house and Odelle walked me back home before dinner. I spent countless afternoons helping health conscious Opal with her garden, cooking what she called "feel good soup" using vegetables and herbs we planted together, while Odelle snuck me pieces of candy.

"Kids need a little sugar to get them through the day."

They looked exactly alike but could not have been more different. I grew to love and trust those women as if they were my own grandmothers.

The day mom went into labor; I was playing on their front porch with Oscar Knickerbocker, their fat orange cat. He was one of many strays the sisters had taken in. All of the cats had names that started with "O" because they had a fondness for the initials "O.K."

They always said, "Everything and everyone is O.K. in this house."

In total, there were eight cats – Oscar, Olivia, Othello, Octavius, Oakley, Ozzy, Otto, and Ophelia. When it was feeding time, all they had to do was ring the little bell mounted on the front porch and yell, "O.K., time for dinner!"

That day, I was tempting Oscar with a feather I had found in the garden earlier when the phone rang. Curious, I sneaked through the front door and listened at the kitchen doorway. I heard the excitement in Opal's voice as she agreed to keep me overnight.

I didn't know if I was more excited about my sister finally being born or sleeping over with my adopted grandmothers. It was that night that everything changed.

At the end of our driveway, I turned around. Steph was shuffling her feet, looking at the ground.

"C'mon, Steph, why don't we find Sandy and go exploring?"

Steph shook her head. "I've had enough exploring for today. Hey, were you crying?"

Lifting the front of my shirt, I wiped the tears from my face.

"No! Why would I cry?"

With a sideways glance she sighed, "Why don't you like those old ladies, Sarah?"

I cleared my throat. "I'll tell you tomorrow when I tell everyone else, okay?"

Steph took off running in the direction of the front door.

"Beat you to the bean bag chair!"

Later after supper, I found Mom sitting at the kitchen table, looking through her sewing basket. I pulled up a chair as she turned a pair of my old blue jeans inside out.

"Looks like you've grown the past few months. I have to take the hem out I put in when we first bought these."

Forcing a smile, I nodded. Mom tilted her head slightly to the left. She did that when she had concerns.

"What's wrong, Sarah?"

Shrugging my shoulders, I mumbled, "Just worried."

She put down the jeans. "Want to talk about it?"

"What if you used to be friends with someone and they hurt your feelings and you stopped talking to them and *then* you were *forced* to talk to them again?"

Mom paused for a second and asked, "Did these friends know they hurt your feelings?"

She could tell I was uncomfortable so she continued. "Sometimes people say or do things that hurt people but they don't realize it."

I shifted uncomfortably in my seat until she reached across the table and touched my hand. "If it's too hard to talk with your friends about it, why don't you start fresh? Forgive and forget."

I looked across the table at my mother and smiled warmly. If anyone knew how to make me feel better, it was my mom.

The next morning was hectic. Dad was getting ready to go out of town for a large auction, and Mom was helping him load a large cooler.

Sitting at the kitchen table with her nightgown on, Steph ran her finger over the highlighted areas of Dad's road map.
"How far away is Sherman, New York?"

"One-inch equals fifty miles." I pulled a ruler out of the junk drawer.
Snatching it from my hand, Steph placed it on the map to figure out the distance. Outside on the driveway, Dad gave Mom a kiss and got into his truck.
"You better hurry, Steph. Dad is going to forget the map again!"

The truck backed out of the driveway as Steph ran as fast as she could after him. Dad stopped so she could hop onto the running board. She threw her arms around Dad's neck and kissed him.

You'd never guess only hours ago she had been screaming in bed from a bad dream. It never seemed to affect her the next day but Mom, who went to comfort her, had been concerned.

"That is the fourth time this week she's had nightmares. I'm worried, Honey." She had said to Dad when she returned to their room.

After we dressed and ate breakfast, Steph and I went the long way around the train yard. Nate was sitting in the grass in front of Ben's house waiting for us.
"It's about time," he signed.
"We're not late." Steph signed with a frown.

Nate seemed surprised. "You're getting better at 'tigning, "Teph!" She grinned from ear to ear.

Making our way to the back door, we noticed the garage door was wide open. We looked in and saw nothing unusual except all the cupboard doors but one was opened wide.
"Looks like Ben began without us." I said with disgust.
"Why would I do that?"
Ben looked barely awake. His hair was uncombed, and there were dark circles under his eyes. Rubbing them, he looked into the garage.
"What happened here?"

I gave him a concerned look. "You okay?"

He nodded and closed the doors one at a time until he reached the only closed one. Bending, he carefully opened the door to look inside. "Aaaarrrgh!" Mike jumped out of the cabinet.

Ben's face went pale as we screamed with surprise and giggled for a long time.

As we left the garage in the direction of the street, I made a suggestion.

"We should visit the Knickerbocker sisters first and go to the library to look for any information they give us."

I didn't hear a peep.

"What?"

Ben tried to hide his smile. Nate had missed what I had just said because my back had been towards him. Steph and Mike looked confused.

"So, we finally know who 'they' are." Ben joked.

"What kind of name is Knickerbocker?" Mike asked.

Steph chimed in, "It's a *weird* name."

We marched single file until Ben caught up with me. His eyes met mine and I understood what they were saying.

"Don't worry about it. I'm not mad," I told him.

He let out a sigh of relief and pulled a pack of gum from his pocket. "Want some?" The rest of us put our hands out with anticipation.

In front of the twins' house, we stopped, smacking our lips and blowing bubbles.

"What should we say when they answer the door?" Mike asked.

Biting my lower lip, I tried to think. We couldn't say we were doing a school project, because it was summer. Besides, they would recognize me.

"We won't have to say anything. They do a pretty good job of talking all by themselves."

I led the way to the front porch.

I ran my fingers through my hair and rang the old-fashioned bell mounted underneath the plaque that said "O. Knickerbocker." A few minutes later, a short, plump old woman answered the door.

Through the screen, I could see she had aged. The wrinkles

were more noticeable and the grey had almost taken over the dark hair I remembered.

"Can I help you?" she asked examining each of us individually.

When her gaze stopped on me, her face lit up. She put her weathered old hand across her chest.

"Oh, my goodness! Is that my Sarah? My little Doodlebug?"

I blushed as I nodded. With a shrill voice she called into the house. "Opal! Come quick! Doodlebug is back!"

The door swung open and the frail old woman wrapped her arms around me in a tight hug.

♂ "Doodlebutt?" I said out loud as the old lady released Sarah. "Did I hear that correctly?"

"No!" Sarah said. "Doodle*bug*!" For added measure, she followed with a swift hit to my arm. I could almost see the bruise forming.

The lady looked to be my grandma's age, but that is where the similarities ended. Her hair had a bright pink streak the color of cotton candy. She had blue eye shadow and bright red lipstick. I knew right away I did not want to be kissed by this person. The lipstick looked like it would stain any surface it touched. She wore a pair of faded blue jeans and an oversized t-shirt with Han Solo's picture on it. She had good taste in movies.

"Guys, this is my friend Odelle. She and her sister Opal are like my adoptive grandparents. Anyway, Grandma Odelle lives by one rule: you can only be young once, but you can be immature forever."

Odelle led us into the house which was a little like entering the Twilight Zone. The living room was a mix of old and new, and none of it matched. There were old oil paintings of your typical flowers or mountain scenes on one wall and on another, were movie posters of Star Wars.

When I wandered over to look at them, I noticed one had a signature on it. Odelle whispered over my shoulder.

"Yep, I got him to sign it for me."

<u>Harrison Ford</u>, one of the coolest actors in the world, had signed this poster for Odelle, most likely one of the oldest fans in the world. How cool was that? My level of respect for Odelle shot up.

In addition to the mix of movie posters and lace doilies, there was an old <u>player piano</u> near the window. It looked like it had been a long time since it was played last, but there was no mistake – it was a player. Kneeling in front of the piano, I looked at the bottom panel. Hidden behind some detailed colored glass was an assortment of other musical instruments. I was just touching the glass when a soft voice spoke from just inside the doorway.

"That was Daddy's favorite."

I looked and there was another version of Odelle. I guess the confusion showed on my face because Sarah laughed.

"Guys, this is Opal. She and Odelle are twins."

Where Odelle was hip and trendy, Opal was refined. Opal wore a summer dress with flowers printed on it. She had on a sunbonnet with the strings tied under her chin. She also wore a red-checkered print apron that had been modified to hold an assortment of gardening tools.

Once the introductions had been made, the tension grew.

Finally, Opal opened her arms and gestured to Sarah.

"Come here, Sweetheart, and give grandma a hug."

It was all Sarah needed to hear. She fell into Opal's arms.

"Okay, enough mush. Why don't we get these kids something to snack on?" Odelle pushed past us.

We heard the sounds of cupboard doors opening and closing. "Opal, where did you hide my cookies?"

Scattered among the knick-knacks on top of the piano were pictures of Sarah at different times in her life. I now understood the warm welcome she had received from these two ladies. Looking over at Sarah, I caught her looking at me. For just a second, it looked as if she was crying and smiling at the same time.

Odelle stuck her head around the corner from the kitchen. "Okay, everybody, get your fannies in the kitchen before the pop gets warm and the cookies dry out."

In the kitchen, I could tell two-different people lived here with extremely different styles. On one side of the sink were multiple boxes of sugar-coated cereal and on the other were two boxes, one of cream of wheat and one simply labeled whole wheat mush.

"Sister, I will not have you rotting out their teeth with liquid sugar junk," said Opal with her hands on her hips.

Odelle turned around with a big smile on her face. "I have been drinking this stuff for most of my life, and my teeth are fine!"

I had to admit her teeth looked fine to me. I was just picking up my cup when Opal said, "That is not the truth, Odelle, and you know it. Your teeth rotted out of your head years ago. All you have now are false teeth."

"Fine sister, you can serve your *pure* apple juice, but they get to keep their cookies. I won't have you chasing off our guest with rabbit food you keep trying to give everyone."

I wasn't going to ask what she meant by rabbit food. I didn't want to know, but apple juice sounded fine with me.

After we ate our cookies and drank the apple juice, it was time to discuss what we had come for. Each one of us kept looking at each other trying to decide who was going to bring up the subject, when Odelle broke the silence.

"Okay kids, what brings you here on a Monday morning?"

Chapter 44
Triple Trouble

♀ The house looked exactly the same except for the newest poster near the ones Odelle and I hung when I was little. It even smelled the same, like fresh garlic, Opal's Avon perfume, and lemon oil used to polish the player piano every day. The couch still had its plastic covering, although it had yellowed a bit, and the heavy curtains had faded from a burgundy to a light pink. Biting my lower lip, I tried to think. If I made it sound like the only reason we stopped was to pump them for information, they might not believe my apology. I looked at their faces and the extra wrinkles that were not there before. I wasted so much time being mad.

My bottom lip quivered, "I came to say I'm sorry."

The expressions on my friends' faces changed from excited to confused. Ben coughed as if he had choked on a cookie crumb. Everyone looked at him. He did it to distract everyone from seeing the single tear that trailed down my cheek. I quickly wiped it away with my napkin. I motioned to the living room where the five of us squeezed together on the couch, and the twins sat in their matching wing back chairs across from us. Taking a chance at forgiveness, I explained.

"When I was little, I spent a lot of time here. But the night Steph was born was the last time I set foot in this house."

Opal shifted uncomfortably in her seat as Odelle gave her a sideways glance.

I continued, "I was sleeping over because my mom was in labor." Looking over at Steph, I smiled. "Sometime during the night, I woke up suddenly. There was something in my room."

"Was it a ghost?" Mike blurted out, jumping up. Ben grabbed him by the shirt and pulled him back to the couch.

"It's okay; they know I see ghosts," I said.
Odelle glared at her sister. "Except, only one of us believed her."
I stood and paced in front of the coffee table.

"I followed the ghost to the piano. When Opal found me, I was crying. I told her I followed a lady who wanted to play the piano. Opal got mad at me! She told me to never make up stories and to never talk about it again."

Odelle shook her head. "And when I came downstairs, Opal had her hand raised like she was going to hit her!"

An awkward silence took over the room as all eyes looked at Opal. She sighed. "There is no need for you to apologize, Sarah. I am the one who is sorry. I wanted to believe, but I was upset."

"Tell her, sister. Tell her *why* you were so upset." Odelle urged.

Opal went to the piano and picked up a picture. Its frame looked like the oldest one in the room. She handed the picture to me. In the black and white photo were three little babies, all in long white dresses and matching bonnets, all three with the same exact smile.

Before I could ask any questions, Opal explained, "We are not twins, Sarah, we are the only two surviving sisters of a set of triplets."
My heart stopped. Odelle stood and put her arm around her sister.

"We lost our sister Olivia only a few months before we started watching you. She was hit by a car walking to the post office. She liked to play the piano."

Now it made sense. The way Opal reacted was not anger at me but grief for her sister. And all this time, I had thought she didn't accept me. All this time, I felt like a freak. Without hesitation, I ran into their arms as we hugged and cried. It was good to know the truth.

"Tarah, did the ghost tay anything important?" Nate spoke up.
I turned toward the piano as the sisters waited anxiously. It was so long ago. I was only three. Retracing my steps from the staircase, I approached the piano.

"I don't remember the ghost saying anything. I just remember it pointing ... *there!*" I pointed to the ornate glass panel near the bottom. Opal moved the piano bench aside and knelt on the floor.

"Here?" She touched the glass panel below the keyboard.

"Yes, there!" I said with anticipation.

"Ben, can you help this old lady out and see if you can pry open the panel for me?" Opal asked.

Ben reached into his pocket, pulled out his Boy Scout knife, and knelt next to her as he pried open the sliding glass panel. He looked inside. "I don't see anything, just a lot of instruments crammed into a small space."

There was a brief period of disappointment.
"What did Olivia like to play?" Steph asked.

Odelle jumped as if bitten and squealed, "<u>Camp Town Races</u>!" She opened the two doors above the keyboard to reveal a long cylinder covered in paper with tiny holes covering it. She flipped a tiny switch off to one side near the bottom, but nothing happened.

"Oh, darn, It has been unplugged for years. Nate, can you plug it in behind those drapes?"

Nate nodded and moved quickly to the outlet. Before I had a chance to warn him, he had plugged the cord in. A large white flash and a zap knocked him off of his feet. At the same time, the piano burst into action as if powered by an invisible player. The piano keys moved up and down, the drum banged, and the cymbal vibrated loudly. It was so loud we had to cover our ears, while staring with our mouths wide open. The melody was quick and cheerful. Just as the song ended, Ben yelled from his spot near the floor. "Hey, I see something!"

He reached into the opening as we waited to see what treasure we had unburied.

♂ I pulled out an envelope and read the front of it.

"Dear Sisters." Handing the envelope to Opal, I again reached into the old piano. I was glad to have long skinny fingers. I was just able to squeeze past the little air powered drum. Hanging from a nail was a long gold chain or necklace. I pulled on it carefully to avoid breaking it, but it was stuck. Something was holding it at the bottom. I applied a little more pressure and it popped free. Hanging from the end of the necklace was a ring. Slowly so I wouldn't drop this little treasure, I withdrew my hands.

Opal had gotten up from the floor and was huddled together with her sister discussing the letter. Once I had gotten the ring from the piano, I stood.
"What is it?" Mike asked.

I had a gut feeling I already knew what it was and was a little bit afraid of finding out. Grabbing the ring from the bottom of the necklace, I brought it to my face. Just what I thought, it was a spider ring just like the one we found in the box, but this one wasn't as big. It looked like it was made for a lady instead of a man.
Sarah could see I wasn't doing too well.

"Ben, are you going to pass out?"
I quickly shook my head and handed her the ring and the necklace.

Over by the couch, the sisters had opened the old envelope.
"Opal, what are you waiting for? Read it!"

All of our attention turned toward Opal as she unfolded the old letter.

"Dear Sisters, if you are reading this letter, it means I am no longer with you and you have found the note in my journal…"

Odelle crossed the room to the old bookshelf and removed a book. As she opened it, a piece of paper fell out onto the floor. Odelle picked it up and read aloud the words written on it. "Dear Sisters, hidden inside the bottom of the piano by the little old drum is a letter. Please read only after I am gone from this world, Olivia."

After Odelle sat, Opal cleared her throat and continued reading:

Dearest Sisters,

If you are reading this letter, it means I am no longer with you and you have found the note in my journal. There are things in my life I have done that I am not proud of. Mr. Robinson promised me by helping him I was protecting the rest of the family.

I don't know how much you will remember of the little business Mr. Robinson had. His business dealings were not all wholesome. I not only worked part-time at his momma's restaurant but I was also called upon to deliver packages to people in other neighboring towns and cities. Being the curious type, I opened one of the packages only to discover it was filled with money. I knew I should have quit and what was going on was not legal, but I had fallen in love with the excitement and the danger. There is a little ring also hidden inside the piano. I was to wear it anytime I made a delivery, it would let the person know I was the real courier and not an imposter. I will not tell you who I made these deliveries to because these people and their families still hold great power in high places even today.

I am also writing this as a warning. My attempt to cut ties with this association after the disappearance of my friend Elizabeth and her sister Katrina, have only brought the two of you closer to danger. I secretly used my membership to continue my search for my dear friend, and in the process have made some powerful people extremely angry. I only hope I can trust the both of you to find out the truth. However, you must be careful, the past is calling for justice and a price has to be paid to bring things back into balance.

In the future, if you are approached by anyone wearing a ring like the one I have, do not trust them. It has only brought me grief and if I am right, an untimely death. Please read my journal to answer more of your questions and use it wisely.

I love you, Opal and Odelle, with all my heart. Please forgive me.

Sisters Forever
Olivia.

A tear made its way down Opal's cheek. She carefully folded the letter and put it back into the envelope.

Odelle broke the silence. "I never did like Mr. Robinson, and if he had something to do with Olivia's death, I will wrap my hands around his neck and squeeze the living daylights right out of him."

Sarah looked startled. "He's still *alive*?"

Ignoring the question, Odelle paced back and forth across the floor. Opal had put the letter with the journal and was wiping her eyes.

"Odelle, you will do no such thing. Now sit. Remember, we have guests and it is not polite to air out our dirty laundry in front of them."

Odelle sat back in her chair. I hadn't realized I was still holding the ring until I could feel it cutting into my hand. I pulled the other ring out of my pocket. I heard Opal squeak once she saw what I had in my hand. She extended her hands in my direction. I gave both rings to her. The one that belonged to her sister, she held softly as if she could still feel the presence of her; the other ring she quickly put on the coffee table as if it were something poisonous or dirty.

While Opal and Odelle were locked in their own worlds of remembrance and revenge, I emptied my pockets of the things we had collected over the past week – the letters, the map, and so on.

Sarah took this as her cue. "We need your help!"

Chapter 45
Deadly Debt

♀ Through their tears, Opal and Odelle looked at me with confusion and worry. "Our help?" Opal finally asked.

Behind me, Mike and Steph had been whispering and it was getting louder. I turned around.

"Is there something you want to say?"

With a shy nod of her head, my little sister stepped forward. "I don't get it, the letter I mean. It used too many big words."

Mike nodded as he grabbed Steph's hand. With a sigh, I tried to explain it a little better.

"Olivia worked for Mr. Robinson even though she knew he was a bad man. She wore the spider ring to deliver money for his secret business. Her friend was Elizabeth. When Elizabeth and Katrina disappeared, she looked for them. She made someone from the Spider Club angry, and she believed they were going to kill her."

"Ooohhhhh!" Mike and Steph bounced with excitement.

The sisters sat quietly and listened without interrupting me as I explained everything that had happened to us in the past week. But several emotions passed over their faces. When I got to the tunnel part with the map and the spiders, Opal covered her mouth.

Odelle folded her arms. "See, I told you, Sister. I knew there was a reason Mr. Robinson never got caught!"

At the end of my story, I plopped myself back on the couch and waited. The sound of the grandfather clock ticking in the front hall and the faint creak of Opal's chair, were the only responses I got.

Nate was fidgeting with his battery pack and most likely had drained it again. He smiled awkwardly.

Odelle broke the silence. "So, if I understand this correctly, Sarah, you see ghosts but can't hear them. Mike hears them but can't see them. Ben faints when a ghost is near and sees the past when he is out. Steph's dreams warn you of danger and Nate has some sort of static electricity thing going that drains and charges things up. Wow!"

I had been focusing on the mystery part and had not paid any attention to what each of us possessed in the way of talent. Last week, we were just ordinary kids. This week, we were a team of ghost hunters. We were almost like...

"Superheroes!" Ben said loudly before I could say it myself.

Nate stood and draped a knitted blanket across his shoulders in an attempt to mimic Superman.

"I thought your battery was dead." I said as he flexed his bicep to form a bulge of muscle. He gave me a devilish smile.

Odelle disappeared into the dining room and returned with a plastic <u>light saber</u> which she used to chase Nate as he flew around the room with my grandmother charging after him. Mike and Steph hid behind the couch waving a white napkin from lunch. Even Opal smiled in the middle of the chaos.

It was strange Ben was not participating in the fun, so I watched him, puzzled. He just stood by the piano, grinning from ear to ear. Nate swerved around him and made a full circle around the dining room table as Odelle hid behind the door waiting to ambush him. It was then, Ben laughed– and it was not just any laugh, either. It was one of those red faced, hold your sides, tears running down your face laughs. I could only guess maybe he was feeling the same way I was at that moment – perfectly happy.

The happiness came to an abrupt halt when the smile on Ben's face disappeared. I followed his gaze to the coffee table where it looked like one of us had knocked a potted plant over. A fine layer of dirt had spread out over the polished surface. I was still smiling as I picked up the pot and reached to brush the dirt into a pile.
"It's okay, Ben. No biggie," I said calmly.
Written in the dirt were the words, "Help them."

My hands flew to cover the scream that was trying to escape from my lips as I heard a loud thud. Ben's body and the ceramic pot hit the floor at the same time.

♂ I was not prepared this time. I was like a puppet that had its strings cut. One minute, I was standing there with my friends, and the next, I was transported back in time once again. The living room looked different – much cleaner. It was missing the posters and knick-knacks; the walls were painted a lighter off-white. The hardwood floors shone as though recently polished. Angry voices were coming from the kitchen, so I headed in that direction.

As I rounded the corner to the kitchen, I saw a large man with his back towards me, talking to a younger version of Opal or Odelle. I couldn't guess which one she was. Her long flowing hair extended past her waist. The strong odor of a cigar filled the air. The man raised his left hand towards his mouth to puff on the end of the fat cigar, and I noticed a large spider ring on his pinky finger. The girl was pressing a dishtowel against the corner of her mouth where it was bleeding. The left side of her face was red as if she had been slapped.

"I promise I won't be late again." she sobbed.

The man leaned forward and lifted her chin, forcing her to look into his eyes.

"Olivia, it wasn't that you were late. You were also $5,000 short."

Pulling back from his hand, she pleaded, "Mr. Robinson, I didn't take the money! I don't know what happened, but I swear I didn't take the money!"

The hand holding the cigar slowly went back to his mouth. As he inhaled, the cigar end glowed brightly until he blew the smoke into Olivia's face making her cough.

"You are going to be working for me for a long time to pay off the missing $5,000, Olivia. Unless you want to involve your sisters in helping you repay your debt?"

Olivia's face revealed her panic. She blurted out, "No! Please don't!"

Mr. Robinson laughed heartily. Leaning back against the kitchen table, he took one last drag on his cigar and threw the still smoldering stub into the kitchen sink. "Get cleaned up. You have another delivery to make."
He left out the back door, slamming it on his way out.

Olivia peeked out the kitchen window to be sure he was gone before she sat at the table and cried.

I came to with a cold washcloth on my forehead and several eager faces looking at me.

"I'm okay," I mumbled as I carefully sat up. I related all that had happened in the minutes I was unconscious.

Sarah grabbed the journal off the table and proceeded to search its pages for any reference of missing money.

"Wait, I have it. Let's see, May 15th.

'What have I done? Why didn't I say no to Mr. Robinson when he first asked me to work for him? The job at his momma's restaurant was fine; I was making good money, so why did I have to be so greedy? What am I going to do if my parents find out? They will disown me! I DIDN'T TAKE THE MONEY!! I don't know what happened. I have retraced my steps from the tunnel under the restaurant to the train yard. The only time I stopped was to talk with Henry.'"

While Sarah continued reading out loud from the journal, I was mentally making a list of the things we were going to need to get back into the tunnels. Eventually, the journal got on my nerves. It was no longer about adventure.

I cleared my throat. "Okay, listen up. We are going to need a few things if we are going to go back into those tunnels."

Even the sisters looked at me with alarm. I was not used to having adults pay attention to me, but I was on a roll. "We are going to need flashlights." I glanced at Nate and amended my list. "With lots of batteries."

Steph giggled as she poked Nate in the side.

"We are going to need a big ball of string or yarn, too." I explained the string was in case we got lost. We could follow the string back to our start point. I finished off the list with snacks and a couple of old canteens of water in case we got thirsty.

Odelle rushed around, putting together the things we were going to need until she had filled a knap sack to capacity. The only thing she didn't have were the canteens, so we had to settle for cold cans of Orange Crush.

Each of us endured several hugs, kisses, and "be careful" from the sisters before we were allowed off the porch. We walked silently in single file towards the old restaurant Opal had informed us was now the town pizzeria.

"Ben, how do we get into the basement?" Sarah asked when we were standing in front of the doors.

I had no clue until I saw a delivery truck pull around back. We both looked at the same time and smiled.

"Follow me."

Chapter 46
Dark Descent

♀ Ben grabbed my hand tightly as he pulled me in the direction of the back alley. The heavy pounding of everyone's sneakers on the hot sidewalk reminded me of the sound of a flat tire on a speeding car.

Rounding the corner, we ducked behind a large stack of crates close to fifteen feet from the back door of the pizza shop. As the delivery truck beeped and backed up, we waited patiently in our hiding spot.

A muscular young man lifted the back door of the delivery truck and loaded a handcart with boxes marked "tomato paste" which he pushed through the back door. Leaning against the brick wall near the dumpster was a faded old sign, "Angelina's Home Cooking."

"How do we get in, Tarah?" Nate asked a little too loudly.

I placed a finger to my lips to hush him.

"I don't know yet, Nate."

When the deliveryman was ready to close the back of his truck, I moved.

"Follow my lead, guys."

Walking with my head held high, I tapped the young man's shoulder.

He spun around quickly. "Whoa! You made me jump out of my skin!"

His hand was on the back doorknob; he started to pull it closed.

"Wait!" I shouted. "My dad said to leave it open. Me and my friends are going to sweep out the storage room for some extra money."

The man made a funny face, as he looked me up and down. "You're Mario's daughter? You sure don't look Italian to me!"

It had not occurred to me red hair and freckles were not common Italian traits when I hatched this plan a few minutes earlier.

"Yeah... I'm... ahhhh... er... *adopted!*" I stammered.

He still didn't look convinced, even though the rest of the group was nodding in unison. Just as it became clear my plan had failed miserably, a loud voice from the front of the building shouted out.

"Bella! Come give me a hand!"

"See, My dad is calling me." I said, thinking quickly. "I'll close the door when we're done," I motioned for everyone to follow me.

The man shrugged his shoulders and jumped back into his truck as he heartily waved out his half open window, "See ya next time, Bella!"

We all waved from inside the back door. Mike let out a huge sigh. "You're a good liar, Sarah."

Looking at my shoes, I felt ashamed. Mom would have been

disappointed in me. Ben nudged me with his shoulder.
"Don't worry. She would understand this time."

Our idle chatting came to an abrupt halt when the voice from the kitchen yelled out again.

"Tony! Grab me another can from the new shipment, will ya!"

Ben shut the door as we scrambled in search of the basement entrance. In the far corner, Steph spotted a wooden door with a sign on it, "Watch your step" and led the way in a mad dash. The sound of Tony's whistling pierced the air as I struggled to pull the door open. With all my weight, I yanked the handle, but it didn't budge. The whistle was getting closer and we were running out of time.

"I can't get it open," I said to Nate in a loud whisper.

Nate reached past me, flipping a metal latch that held the door shut.

"Tilly girl!"

We shoved our way into the stairwell, just in the nick of time.

Tony rushed past the basement door, pulled out a box cutter, and sliced the packaging tape on a nearby box. We peeked through the crack of the slightly ajar door as we held on to each other, not knowing where the landing ended and the first step began. With a large can of tomato paste in his hand, Tony's attention shifted in our direction. He wasn't looking at us but at the floor in front of the basement door. I heard a tiny squeak from Mike as Tony knelt within inches of us and picked up a battery. In the rush, a battery must have slipped out of the knap sack. We watched in horror as Tony processed the fact the basement door was no longer locked.

"What the ..."

He reached for the knob.

The door creaked open an inch as we cowered in the shadows.

"Tooony! I can't wait all day!" The voice from the kitchen filled the air.

With a quick snap of the wrist, Tony slammed the basement door shut and locked it, leaving us in total darkness.

♂ Once I was sure the coast was clear, I switched on one of the flashlights we were carrying. I made a quick glance around the stairwell and saw no light switch. Four sets of eyes were fixed on me, questioning what we should do. Before going down the stairs, I checked the door to make sure we couldn't get it open. There was no turning back now. I pointed the flashlight down the stairs.

"Okay, guys, let's do this."

We headed down the stairs holding on to each other's shirts while trying to balance in the dark. It didn't help matters there was no handrail. Each step screamed out our presence as the old wooden stairs creaked loudly.

"Step softly," I said through gritted teeth.

My imagination made each sound louder than it actually was, and I expected at any moment the door at the top of the stairs would burst open, ending our little adventure before it even began.

Finally, we made it to the bottom of the stairs. Nate pulled out the other two flashlights. He passed one to Sarah and kept one for himself.

"Hey! Why don't Steph and I get one? Is it because we're little?" Mike complained.

"No, it's because you have a more important job, searching," I said. Steph giggled in the darkness as if pleased.

We were standing in a basement similar to the one Sarah and I had been in just the day before. I scanned the flashlight across the cement looking for a floor grate like the one from the Chinese restaurant but had no luck. Sarah and the rest of the group looked for the doorway that would lead us to the tunnels.

"Pssst, Ben," I heard Sarah say somewhere ahead of me.

Turning my flash light in the direction of the sound, I noticed for the first time just how big the basement storeroom was.

"What? Ummm... where are you?" I whispered back.

"Follow my voice," Sarah said. Floor to ceiling boxes and tarp-covered stacks of stuff made a maze even a lab rat would have found a challenge.

"You're getting warmer ... warmer ... you're hot."

I rounded the corner.

"You find me hot, huh?" I giggled as I shined the light into Sarah's face. She rolled her eyes.

"I found it!" Mike shouted. He was opening an ancient looking door set into the wall of the stone basement.

"Shhhhhhhh!" I heard in stereo as Sarah and Steph hissed on either side of me.

"Wal-la," he whispered like a magician as he exposed the interior behind the door. I was expecting a set of stairs, but not this. Behind the little door was an old metal cage, kind of like the elevators in old buildings. The cage was just large enough to hold a 55-gallon drum and maybe one person.

I ducked under the doorframe and stepped carefully on the floor of the cage.
"Be careful," whispered Steph.

It dropped just a little but held my weight. I entered the rest of the way and shined my flashlight upward. It was held by a series of ropes and pulleys. Following the ropes, I found where they came together at one single point. I knew from science class this allowed the person operating the little elevator to ride up and down with whatever cargo they were transporting.

I spied the pull rope wrapped around a metal peg on the wall. Handing my flashlight to Mike, I unwrapped it.

"Ben, pleeeeese be careful. You don't know how old those ropes are. They could be rotten."

I rolled my eyes. I knew what I was doing. Just as I finished unwinding the last of the rope off of the peg, the cage dropped like a rock.

The rope shot through my hands as I tried to slow the descent of the elevator. My body was free falling and my stomach flip-flopped like I was on a roller coaster. It had fallen close to eight feet by the time I brought it to a stop. My hands were on fire. I had given myself a terrible case of rope burn. When would I ever learn? I chided myself as I hauled on the rope bringing the elevator inch by inch back to the floor where I had left my friends.
I grinned sheepishly as I tied off the rope. "See, it works perfectly," I said as if I planned it that way.

Sarah had her arms crossed. She wasn't buying the false macho attitude. "Let me see your hands, Smarty Pants."

I put my hands behind my back as if I had just been caught stealing a cookie. "There is nothing wrong with my hands." My brain told me a different story.

"Ben, let me see your hands," she said louder.

"Sarah, shhhh everyone is going to hear us."

Her face scrunched as she glared at me. *"Ben!"*

I slowly brought my hands forward to show the group. Opening my palms to show them, I looked away. I didn't know the extent of the damage, but from the sounds of Sarah, Nate, Mike, and Steph, it wasn't good.

"Ohhhh," Steph said.

I looked at my hands for the first time. My right hand had a bright red stripe running across the palm. It looked like a bad rug burn. My left hand was worse. It included several broken blisters that were already bleeding. I had seen this once before when I tried to power slide my bike in gravel and ended up skinning my knees. I just didn't remember it hurting so much.

Sarah handed her flashlight to Mike. She cleaned my hands with the first aid kit the sisters had insisted on packing for us. After enduring several agonizing minutes of extensive cleaning, accompanied by a lecture from Sarah, I was ready to continue the adventure with everyone else.

Chapter 47
Underground Unity

♀ Mike shined the flashlight into my face once I had finished cleaning Ben's hands.

"You okay, Sarah? You look kinda green."

Grabbing the flashlight from his hand, I quickly returned to the elevator and shined the light down the shaft.

"I'm *fine,* just a little claustrophobic."

The truth was I wanted to throw up. I was re-thinking becoming a nurse when I grew up.

"Clocker what?" Mike asked.

"It means she doesn't like being trapped in small spaces." Ben explained.

Steph made things worse. "How come you like sitting in your closet with the door closed when you're mad?"

I was in desperate need of a distraction. The beam of light I shined down the shaft wasn't strong enough to see the bottom, so I dropped it and watched it fall. It hit the bottom after only one second and flickered out. "It's not too far, maybe fifteen feet," I exclaimed.

Turning around, the two remaining flashlights shone directly into my face.

"Who made you boss?" Steph asked, clearly agitated.

Mike chimed in. "Yeah! You just wasted one of our flashlights don't we have a say?"

Nate spoke up in my defense. "Tarah know what 'tee doing. You have a better idea?"

It grew silent for a few seconds. Ben seemed unusually quiet as he kept his light directed at my face.

"What do you have to say, Ben?" I asked.

He shuffled his feet and cleared his throat before speaking.

"Well, it *was* a good idea dropping the flashlight to see how far we had to go and we can get it back when we go down, but you should have asked our opinion first. We are a *team*, right?"

Crossing my arms across my chest, I grumbled, "Okay, okay. I won't do it again, but if someone is gonna do something stupid or get hurt, I'm not holdin' back!" I directed my eyes toward Ben. He smiled sheepishly and shrugged his shoulders.

"Let's vote on what to do next!" Mike said excitedly.

We all agreed on one person going down the elevator to make sure the tunnel was not caved in. Since Ben's hands were out of commission, the two strongest left were Nate and me.

"Don't even 'tink about it Tarah," Nate said as if he could read my mind.

Ben agreed. "He's right. He is the only one strong enough to lower us each one at a time."

Nate was nodding so much; he resembled a <u>bobble-head doll</u>.

Setting the flashlight on the floor at his feet so its light aimed upward, he signed something to me. I giggled and shook my head while the rest of the gang remained clueless.

"Hey, what did he say?" Steph asked.

"No fair," Mike complained, "Sign language is not allowed if we *all* can't understand it."

Trying to hide my smile in the shadows, I gave in. "He just said he didn't want my pretty little hands getting rope burn."

Ben stuck his finger down his throat.

"Gag!" he said with a roll of his eyes.

Nate picked up his flashlight and pushed past Ben, knocking him off balance as he headed for the cage. Stepping carefully into it, he reached with one hand for the rope wrapped around the peg.

"Use both hands!" Ben shouted.

Swinging the knapsack from his back, Nate unzipped the top and shoved the flashlight inside where it would be safe. The cage didn't lunge this time and moved effortlessly as Nate lowered it slowly. It took less than a minute before we heard a clunking noise below.

"Here!" Nate yelled. "Oh, wow! The tunnel teems okay. It huuuge."

Excited to get there, Ben yelled, "Do you see the other flashlight? Come and get me!" There was no response from Nate who couldn't hear him.

When Nate came back, he was holding something flat in his hand.

"What's that?" I asked.

"It *was* your flashlight. The edge of the cage came down on it at the bottom, but I pulled it out."

It didn't even resemble a flashlight now.

"Darn, that leaves us with only two." I sighed.

"And this one looks like it needs new batteries." Nate said as his light flickered.

Steph took it out of his hand and replaced the batteries with new ones from the knapsack.

"You're not getting this back, Nate. I don't want to be in a tunnel somewhere and have you drain the batteries."

We giggled, but the thought of being left without one in the tunnels made me shiver. Nate made quick work of lowering Ben to the

tunnel below and returned to take Mike and Steph. I was the last one to go, so I could barely contain my excitement once in the cage. Excited voices echoed up the shaft as we slowly made our way. Half way down, I felt a slight breeze and heard a snapping noise.
"What was that?"
Nate looked panicked. "It the rope! It brea…"

I had no time to prepare myself. The last thing I remembered was Nate screaming.

♂ I was shining my light across the sea of boxes when I heard Nate scream something about the rope. The room we were in was almost full of wooden boxes of different types and sizes, each bearing the name of "Rosalina's Italian Vinegar." My little flashlight was doing its best to cut through the darkness.

With a resounding crash and an explosion of dust, the elevator came to an abrupt stop at the bottom of the shaft. Clouds billowed, filling the room with a choking haze. Our little flashlights could do no more than highlight the dust that swirled in the air.

"Sarah?" I squeaked, coughing hard.

I heard a loud moan. A figure staggered out of the particle filled air. Nate was holding onto one arm and flexing his hand.

"Where is Sarah?" I asked more frantically.

Nate looked like he was going to pass out. I helped him sit on one of the boxes and went in search of my friend. Breathing through my shirt, I groped blindly on my hands and knees until I came to the wreckage that had once been the little elevator. I continued my search forward until I found Sarah's hand. I let out a sigh of relief when she closed her hand around mine. She was alive, but I didn't know how badly she was injured. "Sarah?" It came out more as a plea than anything else.
A low muffled "huh" escaped her lips.

"I need a flashlight over here!" I shouted, as I helped my friend sit. She was coughing. I told her to try to breathe through her shirt.
"Okay," she whispered.
Two nervously held flashlights converged upon me.
"Shine them over here."

The twin beams of light settled on the dust-covered form of my friend. Sarah looked as though she was covered from head to toe in dirty flour. Had the circumstances been different, it would have been funny. Right now, all I was concerned about was if she was hurt.
"Sarah, are you okay?"

I could see the mental processes kicking in as Sarah ran her hands over her arms, legs, and head.
"I think so."

She licked her lips and stuck out her tongue like she was trying to get a bad taste out of her mouth. She coughed.
"Water, please."
Mike handed Sarah a can of Orange Crush.

I helped Sarah stand, lifted her and carried her to the boxes where Nate was sitting. While we waited for our two friends to rest, I pulled out the little map and found where Momma Rosalina's Restaurant was on the map.
"Wait here," I said as I walked down the tunnel.

The floor had the little railroad tracks like the ones we had followed before. Whatever they had been hauling, there must have been a lot of it to need a miniature train to move it. I went another twenty feet when my little flashlight showed another tunnel choked with cobwebs. I was brave, but not that brave.

By the time I returned to my friends, Nate and Sarah looked more human and less like powdered ghosts.

Mike spoke, "How do we get out of here?" His words echoed my own concerns.
"Don't worry, little brother, I will get us out of here."
I shined my flashlight at Nate and Sarah.
"Are you two all right and ready to go?"

They nodded in unison. I cast one last look in the direction of the little elevator, a chill run down my back. The locked basement door, the crashed elevator – it was almost as if something was driving us forward, making sure we couldn't go back.

I took the lead as we set out for the library. My hands were hurting less. I could hold the flashlight with one hand as I used the other hand to knock down dust-covered cobwebs. These cobwebs looked much older than the ones Sarah and I had run into earlier. Still,

I took my time to make sure there were no live spiders.

Before long, we came to the room under the library where Sarah and I had been the day before. While the rest of the group walked around, peeking down the different tunnels, I stood in the center, holding the map out before me. Turning slowly in a circle, I matched the different tunnels to the map. I now had two points of reference with the library and restaurant.

Now that I had my bearings, I called out.

"Okay, guys, we need to go this direction." I pointed towards a tunnel. "This should take us to the X on the map. It looks like it is near the train yard."

Nate was well enough to lead. I was okay with that. The tunnel stretched off into nothingness, and I was tired of wiping out spider webs.

"Mike and Steph, you two get in behind Sarah, and I will go last," I suggested as we headed out.

The tunnel had a slight rise to it. Surprisingly, it was fairly clear of spider webs. As we stumbled along, I played tour guide, pointing out how the tunnels were different ages. At one point we came to a section where the stone walls must have given way and been boarded up. Shining the little flashlight between the boards, I caught a quick glimpse of little red eyes – lots and lots of little red eyes.

The tunnel floor climbed at a steeper angle. We had been traveling pretty much in a straight line since we left the room under the library. Now, we came to a large platform underneath a large trap door in the ceiling.

"This must be what they used to bring the stuff down into the tunnels," Mike said.

An old greasy looking gas motor and chains against the wall looked like it might have been used to raise and lower the platform. Bolted above us, was a ladder that led to a wooden hatch.

Tapping Nate on the shoulder, I motioned.

"Give me a boost."

Cupping his hands, Nate braced himself as I put my right foot in his hands and he lifted me towards the ladder. As I grabbed for the bottom rung, I was reminded why my hands were wrapped and Nate's arm gave out.

"Why am I so stupid?" I muttered to cover for the fact my hands hurt.

I hung there for a few seconds before the ladder lowered to the floor.

Giving me "the look," Sarah grabbed my hands, inspecting them to make sure the bandages hadn't come undone.

"Ladies first," I indicated with a nod.

Chapter 48
Tricky Tryst

♀ With Ben's hands resembling something out of a scary movie and Nate babying his arm, I was the next strongest one in line. From the looks of it, there was a two to three-foot square opening cut out of the tunnel ceiling, covered by a wooden hatch. I stopped on the bottom rung and glanced over at Mike and Steph's faces. They looked scared. I tried to sound upbeat.

"Ready to get out of this place, guys?"

One loud *"yes,"* echoed in my ears as I slowly climbed the rusty ladder.

Stopping near the top, I felt around the edge of the hatch for hinges so I could determine where to shove. There were none. It was not solid wood as I expected it to be and looked like a pallet. I was confident as long as nothing was piled on top of it, moving it should be easy. I pushed with both hands while leaning on the ladder, but it didn't budge. Stepping up a couple of rungs, I bent my head downward and placed my shoulder against it while pushing with my legs. There was a slight shift, but nothing more.

"I need help! I can't do this alone!" I yelled.

My first choice would have been Nate, but the way his arm hung limply at his side, I had reason to believe he had dislocated his shoulder. There would be no way he could hold on with one good arm and push with the injured one. Mike and Steph were too little to do much good, even though Mike offered. Before I knew it, Ben was climbing to help me. His bandages were soaked in blood by the time he reached me. Moving to one side of the ladder, I realized how close together our faces were. With the exception of the time in the library basement when we hid under the tarp, this was the closest I'd ever been to a boy. Our noses inches apart, I looked into Ben's eyes. He looked just as uncomfortable as I was.

"Okay... um... er... what next?" His warm breath tickled my cheek.

I was thankful it was dark and everyone down below could only see our feet. I directed Ben to push with his shoulder while I sat on the top rung and pushed with both hands. On the count of three, we both shoved with all our might. The wooden pallet lifted a few inches and fell with a loud thud, showering dirt on our heads. Ben shook his head like a dog that had been sprayed with a hose, throwing dirt into my face.

"Hey!" I complained.

"Any luck?" Mike yelled up at us impatiently.

"No, not yet, but we're close!" I hollered.

We tried three more times; each time, the door moved a little further. With excitement growing, I got up from my sitting position and stood alongside Ben on the ladder, putting my shoulder against the door too. Using the strength in our legs, we pushed one last time.

"Heave ho!" Ben yelled, almost breaking my eardrums.

The wooden door flew aside and rays of sunshine blinded us as we held on to each other for balance at the top of the ladder. I heard a loud celebration below. We smiled broadly and high fived before clamoring on the metal ladder into the brightness.

The room was small but tidy. It was a long, thin rectangle with rows of dirty windows on the two longest walls and a door on each end. Steph peered out one of the windows directly over a makeshift bed made out of old couch cushions and a plastic beanbag chair. As she stepped on the chair, beads spilled out on to the worn wooden floor.

"We're in a train!" Steph announced loudly.

Sure enough, we were in the train yard. There wasn't much else inside the train car except for a few paper bags full of garbage and the bottom half of a tattered, old calendar hanging from a tack. Ben flipped through its pages.

"1925? Wow, this is *old.*"

Nate placed his finger on a date marked with an X.

"What that for? Hey, what the date tomorrow?" he asked us.

Ben tipped his head sideways. "July 16th, the same day marked on this calendar back in 1925."

Steph jumped off her perch on top of the couch cushions.

"I wonder who lives here? Does Mr. Wilkerson live here, Sarah?"

It had crossed my mind, as soon as I realized we were even in the train yard.

"What if he does and he catches us?" Mike said with panic in his voice.

Ben stepped away from the calendar and walked towards his brother, accidently catching his foot on one of the paper bags, launching it forward. A round Christmas cookie tin rolled out. We watched as it traveled across the floor and stopped directly in front of Mike. Bending to retrieve it, he stopped half way and whispered something. He shook his head and said, "No way! I don't believe you!" Lifting the tin and removing the lid carefully, he smiled, rifled through its contents, and pulled out a crumpled microfiche film. He handed it to me, along with a folded piece of plain paper.

"This is the microfiche film Mr. Wilkerson took from us at the library, Ben!"

Mike unfolded the paper carefully and proudly held it for all to see. The paper was an application for a marriage license. The names on the document were "Elizabeth Victoria Hilliard and *Henry Michael Wilkerson.*"

♂ I was putting the false section of floor back, amazed how the hatch had brought us directly into the train car. Why didn't we see the wheels? I was so focused on figuring it out I neglected to hear what Mike had said.

"What did you just say, Mike?" I asked.

"Henry Michael Wilkerson," he read aloud. I snatched the paper from Mike's hands in disbelief.

"Henry is Mr. Wilkerson – the Henry who was going to marry Elizabeth?"

Sarah took the paper from my hands and scanned it with her eyes. Stuffing the paper in her pocket, she grabbed my hand gently.

"Guys, don't touch anything else," she said as she pulled me to the door.

"Where are we going, Sarah?" I was still in shock from what I had just read.

"We need to get to the library *now!* I want to see what is on that piece of microfiche."

I prayed quietly to myself that the door was unlocked. Stretching my hand out to grab the knob, I flexed open my palm and was painfully reminded of the condition it was in. Sarah playfully slapped the top of my hand away from the doorknob and opened the door. The caboose was indeed sitting on the ground without wheels. Sarah surveyed the area looking for Henry.

Crossing our fingers, we exited the little red caboose into the warm sun. No sooner had our feet hit the ground before Sarah ran.
"Tara, what's the rush?" Nate asked.
Stopping a few feet ahead of us, she almost screamed at us.

"Don't you guys get it? Mr. Wilkerson is the key to this mystery. I bet when we get to the library we're going to find out just what the key will unlock!"
 She waited patiently while we caught up.

"We need to see what is on this piece of film and we need to do it yesterday!"

Sarah snapped out of whatever zone she was in as she looked at Nate holding his arm and me bleeding
. "Oh my, we can't go to the library like this. Mrs. Campbell will call 911 as soon as we walk through the door."
 She redirected our little troop towards my house.

"We should take care of your hands, and we can take a look at your shoulder, Nate."

As if a light went off in her head, she rephrased what she had just said.

"Well, uh, er... Let's take a vote, guys. Who wants to go to Ben's and get cleaned up?"

Nate raised his good hand, Mike and Steph raised both hands, and I just grinned.

209

"We probably shouldn't bleed on the books, so I guess I'm in, too," I joked.

Sarah took Nate and me by our arms and guided us towards the east gate closest to my house.

When we got to my house, both my parents' cars were gone so I wasn't going to have to explain my hands to my mom.

As Sarah and I gathered around the bathroom sink, she took control of the situation.

"Nate, get some ice out of the freezer, wrap it in a plastic bag, and put it on your shoulder. Ben, sit on the toilet and put your hands over the sink. Steph and Mike, watch for parents. *Please.*"

With a grin on her face, she dug into the first aid kit and put it on the back of the sink. She cut away the old bloody wrapping on my hands. I gasped when the last layer stuck to my skin.

Seeing me grimace, Sarah stopped pulling and turned on the water. "Put your hands under here. The water will loosen the wrappings. I will go check on Nate."

The water stung at first but after I got used to it, it was kind of soothing. My mind played over the events of the day, ending at the new mystery. What could have caused this once nice person called Henry, the one I had seen in several visions, become the Mr. Wilkerson of today? It didn't make any sense. Everything up to this point had looked like Elizabeth was going to marry Mr. Robinson. I was still daydreaming when someone directed my hands back under the water.

"Hey, daydreamer, the water doesn't do you any good if your hands aren't underneath it."

Sarah carefully removed the last of the bandages, looking away at the last moment.

"Ohhhhhhh, that looks like it hurts." Mike was peeking out from behind Sarah.

I looked at my hands and wished I hadn't. They were caked in blood, but as the water washed it away, I was happy to see they weren't as bad as I thought. Both had cuts on them and were red, but they didn't look like ground hamburger. Holding my hands out one at a time, Sarah patted them dry with a towel and poured burning red-hot lava on them.

"Ahhhhhh, what the heck was that???"

"Oh, you big baby, it is only a little iodine. It will help keep your hands from getting infected." She gently re-wrapped my hands.

"We need to get to the library. It will be closed in an hour," I announced as I walked out of the bathroom.

Sarah had apparently been busy with Nate. He was sporting a fancy make shift sling made of a bright pink material. He didn't look too happy wearing it.

"Tara, are we ready to go?" Nate said impatiently.

Sarah looked over our group. We were all there but Mike, who appeared holding the small stone I had found under my bed the week before. Raising my eyebrows in a silent question, he just shrugged and put the stone in his pocket.

Chapter 49
Murder Mayhem

♀ I felt a sense of accomplishment as we walked into the lobby of the library. Just over a week ago, we were all just regular kids beginning our summer in search of adventure, and now, we were doing something extremely important – solving a mystery. The excitement grew as we walked past the circulation desk and to the microfiche readers in the back room.

Luckily, Mrs. Campbell was busy helping out a little old man with a cane who was having problems carrying his stack of worn leather-covered books. One other person was in the microfiche room when we entered, a young woman sitting in the corner with her back toward us. I placed a finger to my lips and led the group to the nearest reader. Sliding into the chair, I fumbled with the film as Ben switched the light on. Once the film was in and displayed on the screen, we shoved our heads together as I enlarged the image. A black and white image of Katrina and Elizabeth filled the left side of the screen, while on the right a handsome young man was being led into the police station in handcuffs. The caption read, "Local Railroad Worker Questioned in Disappearance of Sisters." Placing my hand over my mouth, I looked over to Ben as he read aloud in a whisper.

"*Local rail worker Henry Wilkerson was taken in for questioning regarding the disappearance of Katrina and Elizabeth Hilliard. An anonymous tip, placed him at the Hilliard residence the night before Ms. Elizabeth Hilliard was set to marry Mr. Ernesto Robinson. Mr. Robison reported the girls missing. Evidence points to foul play and possibly murder, as personal effects and blood samples matching Katrina Hilliard were found the following day in the train yard where Henry Wilkerson worked.*"

Mike spoke up first. "I don't understand, Ben. Why would Mr. Wilkerson hurt Elizabeth or Katrina?"

We looked to him for answers, as we were obviously just as confused. Ben looked puzzled, shrugged his shoulders, and continued reading.

"*Wilkerson verified a working relationship with the late father of the sisters and a romantic relationship with Elizabeth Hilliard but professed to have no knowledge of the sisters' whereabouts. He was released the next day. In a statement to the press, Chief Miller said: 'We cannot hold anyone suspect for murder without definite proof and bodies.' Mr. Ernesto Robinson, obviously distraught by his missing bride, has offered a large reward for any information leading to her return.*"

Ben shook his head and shut off the machine. "I think something went wrong, *Very wrong.*"

The woman in the corner stood and gathered her things as she shut off her machine.

"It's getting late, kids. Your parents are going to get worried about you." She sounded concerned.

Almost on cue, my stomach growled loudly. It had been hours since we last ate. I motioned for everyone to follow me as I stuck the microfiche film into my pocket and headed to the front desk. Mrs. Campbell was shutting off the lights in the library.

"Oh my, when did you sneak in? I'm closing now. Do you kids need a ride home?"

I was staring at the large painting of Ernesto Robinson above the doors. The small talk continued behind me, but I was mesmerized by what I was seeing. It was the first time I looked closely at it. The portrait was at least ten feet tall and had a dim light mounted on the top of its frame, which cast light across its cracked and aged surface. Sitting in a burgundy leather wingback chair, Mr. Robinson was dressed in a dark suit and his face was partially hidden in the shadows. The hand resting on the arm of the chair had the spider ring on its pinky, while the other hand held a large unlit cigar perched near his mouth. A brass plaque mounted below the painting said, "Ernesto Robinson – Founder of Wall Street Library."

"Watcha looking at Sarah?" Steph asked.
With a chill running down my spine I answered, "Trouble."

♂ Outside of the library, I put my hand inside my pocket and rubbed the large gold spider ring. We needed to find Mr. Wilkerson/Henry. He had all the answers to this mystery. Nate was the first to break away, spotting his mom in front of the grocery store, loading groceries.

"Tee you later. Torry, there no room." His sisters filled the station wagon.

We waved as the car drove past with almost a dozen flailing arms hanging out the windows. "Byyyyyeeeee." we heard as they turned the corner.

The streetlights flickered on above us. Being the gentleman that my mom raised, I offered to see Sarah and Steph home. Walking backward on the sidewalk, I asked. "Sarah, do you believe Wilkerson did it?"

Sarah's lips puckered and went to the far-right side of her face. It kind of reminded me of Samantha from <u>Bewitched</u>.

"I'm not sure Ben, but whatever happened, I believe Mr. Wilkerson was part of it, and he is hiding something."

I couldn't believe how late in the day it was. Mike and Steph had started a little game of kick the pinecone. As I walked, I tried flexing my hands. They were stiff and sore. Sarah must have noticed me grimace.
"How do they feel?"
I shrugged my shoulders.
"They still hurt a little. I will try soaking them in a little water

tonight and have my mom re-wrap them."

In front of her driveway, Sarah reached out and grabbed my left hand gently.

"What are you going to tell your mom?"

"I will tell her I got a rope burn. Hopefully she won't ask how and assume it was from a rope swing or something."

We stood for a few more minutes out in front of the driveway, while Mike and Steph finished their game. I didn't want to go home. I wanted to stay for a minute or two more, and I could tell Sarah felt the same way. Sarah's mom came out on the front porch.

"There you guys are! I was getting worried! Sarah and Steph, your supper is cold. Ben and Mike, your mother has called here a couple of times today looking for you two."

She went back indoors while I smiled at Sarah. "Hey, we are getting closer to solving this. We make a pretty good team."

She smiled back. A flush climbed up my cheeks and my face grew warm. I held out my hands out palms up. "Give me five."

Sarah reached over to slap my palms but stopped short.

"Ben," she laughed.

"Let's go home, twerp," I said to Mike.

As we crossed the street, Sarah and Steph raced each other to the front porch. On the other side, I stood in front of the gate leading into the train yard.

"Ben, don't," Mike whispered.

"I will race you home."

This seemed like a great idea to me. But Mike wasn't up for it.

"Look. I will run right through the train yard. You run down and around, and if you win, you get to use my bike for the rest of the month."

His eyes lit. "Deal, but you have to give me a head start." He took off like he was shot out of a cannon. It was amazing how fast he could run when he was properly motivated.

When he rounded the corner, I slipped through the gate and sprinted through the train yard. The place was especially creepy at night, but I didn't let it slow me. As I came around the last set of rail cars, I heard a loud crash behind me. Instead of continuing to run like I should have, I stopped. I turned slowly, half expecting to see Mr.

Wilkerson coming up behind me, but what I saw was a stray dog that must have lived in the train yard. This little dog was more scared of me than I was of it, so I tried to coax him.

"Come here, boy, come on. I won't hurt you."

He came towards me but lowered his head and slunk away back into the darkness. "That was weird. I wasn't going to hurt him. What scared him off?" I mumbled out loud.

I heard a gruff old voice say, *"Maybe it was me."*

I didn't have time to scream or even move before a large dirty hand clamped over my mouth and strong arms lifted me off the ground.

"Dinneye tell you to stay out of the train yard and outta my business, boy?" I didn't have to see his face to know I was in the clutches of Mr. Wilkerson.

"Now you have gone done messed everything up, so I am going to leave you locked in the shed while I go get the police."

He dragged me to the shed where he slammed me against the wall and held me in place with one hand, while unlocking the door with the other.

My courage overcame my fear.

"You're Henry! You killed those two girls. If you take me to the police, I will tell them!"

I was hoping he would act surprised and would want to make a deal and let me go, but he just looked at me with those yellow jaundiced eyes and laughed.

"You have it all figured out? Well, you are wrong!"

He opened the door and roughly shoved me inside. I was able to turn around in time to break my fall with my palms, feeling the skin on my hands open up. They would soon be bleeding through the bandages Sarah had so carefully wrapped earlier. The door slammed shut behind me, and for an instant, I felt alone in the dark shed. But I heard noises and sparks of light flashed in front of my eyes, like the ones at the end of sparklers on the Fourth of July.

A soft glow filled the dirty old shed. As the glow grew brighter, I saw the back of Mr. Wilkerson. He hung the Coleman lantern on an old nail sticking out of the door frame and pulled a wooden chair from against the wall. Grabbing me by the shoulders, he roughly sat me in the chair.

"What are you doing? You can't do this!" I whined, most of my courage gone.

I watched as he took a length of greasy rope from off the bench. I knew exactly what he had in mind, so I made a break for the door, tripping on the trash that littered the floor.
"Get back here, you little snot," he grumbled.

His long bony fingers grabbed my leg and clamped down like the jaws of a steel trap. I kicked out with my other foot and was rewarded with a solid hit to his face. A string of swear words followed.

I crawled towards the door but Mr. Wilkerson was faster. He grabbed me by my hair, hauling me to my feet. My eyes watered as he grabbed clumps of hair and ripped them from my scalp.
"Stop yermessin." He slammed me back in the chair.

I got up once again, but he backhanded me across the face. I was seeing stars, and my face hurt. The room went dark, and then black.

When I came too, I was sitting in the chair as Mr. Wilkerson finished tying me up. With my arms to my side, he tightly wrapped the rope several times around the chair. Seeing I was awake, he got in my face.

"You will get what's commin to you when I get a hold of the police. Oh, and go ahead and tell the police. I wasn't guilty then and I ain't guilty now."
He left, slamming and locking the door behind him.

The light of the lantern revealed the room was full of old papers, gas cans, oil barrels, and lots of other junk. I stretched out my foot and kicked at a nearby shovel leaning against the wall. I could use it in some way to get out. As I did, the old nail holding the lantern bent downward. I watched in horror as the lantern slid towards the end of the nail. The area beneath was full of lots of things that would burn. I panicked
.   "Help, get me out of here!" I screamed.

Okay, okay, calm down. There has to be a way for me to get out. I just have to think. I wiggled and squirmed enough to move my right hand to my front pocket. I fished my pointer finger inside and carefully pulled out the knife. The lantern slid another half inch down the nail.

I worked both of my arms to the front of me so I could open the knife. Once I had the blade opened, I sawed through the thick greasy rope. Before I could get through the first section of rope, the nail gave way. In slow motion, the old oil lantern spun end over end and hit the floor. With a loud *whoosh* the papers on the floor caught fire. I frantically sawed on the rope.
"I am not going to die, I am not going to die," I kept repeating under my breath.

It seemed like an eternity but just moments later, I had cut through the last strand of rope and was unwinding it from around me. The fire had spread across the doorway, my only chance for escape. I saw no other doors and no windows; I was trapped. The room was filling with thick black smoke. I dropped on to my hands and knees. I was *never* going to see my family again. I *was* going to die here.
"Help me!" I screamed, desperately hoping someone would hear me.
I lay my face on the cool concrete floor and gasped out one last request. *"Help me, please."*

Chapter 50
Anguish & Ashes

♀ Mom took one look at us and shook her head.
"Where have you been running around today? You're both filthy!" Mom lifted my chin with her hand and gave me a stern look. "You haven't been causing trouble, have you?"

I almost gave her possibly the lamest excuse ever when my stomach growled loudly.
"My heavens, go wash and I'll warm your dinner."

Letting out a sigh of relief, I took two stairs at a time to the bathroom, racing my sister to the sink. After a brief battle of elbows and soap slinging, we rushed back downstairs to the kitchen. The table had been cleared except for two plates, each with a slice of meatloaf, potatoes, and fresh green beans. I grabbed the bottle of ketchup and pretended like I was going to pour some on to Steph's plate. She plugged her nose.

"Ewwwww! Mom, make her stop!"

My sister had a thing about condiments. She didn't eat them. Pouring a big blob on my own plate, I quickly inhaled my green beans, stuck my fork into a large piece of meatloaf, and dipped it into the ketchup puddle. My fork was half way to my mouth when the phone rang. Mom picked up the phone and listened intently after the initial hello. Finally, she responded, "No, he isn't here. Let me ask Sarah."

She turned toward me. "Honey, did Ben say he was going straight home?"

I froze in mid-chew, a lump forming in my throat.

"Uh huh," I mumbled with my mouth full. Forcing the food down, I asked, "Why?"

Mom held her hand up as she motioned for me to be quiet. The person on the other end grew louder, so loud we could hear her across the room. "Mike said he took a shortcut through the train yard!"

My heart stopped and I lost my appetite. Mom gave me the kind of look adults give kids when they are trying to hide something and stretched the phone cord around the corner and into the back hall where we couldn't hear her. Steph's eyes were as big as saucers as she stood and pushed her plate away as well. Moments later, Mom returned with a solemn look on her face.

"Ben is missing. He raced his brother home and took a shortcut through the train yard. Mike said he never came out the other side. His parents went to look for him, and the gates were locked tight."

I clenched my fists. "We have to go look for him! I can squeeze through the fence and... "

"You will do no such thing young lady. That is trespassing! Ben's parents are headed for the police station right now."

Steph was rifling through the junk drawer, pulling out a flashlight.

"Where are you going?" Mom asked.

"*We* are going to help!"

Before Mom could argue with her, Dad appeared in the doorway. He must have been listening from his recliner in the living room. Placing his hands-on Mom's shoulders, he interrupted.

"It's the least we could do. They would do the same for us if one of our kids came up missing."

Steph and I were sitting in the bed of dad's pick-up truck with the wind blowing through our hair. Dad and Mom were in the front seats. As we neared the train yard, Dad slowed and pulled up, shining his headlights on the gate. The chain and lock were clearly visible. There was no mistake, it was indeed locked. We quickly backed out and headed toward town to the police station. The Whiting's empty car was parked out front with Nate's family's station wagon pulled in next to it. I jumped from the tailgate before we even came to a complete stop and met Nate on the sidewalk near the front door. He opened his arms so I could fall into them.

"I have a terrible feeling something bad has happened to Ben!" I sobbed into his shirt.

Nate squeezed tightly and tried to comfort me.

"Ben not 'tupid, Tarah, he will be okay."

As Dad opened the door, the loud voice of Ben's mom echoed down the hall. "What do you mean he has to be missing for twenty-four hours?"

We rushed around the corner to the front counter. I didn't expect to see so many people crammed into one space. Ben's parents stood in front of the counter, glaring at an officer who looked bored. I didn't see Mike anywhere. The rest of the crowd was a mixture of neighbors, the mailman, the clerk from the pharmacy, the Knickerbocker sisters, and a few kids from school.

How could Ben have known all these people already? He only just moved here. Pushing through the crowd, I made my way to the front. Mrs. Whiting looked frantic, her eyes puffy from crying. She was still wearing an apron with what looked to be spaghetti sauce smeared on it. She held onto the counter's edge with white knuckles.

"We can't wait 24 hours! What if he is hurt or lying in a ditch somewhere?"

Acting embarrassed, Mr. Whiting put his arm around his wife and calmly spoke to her.

"Honey, you know how Ben is. He gets distracted easily. Maybe he saw something that sparked his interest and lost track of time."

Ben's mom shook her head in disagreement as a small voice in the crowd spoke up.

"My brother hates to lose a race! He's missing!"

It was Mike, although I couldn't see him through the others. The group got loud again as everyone tried to talk at once. Opal's voice rose above them.

"That's what happened to the Hilliard sisters. They *never* found them. We can't sit around and wait."

Cheers of agreement filled the air as the officer behind the counter lost his bored look and tried to maintain order. I fought my way to the counter to remind the officer of Mr. Wilkerson locking my sister in the shed the week before. Looking past the counter, I saw the last person I expected to see.

"YOU!" I shouted as I pointed to old man Wilkerson in the chair on the other side. He was wearing handcuffs. Apparently, they were charging him for locking Steph up.

The room went instantly quiet. Mr. Wilkerson glared at me, the left side of his mouth curving upward in a little smirk, revealing his blackened, rotten teeth. As my blood boiled, I climbed over the counter.

"What did you do to Ben, you murderer!" I screamed as I fell to the floor on the other side and crawled toward him on my knees.

The once-bored officer moved faster than I expected, grabbing me by my foot before I could pounce.

"Whoa! What's this about?" he demanded as he lifted me by the back of my shirt, my arms swinging and feet kicking.

I pointed to him once again. "He murdered the Hilliard sisters and got away with it!"

A burst of excited voices roared from behind me as I stared into his evil eyes. Before I could explain, the police scanner screeched on a nearby desk.

"Dispatch to Unit 3. Fire reported in shed at train yard. Engine Company #1 on its way!"

The faint sound of sirens pierced the air, grew louder as they passed the station, and faded. The old man's expression had changed from evil to scared. The color drained from his face leaving it ashen.

"I didn't mean him no harm, just wanted to scare him, keep

him away... The lantern... The lantern…"

The officer showed no sympathy as he shoved Mr. Wilkerson back into his chair until it balanced only on the two back feet. "What are you talking about?"

Breathing hard as if he just ran a marathon, Mr. Wilkerson spoke in a weak whisper.
"The boy, he's tied up in the shed at the train yard."

Every ounce of strength I had, left my body as I slumped to the floor. I barely heard the screams of the crowd and the rush of everyone out the front door. My dad snapped me out of my trance. Lifting me like a child, he carried me to the truck and placed me on the seat next to my mom. The screech of his tires, as we pulled away from the station, echoed loudly in my ears. By the time we reached the south end of the train yard, the fire department had already knocked down the gate and connected the hoses to a nearby hydrant. The smell of smoke was strong and stung my eyes as I ran to the fence and looked in. The shed was engulfed in flames, the door barely visible through the black smoke. The police were busy keeping the crowd at a safe distance while the firemen aimed their hoses and moved in closer.

Mrs. Whiting clung to her husband with a look of horror on her face. Several people were crying as they held on to the fence, their faces lit up orange by the fire's glow.

"He can't be dead, he can't be dead!" I said to myself over and over again. A news crew pulled up and got out of their van with a large video camera. A petite young woman, holding a microphone, interviewed a young man. I didn't realize the young man was Marcus until he turned his face toward me. Curious, I walked toward them and caught the tail end of the conversation.

"... and when I heard someone screaming for help, I ran across the street and called the fire department!" he was saying proudly.

Once the news crew was done, Marcus walked over to me with a smile on his face.

"Pretty exciting, huh? Maybe it was crazy man Wilkerson in that shed," he joked.

Furious, I swung hard with my right arm and landed a punch square on his jaw with a swift left hook to his nose. Blood gushed from his nostrils and he bent over holding his jaw.

"That was Ben in the shed!" I screamed.

Marcus stood stunned, not sure what to say as blood dripped down the front of his shirt and his eyes watered. Reaching out to touch my shoulder, he apologized. "I'm sorry."

A loud explosion came from behind us and I turned just in time to see the shed turn into tiny scraps of metal and charred wood. There was nothing left. Just as I lost all hope for my friend, someone tapped me on the shoulder. Spinning around, I was surprised to see Mike. He didn't look upset, no tears or concern.

"We need to go, Sarah."

"Go where?"

Mike took my hand and pulled me in the direction of the rest of the gang under a nearby tree. No one looked to be in the mood for an adventure any time soon and they had the same confused looks on their faces. "What is going on?" I asked.

"Elizabeth said to go home to my basement. She has a surprise for us."

Mike expected us to jump at that offer?

"What's wrong with you? You're not even upset! Your brother just died!"

Mike shook his head. "I don't hear him, Sarah. If he was dead, he would talk to me."

I got angry, but Nate stopped me mid-sentence, signing, "He's in shock. Let it go."

I looked at Mike's face – so certain his brother wasn't dead – and put my pain aside.

"Whatever. Let's go, then."

I don't remember the walk back to Ben's house or Marcus joining our little group. It wasn't until I noticed Mike holding Marcus's hand as we walked up his driveway that I came out of my fog. I had no strength left for questions or arguments. I was just going along for the ride. Single file, we made our way to the basement stairs and came to a stop near the built-in bookcase. Mike pointed as Marcus put both hands on the edge of the shelving. Mike pulled a small rock from his pocket and pushed it into a little hole in the stone foundation.

We stood there dumbfounded as Marcus pushed the bookcase aside and the dim light of the basement poured into the opening behind.

There, huddled in a fetal position on the floor, covered head to toe in black soot, was Ben.

It was my turn to pass out.

♂ My eyes still stung from the smoke. I just needed to rest. It seemed as though I had been in the darkness of the tunnels forever. The time creeped by, like I was moving in slow-motion. If I had not heard Sarah's voice calling out to me, I wouldn't have made it out of the shed, let alone found my way here, wherever "here" is. I just wanted to close my stinging eyes, rest my rope burned hands, and sleep. I was so tired.

Just as I was drifting off to sleep, I heard voices again. First it was Mike, then Sarah, and for some reason I heard Marcus. Okay, I had to be dreaming. Marcus was with my friends? This should be a great one. Without opening my eyes, I imagined how they would look when they found me. Mike gave me a big hug. It was realistic. He was saying how he had known I wasn't dead. Steph was shining a light in my face while Nate fidgeted with his battery. Marcus stood there with his giant arms folded across his chest. This dream seemed to be getting better and better. Okay, where was my best friend, Sarah?

Icy cold awareness splashed onto my face. I shivered and looked bleary-eyed into the face of Mike, who was holding an empty water glass. What was with Mike and water these days? He had done it twice in less than a week. Looking around at the group, it dawned on me this was not a dream. What I couldn't figure out, was why Marcus was here.

I attempted to get up but stumbled as the room spun and my vision blurred.

"Relax, Ben," Nate said as he grabbed me under my arms and lowered me to the floor. The old light bulb above his head glowed as the hair on top of his head brushed its surface, making it look like he had an idea.

"Hey, Nate, do that again," I said giddily.

"Do what?" he asked with a confused look on his face.

Making another attempt to stand with Nate's help, I staggered into the open room. It was my own basement, and there was Sarah lying on the floor. Worried, I knelt next to her. As I made eye contact with her, a frown crossed her face. Reaching out, she poked me with her finger and whispered, "Are you alive?"

All I could do was nod my head.

She sat and hugged me, tears running down her face.

"I thought I lost you, Ben," she said between sobs.

This was the best and longest hug I had ever had. My excitement soon faded when I realized it was robbing me of oxygen. It reminded me of a wildlife movie I saw once where the anaconda would squeeze its victims until they died.

"Ummmmm, Sarah, I... can't... breathe," I whispered.

She released me, wiping away her tears.

"What happened, Ben? How did you escape?"

Steph asked the questions on everyone's mind. "Did the pocket knife help you?"

I sat a little straighter, put my hand in my pocket and pulled out my Boy Scout knife. I told them about running into Mr. Wilkerson and being dragged into the shed and tied to a chair.

"I had to think fast because the lantern fell off the wall and caught some stuff on the floor on fire. Good thing I remembered my pocketknife. I used it to cut the ropes."

I smiled at Steph. "You were right about needing my knife."

Steph beamed and looked as if she was ready to cry at the same time.

"The smoke was thick and the flames were... so close. I turned to Sarah. "I almost gave up. Then I heard you calling my name."

Sarah started to talk, but I interrupted. "Let me finish. I followed your voice over to the corner of the shed and found a trap door under a tarp. It took all my strength to lift it. I had no sooner gone down the ladder, when there was this explosion. It felt like a giant hand swatted me, tore me from the ladder, and threw me the rest of the way to the tunnel floor. I didn't have a flashlight, and it was pitch black. If I had not followed your voice, Sarah, I would have never made it here."

As I was telling the story, Sarah, Mike, Nate, and Steph were exchanging glances back and forth like they didn't believe me.

"Ben, I was never in the tunnels," Sarah said. "We just got here a few minutes ago. Mike knew where to find you."

"It was Elizabeth who told me, and it must have been Elizabeth's voice that guided you here," Mike said.

Marcus cleared his throat, "Who is Elizabeth? Where is that music coming from?"

I strained to listen but did not hear anything. A light breeze met my face and brought a distant melody to my ears. Getting up from the floor, I grabbed a flashlight from Mike and pointed toward the opening behind the bookcase. It seemed the tunnel did not end at my house but continued toward our garage. There were lightbulbs dangling from the tunnel ceiling.

"It sounds like it is coming from down there." I said as I pointed toward the unexplored area.

I lifted Sarah from the floor. For just a moment, we continued to hold hands, and to tell the truth, I didn't mind one bit. Nate grabbed the flashlight from Steph and stepped into the tunnel. He hadn't gone one step before it drained.
"Dang it."

Grabbing the one from Sarah, he went into the tunnel again, but it also went dead. "Crap!"

However, the light bulb above his head glowed.
"Nate, stop and reach above your head," Sarah called out.

As Nate reached above his head, his hand brushed the old clear light bulb. A bright spark jumped from his hand to the bulb, causing it to flash like a camera and go out. It took a few moments to blink away the blue dot from my eyes.

"Okay, Nate, this time don't touch the bulb. Just kind of wave your hand around it," Sarah said.

A soft glow formed around the light bulb as Nate waved his hand around it. When he stopped, the glow faded. It was like watching a magician practice a trick. After a few more minutes, Marcus tapped Nate on the shoulder.
"Excuse me, Mr. Magic, are you done now?"

The red color crept up Nate's neck to his face. "I wat experimenting."
With a quick turn, Nate continued to the first bulb and motioned for us to follow him down the tunnel. The effect didn't last long, but it was

225

long enough for Nate to get to the next light bulb and do the same thing and for us to follow him. It wasn't the fastest way, but it was the safest. One bulb at a time, we walked towards the music.

We had only gone close to thirty feet or so when the tunnel turned to the left. On the right was a large metal sliding door. The music sounded like it was coming from behind this door. Nate turned to see if it was okay to continue. I nodded my head. With one final wave of his hand around the light bulb, Nate reached for the handle of the door as the light bulb slowly faded to black.

A loud screeching noise like fingernails on a chalkboard pierced the air. It sounded like the door moved but came to an abrupt halt with a loud clunk.

"It tuck," he said.

The hulking form of Marcus, pushed past me.

"Here, move out of the way and let me do this, ya wimp!"

Nate backed away and gave the light bulb another few swipes with his hands. Marcus grabbed the handle of the door and pulled; the muscles of his back and arms bulged. The door buckled. It slid to the right and finally crashed open. Marcus seemed surprised by his strength. Flexing his hands, he grinned. "That was easy."

The music was louder as it was no longer contained, and a soft glow came from inside the room. Once through the threshold, we saw where the glow was coming from. Fat white pillar candles were scattered about the room. On our left, sitting on top of an old end table, was a wind-up record player which was playing orchestra music. Everywhere you looked were treasures – old toys, a rusty tricycle, someone's deflated red kickball, and one of those wind-up monkeys with cymbals in its hands. The rest of the room was filled with various boxes, an old steamer trunk with clothes hanging out of it, rotting food on paper plates, and coffee cans with loose change in them. The back of the room was covered by a large curtain.

I said to Sarah. "I believe we found out where Henry was living."

As we each explored bits and pieces of the past, Marcus was like a large shadow staying close to me. I spun around. I couldn't stand him just hovering over me.

"What?"

He flinched and took a step back. The way he reacted to being

yelled at, I got the impression he was yelled at a lot.
"Sorry, Marcus."
Marcus squared his shoulders like nothing happened.
"No biggie, I was just doing my job."
Mike spoke up. "I told him we needed protection, Ben."

Marcus nodded and flexed one of his arms as he smiled in Sarah's direction.

"Not sure what you need to be protected from yet," he admitted as he gave me a little more space.

Walking over to the player, I lifted the needle from the record. The silence that followed wasn't much better than the annoying scratchy tune. As I headed toward the bookshelf to see the knick-knacks, the music started again.
"What the heck?"
Sure enough, the needle was back on the dusty record.
"Hey, who put the music back on?"
I was met with blank stares.
Once again, I pulled the needle away and this time for good measure removed the record from the turntable.

Marcus was looking at the main support post in the middle of the room. On it hung all sorts of stuff, from old clothes to old-fashioned black and white pictures which were tacked to its surface.

I looked at the pictures that were stuck on the pillar. Some were of a much younger Henry and Elizabeth together, smiling and happy.

Sarah was over in the corner by the door looking at some type of machine or lift. "Hey Ben, I'm pretty sure we are under your garage."

Curious, I ran to her side. It looked like the mechanical lift was built into the wall and went up to what looked like a trap door, eight feet above our heads. "I bet this comes up under that shelf in the garage."
I lightly smacked her on the shoulder. "Great find, Sarah."
Mike picked up the little monkey with the cymbals.

"Ben, this is so cool," he said as he held it much too close to my nose.

I didn't like the look on the monkey's face. It made the hair stand up on the back of my neck.

"Mike, put that back and don't touch anything else."

Steph climbed off the little rocking horse she had been sitting on.

It was Marcus who pointed out what we had all been missing until that point.

"Hey, guys, is it my imagination, or is it getting cold in here?"

I hadn't noticed until he brought it up, but yeah, it was getting cold. In fact, I could see my breath.

Sarah squeaked, *"Ben!"*

She was pointing to the empty rocking chair in the corner. It moved slowly back and forth as if someone was sitting in it.

"I don't like this." Steph pointed.

The little rocking horse's mane looked like it was blowing in the wind and the sound of pounding hooves filled the air. We jumped when the monkey banged his cymbals together and cowered when an evil laugh escaped its pursed lips. Gathering in the middle of the room by the main support post, we clung to each other. The tricycle came to life. Slowly, it rolled across the room until it picked up speed and slammed into the far wall.

"We need to get out of here," Nate said.

We took off running for the door which slid shut with a screech so loud we had to cover our ears. Steph screamed.

"What's happening?"

Nate's entire body seemed to be glowing with energy. A bright yellow aura surrounded him. The candles' flames shot into the air like fireworks. Soon after, Nate's aura disappeared. Marcus pulled on the door with both hands, his face almost purple.

Sarah stared at the curtain at the back of the room. It was moving like someone had just slipped through the panels. As if in a trance, she walked towards them.

"Sarah, what is going on?"

She motioned for us to follow. Sarah grasped the mildewed curtain fabric in her hand and drew it to the side. The air behind it made me shiver. We seemed to be looking into a little room. The area was extremely dark, but I could make out what seemed to be the outline of a large round table.

The rest of the group stood behind me, panting heavily. As we all peered into the darkness, a white candle in the center of the table flared to life. Nothing prepared us for what we were about to see. Sitting propped in chairs were two bodies. Sarah screamed and instantly turned around to cover the eyes of Mike and Steph. Nate and I stood transfixed.

The one had long golden hair that looked as if it had been brushed and cared for by loving hands. This must have been Elizabeth. Small gifts and handmade things sat in front of her with little pieces of heart-shaped paper. I could almost feel the love Henry felt for her.

The other body had to be Katrina. The almost black hair was knotted and dirty; the hands on the table in front of her looked more like claws. Her skull looked crushed and caved in on one side. Darkness seemed to cling to the body and the tattered remains of her dress. We turned around when one of Katrina's hands moved, making a scratching sound on the table.

"Did you see that?" I asked.

Before anyone could answer, Katrina's head moved. The tendons on her neck stretched, popped, and creaked as her head lifted revealing a large knife lodged in her left eye socket. The jerky-like flesh fell from the side of her face as the head turned to face us. Her face, sunken in like a dried-up lemon almost smiled as the jaw sprung loose, the mouth gaping open to expose blackened teeth. Spider webs coated the inside of her mouth, tunneling towards the back of her throat.

My mouth went dry, and despite the cold I broke out in a sweat. I almost jumped out of my skin when Sarah came along side of me and squeezed my arm. When Katrina's eye socket glowed a deep shade of red, we all joined hands and backed away slowly. The strong wind swirled around us made its way around the room, blowing out each of the candles and plunged us into total darkness.

Chapter 51
Krazy Karma

♀ For a brief moment, the room went dark, including the red glow from Katrina's eye socket, while the smell of blown-out candles permeated the air. Afraid to move, I held Ben's sweaty hand on my left side and on the other side I held a hand even hotter. Nate glowed once more.

I was beginning to see the outline of crates and boxes, when Nate's hearing aid let out a high pitch whine. He let go of my hand. We all watched as he fidgeted with his battery, the sweat running down his face in streams. "Nate! You're *glowing*!" Steph announced.

Nate stopped and looked up. Holding his hands in front of his face he stammered. "What the..."

Nate's yellow-tinged skin was now radiating like the sun. The room was warming rapidly. A trickle of sweat ran down the center of my back.

We heard a clinking sound and faint footsteps. Mike pointed in the direction of the table. His lips moved but no sound came out.

"She's coming!" Steph screamed as we backed up again. Nate's light made a five-foot diameter circle around our group. The more we backed ourselves up, the more of the room before us was obscured by shadows.

"This ain't good, guys!" said Marcus.

"We're trapped!" Ben shouted.

It was only a matter of time before we were backed against the wall with nowhere left to run. It wouldn't be long before the clinking bag of bones that used to be Katrina had us in her clutches. Gritting my teeth with anticipation, I squeezed Ben's hand as tight as I could.

A choking sound made me look to my right. Two bony hands encircled Nate's neck. Struggling for oxygen, his eyes bugged out of his head as his yellow glow faded and his lips turned dark. Katrina had made her way through the darkness.

"Help him!" I screamed.

Before Ben or Marcus had a chance to move, the figure of a

man charged toward Nate.

"Noooo!" he wailed.

He pried the skeletal fingers from Nate's throat, and our friend collapsed to the floor. A gust of wind came out of nowhere and blew through the room, rekindling the candles, lighting the room once again.

Standing in front of us was old man Wilkerson, his hands around the twisted skeletal neck of what used to be Katrina. The body dangled within inches of the floor as Henry shook it frantically.

Henry yelled at the top of his lungs as he tightened his grip on her brittle vertebrae.

"No more! I will not let you do this! You've done enough harm!"

Katrina's body went limp. A rodent crawled out of her eye socket and down Henry's arm. He flinched and threw his arm into the air. The mouse flew into a pile of nearby boxes. After Henry pulled his hand away from her neck, the young Katrina emerged. Stepping out of her mummified remains, she brushed off her dress and primped her hair as the bones fell quickly to the floor in a heap, clinking together like wind chimes. Henry did not act surprised. He stared deep into her eyes as we all rubbed ours, trying to figure out what we were seeing.

"Now, now Henry, you can't kill me again! I'm already dead!" She taunted him.

Furious, Henry reached out, grabbing her by the ruffle on the front of her dress. "You left me no choice Katrina. You killed my Elizabeth!" he said through gritted teeth.

Katrina stood on her tiptoes and leaned in as if she was going to kiss him. "Oh Henry, I loved you so. If only you could have seen that," she said with a smirk.

He shoved her to the floor before her lips could touch him. Henry's body shook in anger. Looking down at her, he grew solemn.

"I loved Elizabeth, and we were going to run away. She would have left *everything* to you. Why did you do it? *Why?"* he cried.

Katrina gazed at herself in a mirror hanging on the wall. Her reflection was not there, but she acted as if she could see herself.

"It was simple, Henry, if I couldn't have you, no one could," she said with no hint of regret.

Henry looked back at us, his face showed the anguish and grief from the past years. A single tear rolled from his eye and traveled down his unshaven face.

"I'm sorry you kids had to get involved in this," he said sincerely.

Katrina's feet floated above the floor as she came back to us.

"I'm sorry too, because now you have to *die!*"

The evil in her eyes was beyond what I could have imagined. My entire body shook uncontrollably. Marcus stepped forward and crossed his arms over his chest.

"You'll have to go through me first!" he said bravely.

Katrina laughed loudly as she floated toward Marcus. Raising his fists, he swung hard with his right hand at Katrina's head. His hand and arm went right through her and came out the other side. She did exactly what Marcus said. She went right through him. Marcus spun around with a shocked look on his face and lowered his fists. Katrina stopped in front of me and pointed her finger in my face.

"You couldn't keep your nose out of *my* business, could you?"

She set her sights on Mike who looked petrified.

"You think you've been helping my sister? Nothing can help her now. I kept Henry away when she was alive and will continue to keep him away in death!"

A bright light appeared behind Katrina. A welcoming warmth radiated through me and a stunning young woman stood before us.

Henry's face lit up. *"Elizabeth!"*

Katrina's rage was unlike anything I'd ever seen as she swung around to face her sister. Elizabeth was even more beautiful than her pictures. Her oval face had a flawless complexion and her eyes were the most vibrant green. Her smile was genuine as she looked at her sister, the kindness undeniable. Turning to Henry, she outstretched her hand to him.

"Never!" Katrina screeched as she picked up a nearby sledgehammer and raced toward them. With a full swing, she aimed directly at Elizabeth. The hammer traveled toward Elizabeth's stomach in what seemed like slow motion. Just before the lovers' fingers touched, the hammer sliced through Elizabeth's frame and hit the center beam behind her. Henry grasped at the air, his opportunity to connect, vanishing as Elizabeth evaporated. The hammer hit the beam hard. A loud cracking sound warned us of impending doom. The

ceiling above us shook and released a shower of blinding dirt and dust. The last thing I saw was the beam breaking in half.

♂ The crack of one of the support beams shocked me out of what seemed to be an old scary movie with zombies and ghosts.
"We have to get out of here!" I shouted.
The candles were like the scorekeeper in this battle between light and dark. One second, they were lit; the next, they were snuffed out. The strobe-like effect of the candles going on and off in the dust, made for an eerie effect, as we watched the figures, Henry and Katrina, fighting. Sarah pulled me towards the doorway. Not until we had our hands on the cold metal surface did we remember we were still trapped.
Mike and Steph were already at the handle, pulling and pounding on it with all their might, in a futile attempt to gain freedom. Tear-streaked faces looked at us as we huddled together and struggled to pull at the door's edge. Another resounding crack filled the air, sounding like thunder following a bolt of lightning. More dust and debris rained down. The first support beam was now broken. It would not be long now before the second beam could no longer hold back the weight of the dirt and cement above our heads and the old wooden-beamed ceiling came crashing down.
"Marcus!" I screamed. "We can't open the door!"
He appeared through the dust cloud and brushed us aside.
"Get out of the way," he growled.
Despite his best effort, the door was not going to come open by pulling on the handle. Marcus backed up ten feet, and like a football player getting ready for a big play, got in a crouch and charged the door.
A tremendous crash followed. The door, although it still held, had buckled in the middle and the track it slid on had pulled away from the wall. Marcus stood to his full height, backed up once again, and aimed for the dented center. This time it was just too much. With a resounding crash, the metal barrier flew off and crashed into the tunnel on the other side.
"Come on, let's go!" Sarah yelled above the sound of the

rushing wind as we scrambled into the tunnels.

The light bulbs in the tunnel were flashing on and off just like the candles. Sarah turned back around to take count of our little group. "Nate!" she screamed.

Sure enough, Nate was not with us. Pushing us aside, Marcus again came to the rescue. "You guys stay here."
None of us listened and we followed him down the hallway.

Nate was standing in the middle of the room, obviously confused and without battery power to his hearing aid. With the glowing he had done earlier, the battery had no chance of recuperating.

Henry threw Katrina to the ground, and raced to hold the last pillar together.

'Git out of here!" he yelled as Marcus charged forward, grabbed Nate, threw him over his shoulder, and raced back into the tunnel.

The support post gave out. In an explosive crash, it split in two. The last I saw of Henry, he was holding his hands above his head as tons of rocks, boards, and other debris cascaded on top of him.

"Nooooooooooo!" Sarah and I screamed in unison.

Large meaty hands grabbed both Sarah and me by the shoulders and dragged us through the tunnel towards the basement entrance. I was mumbling that we needed to go back and rescue Henry, but I allowed Marcus to lead the group out of the basement and up the outside stairs to the back yard.

The flashing lights of a police car drew us to the back of the house. The garage was a complete devastation. The walls had buckled and the roof was now sitting on a pile of rubble. My parents stood holding each other. Mom was sobbing.
"Mom, Dad!" I yelled as I raced to them.

At first, they looked at me as if they didn't know who I was. I was covered in soot from head to toe.

"Ben!" my mom screamed as she stumbled and ran toward me.
Dad fell to his knees as if he was praying.

Mike and Steph were talking excitedly to one of the police officers. They were trying to convince him to hurry and help Henry. I broke away from my mom to lend them a hand, telling them we had to hurry because he could be badly hurt. The one officer looked at the other and looked back at us.

"Okay, quiet!" Officer Hemphill yelled. "I can't understand when you are trying to talk all at once!" Pointing at Sarah he frowned. "You tell me what is going on, and the rest of you shut up."

Sarah began with the shack exploding, the tunnels, and the room under the garage. She continued explaining about Henry being Mr. Wilkerson, the dead bodies of Katrina and Elizabeth, and how he saved us from the cave in.

One of the officers had gone back to the police car to talk on the radio. When he came back, he whispered something to Officer Hemphill. "Are you sure Mr. Wilkerson saved you?"

We nodded in unison. Looking uncomfortable, the officer cleared his throat.

"I'm afraid that is impossible, kids. Mr. Wilkerson died of a heart attack in jail close to an hour ago."

Chapter 52
Alliance & Aftermath

♀ The police roped off the garage with "CRIME SCENE – DO NOT CROSS" tape. When they left, the reporters and neighborhood gawkers eventually went home. We sat around the Whitings' big, round kitchen table. We were all slightly bumped, scratched, and bruised, but otherwise in good spirits. None of us were sleepy even though the night was almost over and the sky was beginning to lighten. The adrenaline was still pumping through our veins. After the shock of the news that Henry had died an hour before he came to our rescue, I was numb.

Opal and Odelle took over the kitchen, busily making coffee and hot cocoa while my mom and Mrs. Whiting escorted each of us to the bathroom to scrub us as clean as they could without hosing us down. Ben donated some of his clean clothing. I giggled at my reflection in the mirror as I admired the two-piece pajamas I remembered Ben wearing the first night he sneaked to my house with his flashlight.

Steph had rolled up a pair of blue jeans and looked lost in a large grey sweatshirt while Nate looked the opposite with the legs of his sweatpants ending just below his knees. My mom made sure each one of us was properly bandaged. Ben's hands were wrapped in fresh gauze. Nate had a Band-Aid across his forehead, and the rest of us looking like we just stepped out of a boxing ring. The only one of us who seemed to have escaped without a scratch was Marcus.

As I carefully sipped my cocoa, I glanced over to the kitchen sink where both our moms peeked out the back window at our dads. They were scratching their heads and complaining they were not allowed to cross the yellow tape.

"Look at them! It's just killing them not to touch." my mom said.

Mrs. Whiting nodded and let out a big sigh, "I know. Thank heavens the kids are all safe."

I smiled across the table at Ben who was trying to lift his cup with huge bandaged hands. Mike ran to a nearby drawer, returned with a straw, and dropped it into Ben's cup. This set off a bout of uncontrollable giggling and demands for five more straws. Opal carried trays of hot beverages to the living room where Nate's entire family and Marcus's mom sat in front of the television, waiting for the morning news.

A loud knock at the front door turned out to be our sweet Mrs. Campbell, the librarian, with the morning newspaper. The library always got the first delivery.

"Everyone, wait till you hear," she squealed with excitement.

I never knew Mrs. Campbell to bounce, but she was bouncing up and down. We all, including the dads, congregated in the kitchen and waited with nail-biting anticipation.

"It took up not only the entire front page, but the back page too!"

Holding the paper for us to see, I spotted several large photos and the headline: "Local Authorities Solve 60-Year-Old Mystery!"

Mrs. Campbell held her hand up to hush the loud outburst. I was amazed how such a little woman could take charge of the room. Once the room was quiet enough to hear a pin drop, she read.

"For more than 60 years, the whereabouts of Elizabeth and Katrina Hilliard have been a mystery. The wealthy sisters vanished shortly after their parents' tragic death in the mid 1920s. Elizabeth, who was 18 at the time, was named sole guardian of her sister Katrina and heir to their parent's fortune. Henry Wilkerson, a local railroad

worker who did odd jobs for the Hilliard family was originally considered a suspect, but after extensive questioning, charges were not made due to lack of evidence and bodies. Through the years, the mystery remained unsolved but was never forgotten.

Little did our local authorities know when they responded to a random fire at the old train yard between Maple and Vine Streets last night, they would ultimately solve this mystery with the help of six local kids."

Mike spoke up. "They didn't solve it! We did!"

Opal patted Mike on the shoulder and hushed him. "We know, Honey, we know."

The article went on to detail the events that followed and revealed how they found the mummified bodies of the sisters in the rubble beneath Ben's garage. It also mentioned finding five thousand dollars in cash in a knapsack belonging to Mr. Wilkerson. Odelle's sudden cry caused everyone to look at her. She blushed with embarrassment and whispered to her sister.

"It's the money he stole from Olivia! He must have taken it from her. Why?"

Mrs. Campbell burst with excitement. "Wait, wait! You have to hear this!" She continued reading.

"Who killed the Hilliard sisters and why? If it were not for the arrest of Henry Wilkerson early last night, we may have never known this answer. Brought in on charges of endangering the welfare of a minor for locking Stephanie McNally in a shed at the train yard last week, Wilkerson suffered a heart attack in his jail cell. His dying confession told the true story of what happened.

"As Henry Wilkerson clung to life, he revealed the tragic events of the past. He admitted his love for Elizabeth Hilliard and the couple's desire to run away and avoid her impending marriage to Ernesto Robinson. According to Wilkerson, a bizarre love triangle and Katrina Hilliard's jealous rage led her to intervene in their plans and murder her own sister. He arrived to find his true love dead with her sister looming above her holding a knife. Distraught and angry, he charged at Katrina and violently pushed her aside causing her to fall on her own knife. He hid the bodies and his secret for all these years. Officers explained he seemed mentally traumatized and unstable when he

explained, 'Katrina has haunted me ever since.' Once his confession was done, the will to live was gone. His last words were, 'I didn't mean no harm to the boy.'"

Mike interrupted again, "Hey! They didn't say anything about Henry saving us and ..." Steph elbowed Mike in the ribs to shut him up as he looked to Ben for answers. Winking at his little brother, Ben shook his head. Mike crossed his arms across his chest and dropped his eyes to the floor.

Mrs. Campbell pointed at the article. "Look! They are donating the money they found to rebuild your garage," she said to Mr. Whiting.

Ben's dad smiled widely, and for the first time, I realized how much Ben looked like him. "Well, well. That's nice of them!"
"What do they say about us, the kids?" I asked.

Mrs. Campbell searched eagerly until she got to the bottom of the back page. "Oh, here's something. "The kids were obviously shaken, but not seriously injured."

♂ Not only did our hard work go unmentioned, but the police had taken most of the credit. Disgusted, I nodded to the gang and we headed toward the back door. The kitchen was still buzzing. My dad received several backslaps and a discussion began about his future garage plans. Marcus grabbed the newspaper off the counter on his way out the door and followed us to the shady spot under the large tree. Sitting in a circle on the ground, we passed the paper around, admiring the photos with our names listed beneath.
When it got to Nate, he screamed.

"Tay! There another article about Mr. Robin'ton!" Sure enough, in the bottom corner of the front page was another article titled "Hilliard Fiancé Ran Secret Spider Society." Sarah read it out loud.

"Discovery of the Hilliard sisters' bodies and the secret of eight tunnels below our city, refocuses attention on Grayson Mills' Secret Spider Society. Shortly after the end of prohibition in the early 1930s, this newspaper reported breaking news about businessman tycoon Ernesto Robinson's illegal activities, exposing him as the alleged ringleader of the secret society that sold alcohol to speakeasies in seven counties. Robinson came to America as a small child and spoke

barely a word of English. He helped support his family by working as a corner shoeshine boy. His mother worked at a restaurant, which was eventually willed to her when its owner passed away.

"Angelina's became the front for selling bootlegged alcohol disguised as cooking vinegar. A spider, symbol of the bootlegging operation, was embossed on the bottle.

"Charges were not filed against Robinson because prohibition was over by the time the secret society was unveiled. Shortly after the disappearance of his fiancée, Elizabeth Hilliard, Robinson dropped out of sight. If he is still rumored to be alive, he would be close to 100 years old. There is no record of his death."

I plopped myself down on to my back and let out a huge sigh. Marcus shifted uncomfortably as he pushed his hand deep into his pockets like he was searching for something.

"It makes sense now," I said as I looked into the tree's limbs.

A dark shadow crossed my face. Before I had a chance to focus on where it came from, a pile of old money landed on my chest. Marcus stood over me.

"I want to give this back."

I grabbed the money and sat up. It was the money from Elizabeth's box Marcus had stolen. I was shocked. I almost missed the miracle of Marcus *smiling*. Before I knew it, we were all grinning from ear to ear.

My mom interrupted when she yelled from the back door. "Kids, you need some rest! The McNallys are getting ready to leave, so say your goodbyes!"

I waved to her. "Okay, Mom! We just have something to finish super quick!"

We inducted Marcus into the group as an official member. After our oath of silence, we pinky swore to always be friends in a world of ghosts, mysteries and teamwork. Where being different was way better than being like everyone else.

Our circle joined hands as the wind suddenly picked up and swirled around us. I had the strange sense Elizabeth and Henry were finally together, and what we accomplished not only set them free, but also brought the six of us together for reasons we still didn't understand.

I had an even stranger sense someone was watching us. My eyes were drawn to a long black car at the curb with the window slightly open. Sticking out was the glowing end of a large cigar.

<u>The End</u>

Sneak peek- The Wandering
To be released 2019

"The crackling fire was much larger than we had earlier. Its color was odd as well, almost orange with a hint of green. In the center, he appeared. Untouched once again by the flames, he stepped out of the fire and walked toward the center of our circle. With each step, he left behind a footprint of fire."

Copyright © [2018] by [Cristal Sipple-Underwood & Andrew Underwood]
All rights reserved. No part of this book may be reproduced, scanned, or distributed in any printed or electronic form without permission
First Edition: [September] [2018]
Printed in the United States of America
ISBN-10: 1642545155
ISBN-13: 9781642545159